BEYOND RESOLUTION

Book 2 of the Resolution Series

ROSE DEE

HOLE IN THE WIND PUBLISHING

Beyond Resolution - Copyright 2016 – Rose Dee

All rights reserved. Without limiting the rights under copyright reserved above, no part of this publication may be reproduced, stored in or introduced into a retrieval system, or transmitted, in any form, or by any means (electronic, mechanical, photocopying, recording, or otherwise) without the prior written permission of both the copyright owner and the above publisher of this book. This is a work of fiction. Names, characters, places, brands, media, and incidents are either the product of the author's imagination or are used fictitiously.

Scripture references are taken from the HOLY BIBLE, NEW INTERNATIONAL VERSION. Used by permission of Zondervan. All rights reserved.

Re-edited for the US eBook market.

Formatting by: Wild Seas Formatting (RikHall.com)
ISBN Ebook: 978 – 0 – 9944011 – 5 – 1
ISBN Print: 978 – 0 – 9944011 – 6 – 8

Hole in the Wind Publishing

Acknowledgements

Firstly, I wish to thank my Heavenly Father – my eternal source.

Thank you to my family and readers.

Thank you to my editors, Wendy Noble and Iola Goulton.

This book is dedicated to my friend, Pat Casanovas who once shared with me the feeling of God's peace that surpasses understanding, and whose words and loving heart has contributed to my peace.

CHAPTER 1

Samara lifted her face to the breeze as she stepped out of the pick-up truck. The smell wafting from the louvered window of her unit was undeniable. Marijuana.

She set her jaw and pulled her shoulders back, preparing for a showdown that had been a long time coming.

The commotion in the two-bedroom duplex grew louder as she made her way to the door. The click-clacking of her stiletto heels on the concrete beat in sync with the pulsing beats inside her chest.

She glanced over to the adjoining flat before turning the knob of her own door. The unit had been vacant for over a month, a relief, as it meant there was no one to report the party den her unwanted guest had established in her unit.

The second she pulled the door open, a grey plume of smoke enveloped her. She coughed before moving further into the room.

"Here she is. The lady of the house." Ricky had made himself a nest on the two-seater sofa. One of his stocky little legs draped over the cushions, and the other was cocked up on the coffee table.

"Get your feet off my furniture." Samara threw her handbag at him, but missed.

Ricky gave his two friends seated opposite a withering glance. One scruffy young man was lolling on a recliner chair, and the other had sunken deep into a beanbag. Ricky took his time adjusting his sitting position.

Samara eyeballed the louts. They were well-known drug-affected youths in the small seaside town. "What are these two drop kicks doing here?"

The one in the chair frowned. "Hey, chill out, Sam. We're in the middle of a business meeting." He glanced over at the empty beer bottles and drug paraphernalia strewn across the coffee table. His lopsided grin said it all.

Samara turned to Ricky and gave him what she hoped was the most intense death stare in history. His return smirk fired her anger.

"This is my home, not an office. And this is no business meeting. Get out." She pointed to the door, and kicked the shin of the lout in the beanbag.

"Yeow."

Sam squinted at the slacker, who jutted out his bottom lip in pouting response to her aggression.

Both men sought direction from Ricky, who rolled his eyes and reached for the half-empty bag of dope on the table. "Party's over, boys. Take this for your trouble."

Beanbag boy leaped from his position like a gazelle. "Hey, thanks man." He snatched the bag from Ricky and sniffed its contents. "This is the best stuff we've had in ages."

Ricky gave him a close-lipped smirk, his ungroomed, bushy eyebrows dipping over glassy blue eyes. "No worries. You know where to buy in the future, right?"

The other teen reached for a pipe on the table.

"For sure. We won't go anywhere else. You got the best stuff."

Ricky rose and stumbled around the furniture. "Don't go yet. I'll get you a beer for the road."

He made his way to the kitchen. Samara followed him. He wasn't going to help himself to anything else. She could feel the fire in her gut grow, along with the overwhelming dread at the situation she found herself in. She didn't wait until they were in the kitchen to explode.

"I told you I didn't want you here if I wasn't home." She clenched her teeth at Ricky's back.

He didn't answer her until they were both in the kitchen. "I don't care what you want. This is business. You're in business with us, so you're going to have to deal with it."

Sam could feel her breath, shallow and rapid. "My agreement was with Karl, not you, and it was for use of my landline telephone, not the entire unit."

Ricky leaned over the kitchen bench that stood between them. His lip curled. "These guys are sellers. They have a lot of buyers. I checked with Karl. He's cool about it."

Samara reached for the cordless phone on the bench. "We'll see about that." She dialed the number.

Karl answered in one ring. "Somers."

"It's me." She knew he would recognize her voice, especially after all the long flirty telephone conversations they'd had recently.

"Hi." Karl's voice was as smooth and slick.

"We've got a problem."

"Let me guess. Ricky is being difficult?"

There was just enough agitation in his voice to

pacify Samara, but the situation still had to be addressed. She didn't want to squash the attraction between her and Karl, but she had to put a stop to Ricky's abuse of the limited privileges she had agreed to.

She took a breath before continuing. "The deal I made with you was payment for the use of my telephone, not full access to the unit for drug dealing. I can't be involved in that, Karl. My dad's the local cop and he knows everything that goes on here at Kiisay Point." She paused for another breath. "You've never been here. You don't know how small this place is."

"Well, that's about to change, because I'm an hour away."

Sam bit her lip and lifted her long dark hair off the back of her neck. How did she feel about seeing Karl again? When he and Ricky had taken a table next to her at a cafe in the nearby town over a month ago, she had been both instantly attracted to, and wary of Karl. As interesting as he was, she had judged that the suave, sophisticated city man wasn't someone she could fully trust. She had encountered his type in her modelling days. They were after a trophy girl, fun with no substance. Maybe her attraction to him was because he was so different from her last boyfriend.

Her still fresh uncoupling fiasco pricked her conscience, and sent a rush of fear through her. "If Flynn comes back and finds out what's been going on in his unit, he's going to freak out."

There was a pause at the end of the line before Karl spoke. "I thought you said you had broken up with him."

Samara wet her lips and turned her back to Ricky. "We are broken up—have been for a while. He has every right to kick me out."

She dropped her hair and let it swing down her back, unsure how much she wanted to disclose about her situation. The new realization concerning her mistakes was still raw. If only she had taken the harder road and worked as a checkout girl at the local store, instead of making this deal with Karl. Sure, it provided some easy cash, but now it was blowing up in her face.

The heavy pause at the end of the line required her to say something about her situation. "I owe Flynn some money, and I need the deposit for my next rental when I move out. Flynn's away working, so he said I could stay here until he gets back into port. The only reason I agreed to let Ricky use the phone is because I need the money. I didn't agree to Ricky practically moving in, or dealing drugs from here." She could feel a resurgence of indignation over the way she was being used.

Just like you used Flynn?

The thought sent a rush of heat into her cheeks. She had used Flynn, and she had vowed to pay back every cent she had taken from him over the few months they had been together. The epiphany that she had been spending money to fill her broken heart didn't mean a thing unless she did something to fix her mistake.

"Sit tight. I'll sort it all out when I get there. Your ex isn't going to be back anytime soon, is he?" Karl's voice had an impatient edge.

Sam could hear noises behind her. She turned around to see Ricky opening the refrigerator door. "No, he's still at sea. His fishing boat's not due into port until tomorrow or the next day."

Ricky pulled out a six-pack of beer and closed the door as Karl's cell phone line crackled. "Cool, then don't stress. Put Ricky on so I can talk to him. And princess?"

Samara softened a little at the sound of this new pet name. "Yes?"

"I can't wait to see you again. Face to face." His voice broke off with the air of an unsaid promise.

A swirling mix of anticipation, regret, and wariness tumbled in her belly. Was getting romantically involved with this guy a good idea?

She handed the phone over the bench and attempted to grab the beer, but Ricky moved the pack out of her reach. He then made a point of caressing her hand as he took the phone from her. All contemplation of her feelings about Karl was squashed in a wave of disgust. Ricky was the most unattractive man she had ever met.

Since she had returned to her hometown of Kiisay Point over eight months ago, Ricky, a local loser, had displayed blatant interest in her. Not even the devastating heartbreak that had driven her home would have inspired her to fall into the arms of this repulsive individual. She had unwisely reserved that rebound relationship for Flynn, who had restored her faith in her attractiveness to men, and had also provided satisfying revenge to the man who had broken her heart—or so she had thought.

Now here she was in a different heart struggle.

This time it was between keeping her policeman father's love, and getting enough money to maintain her independence from him. If she couldn't make it on her own, she'd be forced to move back in with her dad. After over five years away from home, she had no desire to play the child again. And he was the best option. Moving in with her hypocritical mother and pious stepfather didn't bear thinking about.

Ricky cocked his head to the phone. "Hey, boss." He played with the plastic wrapping of the beer pack while he listened.

Samara couldn't hear what Karl was saying, but it certainly didn't seem to be instilling any fear in Ricky. He started pulling off bits of plastic wrapping.

Eventually he spoke. "But I told you, my place is too hot, and this is the perfect joint. Her old man isn't going to bust his little girl. Besides, it's in the middle of nowhere, no neighbors around, not even a crow. Don't worry, I've covered my tracks, and we got heaps of business outta it." He paused to throw a piece of plastic on the floor. "I can't cool it now."

Karl must have forced his 'cooling it' point because Ricky groaned, said "I just wanted a few beers for my customers but alright," and held out the phone. "He wants to talk you again."

Samara rubbed the handset on the leg of her jeans before putting it up to her ear. She could see the sweat beading on Ricky's forehead, and she didn't want any part of that grossness. "Is he leaving?" She waited for Karl to confirm what she was sure she already knew.

"He sure is. Let him have the beer. I'll pay you back. Now go and pack your bags. When I'm finished my business there I want to take you away for the weekend. Maybe to one of the islands. Would you like that?"

Samara felt her spirits lift. Escape to one of the nearby tropical island resorts sounded like a dream. Maybe if she wasn't around when Flynn returned, he'd let her stay a bit longer. An additional tour at sea on his reef fishing boat would buy her another six weeks. She would definitely have enough money to pay him back by then. And hopefully enough for a flat as well.

Apart from that advantage, Sam was sure Karl was looking to advance their romance with his offer, and why not? It wasn't as though she had a lot of other men beating down her door to spoil her. She was in a precarious position, and Karl was looking like a welcome distraction.

May as well give a bad boy a go. The so-called good one was a disaster.

She smiled into the receiver. "Sounds awesome."

"I'll be there to collect you in an hour. Tell Ricky to meet me at his place. That'll get him out of your hair."

Samara breathed a sigh of relief and glanced up at Ricky, who had pulled a beer from the packaging and was sucking on the bottle. His pouty expression was indication of his dislike at being reprimanded.

Samara pressed the red disconnect button and put the phone back on its charging cradle. "You have to go home. Karl's meeting you there."

Ricky's eyes narrowed. "You really got tickets on yourself, don't you?" His mouth drooped on one corner. "You do know your boyfriend's just a fisherman and Karl's got chicks like you lined up back in the city. Just because you went to university and posed for a few photos doesn't make you some sort of prize."

She rolled her eyes at his attempt to bring her down a peg or two. "I'm a qualified nurse. I don't need to associate with lowlifes like you to make a living."

He leaned over the kitchen counter barrier between them. "Then why are you?" His smirk was so high it made his jaw jut out.

Samara's gut dropped. Why was she? She could go back to nursing, but that would mean having to face all the emotions surrounding the time before she left, including the relationship that broke her heart.

The sound of the front door opening and slamming against the wall forced a stop to any further contemplation. Samara could feel her eyes widening, and one look at Ricky, beer paused in midair, made her entire being freeze.

Sam tried to move, but felt glued to the spot. Not a sound could be heard from down the short hallway. Someone had discovered the party drug den.

"What are you two turkeys doing in my unit?"

"Flynn." Sam could feel her legs turn to jelly. He was back early.

Ricky's eyes widened as he placed his beer on the counter. "I'm outta here," he whispered, then moved as fast as his stocky legs would carry him down the hallway.

Sam followed, not sure what was going to happen, but certain that she needed to face up to

Flynn. This was his home, and she had put him through enough. Every attempt she had made to get out of his life had backfired.

A mass of red hair appeared a few feet in front of Ricky. "Hold on. Where do you think you're going?" In an instant, Flynn had him in a headlock and was forcing him into the small lounge room.

His massive red curly beard shook as he glanced behind at her. "You get your butt down here too. I want to speak to you."

Sam cringed at the ferocious glare in his grey eyes. Flynn didn't have red hair for nothing. She was younger than him, but had known him as a child when staying with her father at Kiisay Point during her school holidays. Even back then, Flynn McKenna's fiery temper and subsequent fighting skills were renowned.

She followed back down the hallway, watching Ricky squirm under the taut muscular arm that held him in place.

Flynn didn't release him when they entered the lounge, and there were no sign of the two youths. They had no doubt taken advantage of the open doorway.

Flynn used his free hand to point to the incriminating evidence on the coffee table. "What's this?"

Ricky had given up trying to get out of the headlock and was now set rigid with his fingers digging into Flynn's arm. "It's none of your business, Mate so just go . . ." A tirade of abuse followed.

Flynn looked at her. The wild fire in his eyes, and the set of his jaw made Sam cringe inside like a beaten dog. She blinked hard and felt her teeth chatter, which was ridiculous in the North Australian tropical heat.

Flynn pointed to one of the makeshift drug devices. "Get me that."

Sam moved as fast as she could to the table, retrieved it, and deposited it in his free hand.

Flynn popped the top off the bottle to expose the dirty water. "Here. You don't want to waste this." He proceeded to tip the contents onto Ricky's face.

The captured man thrashed around trying to escape. His thick torso and squat legs were no match for Flynn's superior physique. Foul language accompanied the display.

Flynn pulled Ricky towards the door, dripping all the way. Samara didn't dare intervene. In one swift motion, Flynn released his captive and kicked him hard up the rear. Ricky stumbled outside and fell with the force.

"Don't come back." Flynn pointed a finger as Ricky stumbled to his feet. "You got it?" He didn't wait for a response before turning and slamming the door.

Sam held her breath and waited for Flynn's next explosion, this time directed at her. She knew she deserved a whole lot more than Ricky had endured.

You got it coming.

She steeled herself for the onslaught, but Flynn didn't move. He stood in the doorway clenching and unclenching his fists.

Sam took the opportunity to try and explain. "I'm so sorry. I am. I had no idea this was going on. I didn't. You know I don't do drugs." She took a step towards him, but froze when he looked up at her. His grey eyes cut through her as sharp as razors. "I know I've made some horrible mistakes, but I never meant for this to happen. I can't seem to get it together." She heard her voice crack, and a hot rush of liquid welled in her eyes. "I just can't." The tears flowed hard and fast. "I can't seem to make anything good happen."

It was exactly how she felt, like a complete and utter loser. Everyone said she had great potential. She was smart—one of the top students in her nursing program. She had beauty, modelling her way through her university years and making great living in the industry. Her family loved her. Even though her parents had divorced when she was a child, she and her brothers had never wanted for a thing. But none of it mattered, because the one person she had loved and wanted more than anything in the world had rejected her. Since then nothing had mattered; not her family, not Flynn, not even herself.

She looked up through her tears to see Flynn shake his head. "Well, it's done now. Go pack your stuff." He shifted towards her, his stare no longer as hateful as it had been a moment ago. "Go to your family. When things fall apart, they're often the only ones that can help."

Samara rubbed her wet cheeks and nodded.

CHAPTER 2

Ten months later

The incoming alert on her cell sounded as Samara entered the modelling agency. She paused to make sure the text wasn't from Karl before fumbling with the password and opening her messages. It was from her father.

Thinking about you. Hope you are doing OK. Love Dad.

She plonked down on the closest seat, outside her agent's office.

A stabbing pain of guilt pierced inside. It had been ages since she had spoken to her father. The last time was over ten months ago when she had called to inform him of her decision to move with Karl from Kiisay Point to Sydney, after Flynn had kicked her out.

She looked up as a middle-aged lady with wide-rimmed glasses took a seat beside her. "Sam, I'm glad I've caught you."

Sam racked her brain for the woman's name, but came up with a blank. They had met a few days ago. Ms. Glasses was her third new representative at the agency, and her fifth since re-entering the modelling industry after her move to Sydney.

The woman carried a clipboard with a list of names. She peered through her glasses. "I'm sorry to have to tell you this, but the client ruled you out this morning. They're going for a younger model."

Sam flipped her cell phone case closed. "I'm twenty-six. How much younger do they want?"

The woman gave her a tight smile that warped her lips. "Unfortunately, much younger." She glanced down at the board before continuing. "There was also something about the color of your eyes being wrong. They're looking for brilliance, not dark brown, and they want white skin tone, not naturally olive. Everything about you was wrong." She looked up from the clipboard, turning the fake smile into an undisguised cringe. "Sorry. We don't have a lot on the books for you. Period."

Sam recognized the kiss of death when she saw it. Prolonging this not–so-gentle shove out the door would only extend her agony.

She tucked her cell phone back into her purse and rose. "Thanks for the representation."

They shook hands. "I'll call if anything comes up."

Sam smiled, knowing full well that this was the way girls were ticked off the agency's books in order to make room for newer, younger faces. Much younger.

The drive back to the apartment she shared with Karl seemed to take longer than normal. Each red light meant more time to contemplate her situation.

She didn't love Karl, and he certainly didn't love her. She was a trophy on his arm, and he understood that, as long as he let her do what she wanted, she would turn a blind eye to the nature of his business, and his womanizing. Now, ten months into their relationship of convenience, the obstacles were becoming unbearable. All they did was fight, break up, and fight some more. If only she could work out her next step, she would be out the door in a heartbeat.

Samara had full knowledge of all Karl's drug wheeling and dealing. She knew her situation was untenable, but she also had no idea what to do. Karl held all the cards. While she had no money, no friends, and nowhere to go, he knew he could control her.

As she punched in the security code to the underground car park, she wondered at her lack of ambition, her disinterest in wanting more for herself. She hadn't always been this way. Somewhere along the path she had settled for existing. Then she had morphed into existing in any easy form it was offered to her.

Another resident's car alarm ran out. The shrill ringing echoed off the concrete walls as she found Karl's spot, and parked his BMW. She made her way to the elevator and up to the apartment.

Sam placed her designer handbag on the foyer side table on her way through to the bedroom. The door was slightly ajar, and the grunts and groans of a passionate tryst echoed in the hall.

A flutter of anguish worked its way through her body as she pushed the door open. Karl was in a precarious position with a woman she recognized as a much younger model from her agency. A week ago the girl had tearfully confided that she had no family or friends in Sydney, having only moved there recently. Clearly, introducing her around at Karl's last party had been a bad idea.

As they clamored to untwine, all Samara could

think about were what they were doing to her new expensive sheet set.

"Couldn't you have done this at a hotel, Karl? I spent ages picking out that bedding."

He jumped from the bed and turned to face her. The blonde hair and boyish features she once found attractive had come to repulse her. The wide-eyed girl pulled the covers over her body.

A sneer appeared on Karl's handsome face as he reached for his pants. "You're just nasty, Samara."

Sam rolled her eyes and walked back out to the living area.

Karl followed her. "I want you out of here. All you do is whine and moan about everything. I'm through having to deal with you. You go through money like its water, and I'm not getting anything for my investment anymore."

His voiced grated on her. Samara whipped around to face him. "You make out like you're some sort of businessman, Karl, but your money's as dirty as you are."

He slapped her cheek, sending her staggering back.

"Get your stuff and get out. Your replacement's already moved in."

With that he retreated to the bedroom, slamming the door.

That was it. She moved out within hours.

The lights of the Sydney Harbor Bridge beamed down as the bus made its way underneath the high arches. Samara stared out her window at the black water. The surface shimmered with flashes of light reflecting off the overpass. A procession of harbor ferries broke the surface as the expanse of water snaked its way out to sea.

Samara recalled the first time she had crossed the iconic bridge. She had arrived in Sydney with Karl and he had taken her on a tour of the city. They had whizzed over the bridge in his BMW convertible, with her jumping in excitement as the Sydney Opera House came into sight.

She huffed and shook her head at the contrast to her present situation—riding in the back seat of a police car.

Sam closed her eyes and tried to control her breathing from a shallow intake to a long expulsion. "Drop me off a block from the hotel."

The uniformed underling looked back from his passenger seat. "Is that wise? Karl may have one of his cronies tailing you."

Even in the dull light of the sedan cab, Sam could see the man give his driving partner a cursory glance. The uniformed driver turned his head slightly to address her. "We have orders to drop you directly in front of your accommodation."

Sam closed her eyes for a second and took a long, hard swallow. "Listen here, you pair." Her voice was louder than she had planned. "My father's been in the force longer than you two have been alive, so I'm no idiot. I've been hauled in by your detectives three times in three weeks and I've told them everything I know. It isn't my fault that I couldn't tell you anything new." She stopped to take another breath. "I know why they told to drop me outside my hotel.

It's because if Karl is having me followed, you want to agitate him. But I'm not your bait. I know my rights, and I know you have no right or cause to even have me in this vehicle. So do as I say and drop me where I tell you, or you can forget about me coming to you in the future."

Her words sounded far more forceful than she felt. The cops knew Karl was only a lackey in the drug ring. They police were after bigger men than him, and those guys were a lot smarter about covering their tracks. They were hard targets to nail, but she knew the tactics. She wasn't going to be a pawn in their game.

The men in the front seats glanced at one another before the younger in the passenger seat turned back to her. "We'll have to clear any other drop off points with the base."

Sam stared at his profile. "I don't care what you have to do, but if you drop me anywhere near my hotel you'll never get another piece of information out of me." She sat back and stared out the window, concentrating on the flashing lights of Sydney while the call was made in the front.

After relaying her wishes to the detective in charge of the case, the driver called out from his front seat. "We'll drop you off where you want."

Sam breathed a sigh of relief. She had no idea if Karl knew she had been talking to the police or not, but any distance she could put between her and her ex, the better. At least she was calling the shots in her own life. Not that the dingy hotel room she was living in was anything to get excited about.

Since leaving Karl three weeks ago, she had been

forced to take shelter in the cheapest accommodation she could find in an outlying suburb. The low-standard room was at odds with the high-class possessions that filled it. The amount she had spent on expensive designer gear during her relationship with Karl could easily have paid for a month in a five-star hotel. Ironic. She looked like a million dollars, but had nothing in the bank.

Walking away from Karl had been a huge relief. Leaving the lifestyle he provided was a completely different story. While she was with him she had enjoyed the latest and best of everything, all designer products and nothing second-rate. Now all the stuff meant nothing.

She was free of a bad relationship, but still didn't know what to do, where to go, or which road to take. Ex-girlfriend of a drug dealer. How low could she go?

The cop car rounded a corner and stopped at the intersection she had specified. The younger officer exited and opened her door. "Are you sure you're going to be OK?"

Sam detected real concern in his countenance. Was she going to be OK? She didn't know, and had to acknowledge there was a part of her that didn't care.

"I'll be fine. Don't hang around." She turned and walked down the street. After a while she heard the vehicle drive away.

A sudden chill descended on the street. Sam checked her watch. Ten o'clock. The click of her shoes echoed on the pavement of the deserted road.

She rounded a corner and saw the dilapidated

building that sat at the end of the same street as her hotel. In the daylight it looked pathetic, its neglected structure crumbling, glass broken and graffiti covering every inch of its surface, but the night light made it look eerie. She shivered.

A scuffling noise sounded behind her. She whipped around to stare into the darkness, half expecting the cop car to appear. It didn't. The shadow of a tree moved as its branches swayed in the wind. She wrapped her arms around her body and picked up her pace. It was another block before the hotel would come into view.

The shadow of a person stepped out in front of her. She froze for a second before continuing on her way. The shadow loomed larger as the man drew closer. It was impossible to see his features in the dark.

Sam could feel her heart beating so fast she felt short of breath. She tried to maintain her course with purpose, expecting the man to pass her by, but he veered into her path. Sam halted and stepped back a few paces, only to slam hard into something behind her.

A forceful jolt to her back sent her to the ground. Pain stung as a foot connected with her stomach. Seconds later she felt the air in her lungs drain, and pain pierce her insides. Another blow struck her side. Several blows ensued, each one inflicting pain to her abdomen. She felt herself being pulled to her feet as she struggled for breath.

There was no time to think, no time to plan, no time to take a breath. Strong arms wrapped around her waist and heavy breathing sounded against her ear. The heat of the man's breath made her ear moist and pain coursed through her again.

The man ran a wet tongue up her neck, licking her from her collarbone to her ear. The sticky wetness did something to her awareness, and she found her voice. The scream was firmly muffled by a heavy hand. A sudden shot of reality broke through her pain and the sting of despair paralyzed her.

A soft whisper sounded in her ear. "Stop talking to the cops."

With that, she was dropped back to the pavement.

She hit the concrete and doubled up in pain as the heavy footsteps of her retreating attackers sounded behind her.

CHAPTER 3

Four months later

Samara made her way to the stage, taking extra care not to stumble on the uneven staircase. The twelve-inch thigh-high boots were impossible to walk in. A tattered edge of the stage curtain wrapped around her heel and she shook her foot to free it. She peered around the heavy linen to gauge the atmosphere inside the club. The yelling and foul-mouthed comments circulating the room made her cringe. It was a rowdy night.

One of the model assistants, a grossly overweight lady with inch-thick makeup approached her. She handed her a glass of cheap champagne. "Get this into you, love."

Sam took it from her, but didn't drink. She had been at this job long enough to know how bad it tasted.

The woman reached under the collar of the silk wrap Sam was wearing and pulled at the straps on her lacy bra, forcing the Karl-funded breast implants to burst over the seam. "You know the rules—serve it up as sexy as you can. You may not have to take all your clothes off, but it's still stripping. We want the patrons to see the goods." She positioned her face close to Sam's, invading her personal space. "Unless you want to upgrade your paycheck, like Layla?"

Sam peered up at the woman from under her massive fake eyelashes. "No thanks." She was careful to inject enough sweetness in her tone so as not to upset the woman. She needed this job. Staying away from Karl and his cronies had plummeted her lower than she had ever thought she would go. Could go. This was supposed to be catwalk lingerie, but instead it presented as flesh flashing with a hint of modesty, specifically to fool the girls and arouse the crowd.

The woman rolled her heavily lidded eyes. "Oh, I get it. You're a real model!" The emphasized sarcasm in the word 'real' indicated exactly what the woman thought of her.

Sam found it hard to keep her cool. She knew she was either on the verge of hitting the woman, or crying inconsolably.

"How long have you been here?" The woman pulled at her straps some more.

Sam tilted her long stemmed glass, and wished she could find a place to put it down. "Over three months."

The woman steeped back to give her body a full once-over. "Just as well you're a favorite with the crowd, or Jamal would have moved you onto one of his other places ages ago."

Sam felt a cold shudder down her spine as the woman turned her attention to the girl lined up behind her. Jamal owned several nightclubs. This was the only one specializing in catwalk modelling lingerie and swimwear. All the others were strip joints. He was open about his business plan to lure in the unsure models and customers with the ploy that it wasn't 'stripping', and then promote his other, more lucrative clubs.

Sam shook her head. She had considered herself

lucky when she had found a reasonably priced room to rent, and had liked her flatmate, Layla, immediately. Layla had helped her get this modelling job. But there was heavy pressure on the girls to move into the stripping clubs. Sam now realized it was also how Jamal managed to get the best looking girls into his employ. He also plied the models with alcohol and drugs to get them to a point of compliance. Sam was sure Layla wouldn't have succumbed to the pressure to strip if she hadn't accepted the drugs.

Layla had made the modelling job sound glamorous and profitable. At the time Sam had reasoned that it couldn't be too bad. Layla had explained it was just like the dancers in the rap music videos. All she would have to do was walk the runway, remove several outer layers, but keep the bikini or lingerie underneath on.

What Layla didn't tell her was how utterly degrading the job was, how worthless it would make her feel. It wasn't modelling. It was glorified stripping. She cringed at her foolish thoughts of glamour and glory. She wanted to cry every time she saw a rap video with gyrating semi-naked women. That was her.

She also hadn't envisaged the men would treat her like a piece of meat. It certainly wasn't the Hollywood fantasy. Since working at the club Samara had been obscenely yelled at, groped, and a few times, spat on.

So much for glamour.

Sam moved to the side of the backstage area as a model from the current set appeared behind the stage curtain.

"Is it as bad as it sounds?" she asked the girl, taking a deep swig of the bad champagne. The Dutch courage was horrible, but at least it was free, and not the drugs flowing free down the line behind her.

"Worse." The girl was clutching her discarded sailor costume. "Three bachelor parties and that creepy guy in the raincoat."

Sam grabbed the edge of the curtain and peeked out. The man in the corner of the room sat as still as a statue, peering out from under the hood of the old raincoat. The girls had nicknamed him, Mr. Hood. Tonight he was just one unsavory character amongst hundreds.

"Great. The nasty and the crazy." She dropped the curtain and turned back to the girl, who gently touched the top of her arm.

"At least Rocco's out there to keep them in check." She grinned and winked one smoky eye. "He'll look after you. We all know who his favorite is."

"Ugh." Sam rolled her eyes. She didn't know what more she could do to convince the massively overweight bouncer, with poor personal hygiene, that she wasn't interested in him. After he had playfully thwacked her bottom as she passed him earlier in the night, she was certain his unwanted advances were building to an unpleasant confrontation.

"Have fun." The model gave her a shrug and disappeared down the short line of skimpily clad girls.

Sam downed the rest of the drink and handed

her empty glass to the assistant who had reappeared as her musical introduction started.

The onslaught hit her the minute she stepped out onto the catwalk.

"Woo hoo, come on over here love and I'll—' A list of obscenities broke out from one of the men in the bachelor party group. The lewd comments made her cringe. She looked up to see Rocco addressing the group. His sheer bulk subdued the men.

Samara had seen enough of Rocco's scare tactics to be convinced the rumor about him beating up his girlfriends was true.

He gave her a dense, lopsided smile as she reached the end of the catwalk. Samara returned the gesture with a tight-lipped nod and finished her walk.

Mel, another leader model with thick red hair and the biggest breast implants Samara had ever seen, stood waiting in the wings. "Bunch of mongrels tonight, hey Shanny?" She took a swig from a champagne bottle.

Sam sighed. On the odd occasion it was still strange to be called by her adopted stage name. No one in her current world knew her as Samara. After she had been attacked in the street, she had assumed a false name for her own security. She had decided upon Chanel, hoping the associated class of the word gave her an aura of exclusivity, but they had all soon shortened the word to Shanny. The nickname only served to cheapen her further.

"You're not wrong." She moved aside so the models exiting behind her had room. "Be careful out there. It's dangerous."

"Just as well you got Rocco for protection."

"You can have him." She gave Mel a hopeful look.

"No way. That guy is solid bone from the jaw up. I like my men to be capable of stringing a sentence together." Mel opened the curtain to peek out onto the platform of the main stage area. She pulled her huge breasts into place behind the tiny folds of her bikini top.

"Well, here goes nothing. I hope they're too drunk to tell the difference between a twenty and a fifty." She stepped out onto the stage as the DJ began her introduction.

Samara made her way down the uneven staircase and back down the narrow hall to the leader model's dressing room. The other, lesser-known girls had a larger room further down the hall.

There were three out of the five top girls here tonight. With Mel on stage, their tiny dressing room was empty apart from Kelsey.

The older lady looked up as she entered. "Still rotten out there?"

Samara took her seat in the cramped conditions. Dressing chairs and tables were crammed into the space, along with a variety of lingerie, swimwear, and an unprecedented number of feather boas.

Sam pushed aside a pink fluffy wrap from the corner of the small mirror. "This has got to be the worst night I've ever had."

She looked at Kelsey's mirror image.

The older model abandoned her makeup procedure to focus on her. "At least you're done. Spare a thought for me. I've got another four sets before I can get out of here."

Samara closed her eyes and blocked out the other lady's face. It was difficult to feel sorry for anyone but herself.

She opened her eyes. The woman in the refection stared back at her. She hardly recognized her own face. Heavy makeup clung to her skin, making her natural features almost unrecognizable. Her huge brown eyes were dull and lackluster. During her modelling days, photographers had gushed over her ability to convey emotion through her eyes. Now she could barely manage a smile with her mouth, let alone convey one from the inside.

It wasn't only her face that was unfamiliar. Who was she? She didn't know anymore. *What are you doing?* She closed her eyes again in an attempt to quiet the voice inside her head that had been niggling for weeks. It was getting louder and louder.

"What's wrong, love?"

She opened her eyes to see Kelsey's reflection in her mirror. Sam shook her head and threw the tissue she had in her hand onto the makeup counter.

"I don't know who I am anymore." Her friend gave her upper arm a brief rub "I used to know. Once." She pulled another tissue from the box. "I was always such a tomboy growing up. I used to drive my two big brothers crazy."

Kelsey took the seat beside her. "How much older are your brothers?"

Sam turned to her and smiled. She was a sweet woman, who had clearly picked up on her depressive state and need to confide in someone. Despite being careful about her past, she trusted

Kelsey. Ten years older made her close to a mother figure.

"Andy is nine years older, and Mitch is five years, so you can imagine what they thought of their younger sister tailing them all day." She smiled at the memory. "I was good at patching up their scrapes, so the only time they would let me near them was when they were hurt. Which was often." She gave Kelsey a withering look, making her friend laugh.

"That's men for you." Kelsey rolled her eyes. "Is that why you wanted to be a nurse, because you were used to cuts and scrapes?"

Sam nodded. "That, and I was never worried about blood. In fact, I can't remember a time when I didn't want to be a nurse."

Kelsey ran one finger over a wrinkle on her forehead, examining it for smoothness in the mirror. "So how did a girl who always wanted to be a nurse end up being a lingerie model at a joint like this?"

"A scout gave me his card when I was in my first year at uni. I made a good living in fashion modelling all through my degree." Sam recalled the first time she had stepped onto a shoot. She had no idea what she was doing. "You can imagine what an impact the fashion world had on a tomboy who never thought she was attractive. I got so wrapped up in it."

Kelsey turned to her and frowned, her blonde bobbed hair bouncing with the movement. "Yeah, but I didn't have your smarts. I've only ever been a pretty face. I never had a problem until I got old. Now I know a pretty face only gets you so far." Kelsey looked away and sighed, then turned back. "You finished your degree?"

Sam wiped her forehead clean of foundation. "Yeah. I'm fully qualified. I even did a stint in a hospital after Uni. I loved it."

The other lady shrugged her slim shoulder. "So, hello? What are you doing here? If I had a profession to fall back on, do you think I'd be doing time in this hole?"

Sam looked into her reflection. It didn't make any sense to her either, but that part of her life was too painful to address. Her silence didn't stop Kelsey from prodding the issue.

"So why did you leave nursing?"

Sam continued to remove the makeup from the rest of her face. Her aggressive wiping was so hard her cheeks stretched with the pressure. She could feel Kelsey's eyes on her, waiting for an answer. Finally she caved.

"A man broke my heart, and I went back home to get over him. I've guess I've just never found my way back. Maybe it's not really who I am after all." She twisted in her chair to face Kelsey. "Maybe this is who I really am."

Her friend reached out and squeezed her hand. "Baby, this isn't who any of us are." She reached for a brush. "This is where we find ourselves. Some of us through bad choices, others because we don't think we deserve any better, and then there are those who, like you, get lost and forget who they're supposed to be. Me? I just ran out of options. No room for an old lady in the modelling world. Anywhere past thirty is ancient." She looked in the mirror and ran the brush through her already straight bob. "You know, we all think stripping is the way to go, or the only way, but it never is. It's just the way we fall into because we don't know the way we should go."

Looking at her refection, Sam knew Kelsey was right. She didn't know the way she should go, and she hadn't known for a long time. She hardly even recognized herself. Her straight, dark brown hair hung down her back. It had thinned out due her recent weight loss. In her opinion, she looked older than her years. She felt older. She ran her fingertips over high cheekbones jutting out on her thin face. Her weight loss had been slow at first, but in the last few weeks even she had noticed a dramatic difference. Her stomach caved in and hip bones protruded. Her thighs, which were never big, looked like twigs holding up her body. The only curves she had left were her cosmetically enhanced breasts, their shape barely affected by her weight loss. They were a permanent reminder of her dysfunctional relationship with Karl.

The sound of the door opening drew her attention and she looked up to see Rocco's massive bulk filling the doorway.

"Hi there, sweet cakes." His deep booming voice bounced off the thin walls of the room.

Fear swelled the pit of Samara's stomach. Rocco had never ventured behind the main bar area before. She felt him closing in on her.

"Rocco, get out! You know you're not allowed back here." Kelsey came to her rescue, yelling a string of obscenities at the huge man.

"Settle down." Rocco's bushy eyebrows drooped at the rebuke. "I just wanted to make sure my girl's alright."

Samara felt her stomach drop. What was she going to do? There was no way she was going to be his anything.

Rocco wiggled his monobrow up and down and gave her a lopsided grin before exiting the room.

She looked to Kelsey, who must have recognized her terrified expression because she frowned with concern. "You're going to have to make your dislike crystal clear to him, because he's really gone on you."

"I know. I've been putting it off, hoping he'll get over me and move on to someone else." Her plan to ignore Rocco hadn't worked. The thrill of the chase had encouraged his interest in her.

"You just make sure there are plenty of people around when you set him right. You don't want him getting nasty with you."

Kelsey's words were wise. Rocco's bad temper was another reason she had been delaying the inevitable talk. She added the unavoidable confrontation to the list of fears plaguing her. She had already suffered one beating this year, and the thought of having to go through another scared her senseless.

The break in the music signaled the end of Mel's routine.

"Got to go." Kelsey took one last look at her face and got to her feet. She was out the door in seconds.

Sam went through the mindless motions of cleaning up. This night couldn't end soon enough.

Samara breathed a sigh of relief as she made her way down the hall towards back door of the club. A chorus of goodbyes sounded as she walked past the larger dressing room. She returned the sentiment and kept on walking.

I'm not spending one more minute in this place. Her vow was the same every night.

She reached for the back door handle, but it swung open, almost hitting her. She stumbled back as Jamal walked through the door.

"Is it that late?" He looked at his watch, then set his beady eyes on her. He had to look up due to her height and his small stature. "You want to get a drink? My shout."

Sam fingered the strap on her handbag. "Thanks, but I have somewhere I need to be." It was a lie, but she wasn't accepting a thing from this crooked little man.

"Maybe next time." He licked thin lips and looked her over her from head to toe. "You know, we're starting to get complaints about your bones sticking out. You might get more work in the model world looking like that, but in my clubs, it's all about the curves." He moved past her and walked a few paces down the hall, calling over his shoulder. "Get a hamburger. I've got plans for you."

Sam had a good idea what plans Jamal had. Rumor was he had opened a side business as a pimp for five of the girls who had previously stripped at one of his clubs. Sam was certain one of them was her flatmate. Layla had been vocal about Sam getting a better cut of Jamal's action, like she had.

"No worries, Jamal. I'll put on some weight, okay," she called to his retreating back, then raced out the door.

The lane was dark, but she stopped to take a deep breath. Freedom. How long was she going to do this? Live this way? Act this way? Feel this way?

She ran past the industrial bins scattered in the laneway. The stale smell of rubbish was almost a relief from the putrid stench in the club. As she reached the end of the lane, a dark shadow emerged from behind the last dumpster.

"Hello there. Remember me?" The voice was familiar, but Samara couldn't see his face in the dark.

The situation brought back memories of her horrific encounter with Karl and his henchmen. She quickened her pace as she passed the man, ignoring his greeting. The main street was a few meters away, so close she could see pedestrians walking past the entry to the lane.

Samara's heart pounded in her chest and she could feel the panic rising up to engulf her. The man's heavy footsteps echoed on the pavement behind her.

"Hey, wait up," he called.

She escalated her steps from a power walk to a run. The man lunged and grabbed her arm, stopping her short. She screamed with what little air she had left in her lungs.

"Shut up. I'm not going to hurt you." He loosened his grip on her arm.

Samara could feel her chest heaving, hyperventilating. She looked up the street for a way out. A passerby had stopped at the entrance to the lane and was peering into the darkness.

"Are you alright, love?" a male voice called to her.

Her arm was released. She ran the few meters out of the lane into the safety of the well-lit main street. The area was full of Saturday night revelers.

She turned to face the man who had grabbed her. Samara recognized him in the light—Ricky. Karl's lackey.

His low-slung jeans made him look like a giant midget, and his greasy brown hair looked worse than last time she saw him, if that were possible. Large fake diamond earrings and a heavy gold chain around his neck reinforced the gangster look he was clearly trying to emulate.

"You good?" the pedestrian repeated.

Ricky held his palm out. "I'm not here to cause you any trouble. I just want to talk."

Samara squinted at him. What did the snake want with her? She took a moment to control herself and looked up at the kind pedestrian. "Thank you. I'll be okay."

He nodded then continued on his way. She turned to Ricky and stared him down. "What do you want?"

"I was in the club. I thought it was you up there, but you look so different I wasn't sure." Ricky had a sly smirk on his face. Samara wanted to slap it off.

"So now you've seen it's me, you can go." She turned on her heels and took a few steps down the street before he caught up.

"Oh, come on. Don't be like that. Not to an old friend like me." Ricky came to stand in front of her, blocking her path.

Samara darted to the right to get around him. Ricky was quick enough to preempt her. They danced back and forth for a few seconds, her making attempts to get around him, and he successfully stopping her.

"Look, Ricky, leave me alone. You were never a friend of mine and never will be. Go away." Samara's anger escalated.

"I was thinking that now you're a little more approachable we could get together. How much do you charge?" His large mouth tipped at each end in anticipation.

"I'm not a prostitute, so leave me alone." She regretted dismissing the stranger. Ricky didn't budge.

"Well, I'm sorry." His sarcastic tone suggested he was anything but. "I assumed Daddy's little girl must have fallen a little further from grace. Taking your clothes off is as low as you got, hey?"

Samara didn't know what she wanted more, to punch him, or cower like a wounded animal. Thankfully she was saved from making the decision by Rocco, who came out the main entrance to the club and saw her predicament.

He waddled over to them as fast as his huge form would allow. "Everything okay here, Shanny?" He stared down Ricky, who sat back on his heels.

Regardless of the issues she had with Rocco, Samara was relieved by his presence. She felt a power wash over her.

"He was just leaving" She turned to Ricky. "Weren't you?"

Ricky looked Rocco up and down. "Sure. I'll see you again very soon, Shaaaannnny." He smirked, then turned and left. She watched him get into a taxi before she turned to face Rocco.

"Thanks." She managed a small, noncommittal smile.

Rocco squinted. "He's not your boyfriend, is he?"

She shook her head. "Definitely not. He's just some guy I used to know."

Rocco leaned into her. His strong body odor filled her nostrils.

"Good, because I don't like competition." His bushy monobrow furrowed in the middle.

Samara turned her head and took a deep breath. No time like the present to set him right. At least she was in a public place.

She looked at her feet, not willing to meet his eyes. *Here goes.* "Rocco, while I think you are a lovely man, and a great catch. I'm not in an emotional state right now to have a relationship. I know I wouldn't make you happy." Sam peeked at him from under the veil of her fake eyelashes. Would he believe her?

He looked confused. "What are you saying?"

"Well. . ." She searched for a clearer definition. "I'm emotionally fragile right now and it's much better for me to concentrate on my own well-being." It was the truth. Even if it left out the fact she found Rocco repulsive and dangerous.

Rocco still looked confused.

"Huh?" He pulled a goofy face. Mel's character analysis might not have been too far off the mark. Solid bone from the jaw up.

Samara could see she needed to put it in the simplest terms. "I'm screwed up and would make a crappy girlfriend."

Rocco scratched his head before understanding registered on his face. "That's okay with me. I make a crappy boyfriend. So we should get along good."

What? This was not going to plan. Not that she had a plan to start with. Sheer frustration took over. "It's not going to happen, Rocco."

Rocco slowly transformed from dim-witted to scary. His face burned a bright red and he lunged towards her.

"So that's how it's going to be then. You think you're too good for me?" His voice was deep and low.

Samara recoiled under his gaze. "It's not like that Rocco. I don't think that."

"Yes you do. You're going to pay." He waved a pudgy finger at her. "You wait and see. I'm going to make you sorry you turned me down." He closed the gap between their faces, his eyes beaming undisguised rage.

Samara froze, but wanted to run. She broke from his glare and looked around, seeking relief in the number of passersby.

Rocco must have also remembered they were in a public arena, because he gave her back her space. He grunted, pulling up his enormous pants as he turned away and walked back into the club. He didn't look back as he went through the door.

Sam made her way down the street, looking behind every few meters to make sure she wasn't being followed.

CHAPTER 4

The clicking of the train on the tracks synchronized with the pounding in Sam's head. No matter how much she mulled over her predicament, there was no solution. Every possible plan of attack morphed into a dead end.

Samara rummaged through her massive bag, trying to find some headache tablets. She pulled out a huge wad of papers in an effort to recover the packet. A booklet dropped to the floor.

Sam picked it up and looked it over. *Where has this come from?* That's right. She'd got it yesterday, from a man who stood at the corner of one of the crossings she negotiated on her way to the club. He'd stand there, every Friday afternoon, holding out a little magazine, offering it free to passersby. She had ignored him for months. Yesterday, instead of looking down as she crossed the road, she looked ahead, straight at the man. His greying, three-day growth matched the salt and pepper smattering of color atop his scruffy unkempt head. His lanky body looked malnourished under the faded blue t-shirt, and his baggy cargo pants and thongs completed his homeless look. However, it wasn't his attire or physique that kept her gaze.

It was his eyes.

They were light grey and piercing. Sam had been convinced he saw right through her. The connection was so unexpected that she was drawn to him, accepting the magazine before averting her gaze and continuing on her way.

She had shoved the little book into her bag, and forgotten all about it. Now she opened the first page. It looked like some sort of religious devotional. Each day and date was listed, and a short paragraph was written under each. Sam rolled her eyes in disappointment and threw it back into her handbag.

Half an hour later, boredom drove her to the point of reopening the book. The current date was halfway through the first month. She read all the past days for that month. One made her hair stand on end.

The passage was about fear. It was like the words were jumping off the page and directly down her throat. It ended with a Bible verse: *God has not given us the spirit of fear, but of power, and of love, and of a sound mind.*

The announcement of her stop jerked her out of further contemplation. The train came to a halt and the doors slid open.

Her flat was a short walk up the hill and around the corner from the train stop. The shrill ring of a police siren sounded a short distance away. It wasn't the best neighborhood, and she took comfort in the police presence. It would ward off any potential threats for a while.

She was accustomed to commuting alone as she always finished work early in the morning, but no matter how many times she walked up this hill, fear gripped her.

A scuffling noise sounded behind her and she whipped around to see a black cat disappear into the shrub at the side of the road. She picked up her pace, speed walking to reach her flat as fast as she could.

The three flights of steps up to her door was the final leg of her journey. She stood for a second at the top level to catch her breath.

No wonder I'm so thin.

She looked up and found the front door to her flat wide open. The blackness made it impossible to see any potential threat inside.

Samara was conscious of being alone. She looked back down the stairs, then walked up to the open doorway, ensuring she was still close enough to the staircase to flee if needed.

Her heart beat so fast in her chest she thought it would burst right out. Goose bumps surfaced on her skin as the natural instinct to run kicked in. She could feel the adrenaline course through her body.

"Layla?" she called into the blackness. "Are you in there? Are you alright?"

Samara was rooted to the spot, petrified. She wasn't willing to venture further into the doorway, but was also frightened to take the staircase back down onto the dark street.

A scuffling noise came from inside, then an enormous thud followed by the high-octane smash of breaking glass.

She jumped to the doorway, reaching in to flip the light switch to illuminate the room and reveal the cause of the noise. The tiny living room was in disarray. A chair lay upturned and there was a spill on the carpet.

Samara looked past the mess to see Layla half-naked on the floor, pushing herself up by sheer determination. She stumbled back, landing on the upturned coffee table. Samara winced and ran to help.

Layla was using hard drugs. In the short time Samara had rented the spare room in Layla's flat, she'd seen the evidence of more than a few drug sessions. When she had moved in, Layla had been open about her use of party drugs, but this was hard core. Much worse than the party scene.

Sam sat on a chair next to her flatmate's bed and stared at her sleeping friend, noting the prominent injection marks jutting red on the inside of her arm. Layla's black hair was lackluster against the pillow, and her skin had the telling yellow tinge of ill health. She was more heavily-built than Samara—short and muscular, with a sporty frame. Sam had always been envious of Layla's incredible almond-shaped eyes that made her look mysterious, exotic. In recent weeks they had been low-lidded, the whites an unattractive red.

Sam got up and detailed the room. She opened draws as quietly as she could, and shuffled piles of Layla's clothing around as she searched for a hidden drug stash. Since she had started working on Jamal's 'special project' a month ago, Layla had lost all sense of self, and Samara rarely saw her. Her time as a nurse and months with Karl meant Samara had seen it before. Karl had exposed her to many in a similar state to Layla. Addiction was a vicious, destructive disease she vowed never to get involved in. Karl himself had occasionally used party drugs and, although he dealt in all drugs, he never used the hard stuff, and wouldn't let Samara anywhere near them. "I refuse to have a junkie for a girlfriend," he'd said. Sam knew drug use was a crutch she could have easily fallen into. Forgetting her problems and replacing her fear with a drug-induced euphoria had been an appealing proposition on numerous occasions.

But she had managed to avoid drugs, even living with Layla. Doing drugs was only going to add to her problems.

Sam sat back down as Layla stirred and opened her eyes. She hadn't overdosed—she was just on a particularly numbing trip. In any case, Samara had stayed by her bedside for the rest of the night to monitor her.

"Man. What a night." Layla sat up in bed and rubbed her face. "What happened?"

"I have no idea." Samara stretched as well as she could in the uncomfortable chair. "I came home to find you out of it."

Layla shook her head. "Jamal came around. He told me the stuff was pure. Boy! He wasn't kidding." She scanned the room as she spoke. The entire bedroom was a mess.

"If you think this is bad you should see the lounge." Sam raised her eyebrows at her flatmate.

"Ow." Layla rubbed her forehead with her hand for a long time, her eyelids heavy, the corners of her mouth drooping. She looked down at a spot on the blanket, then stared up at Sam. "Don't let yourself get like this, Shanny. I know I've been trying to get you to work for Jamal, but don't do it. I told myself I'd never become a junkie like my mother. Now here I am, whoring myself and sticking needles up my arm."

Layla fell back down on her pillows. "A year ago I had a good job working at a factory. It was hard, but decent work. I convinced myself it was a dead-end job. Now dead end is where I'm at." She turned to grab one of Samara's arms. "Don't be like me. Take a job in a supermarket if you have to. Hard work is better than chasing the dream of more money." She released her grip and frowned. "To be honest, I've never been able to understand what you're doing here in the first place. You're not like the rest of us. You have options. Why would you want to live like this?" She waved one hand in the air.

How did I get into such a hopeless situation? Her mother wasn't an addict who had abandoned her like Layla's had. She hadn't suffered the childhood hardships Kelsey had shared during their heart-to-hearts. What was her excuse for living the way she did?

She looked at Layla and knew the answer. Because things didn't turn out the way she had expected. Because she hadn't gotten what she wanted. So she had rebelled, taking every easy out that came her way. Now here she was, in the muck and mire, living every day consumed by fear.

A loud knock on the door drew her attention. Layla groaned and threw her arm over her eyes. "Go away," she yelled.

"Police. Open up." The male voice was loud and commanding.

Layla flew up in a panic. A flow of curse words fell from her mouth as she gave Samara a terrified look.

Sam felt panic rise up inside her. "Oh, no. Layla, you don't have any drugs in here do you?"

"I don't think so." Layla put her hands up to cup her face. "I mean, I can't imagine Jamal leaving any here."

Nor could Samara. There was no way he would leave anything extra for Layla.

The knock sounded again, with force this time. Samara startled at the thud. "Layla, what about pipes or needles or stolen prescription drugs?"

Layla's eyes were wide and darting from side to side as her drug-slowed brain tried to digest the situation. "I don't think so. Why do you think I let Jamal in? I was desperate for a hit. If we're really quiet, maybe they'll think no-one's home."

Samara gave her a withering look. "That's going to be a bit difficult for them to believe after the mouthful you just yelled at them."

Layla covered her face with her hands. "Great. The lockup is just what I needed today."

The knock sounded again, but a little quieter this time. Sam held her breath and racked her brain for an effective plan of attack.

"Samara, it's Delaney. I need a few words with you." This was a different voice, one she recognized.

Layla gave her a confused look. "Who's Samara? Maybe he has the wrong place."

Sam stood up and walked to the door. "You stay in here. If they see the state you're in, they'll do a sweep of the place. I'll try and get rid of them."

Layla nodded "No problem. I won't come out." She was clearly happy to delegate the situation. It meant Samara didn't have to explain her name change.

She closed the door to Layla's bedroom and picked her way over the mess in the lounge to reach the main door. She checked her appearance in the mirror on the wall next to the locks as the soft knock sounded again.

"One moment." She smoothed back the hair escaping from her pony tail. It still looked a little messy. The bags under her eyes were tinged with a shiny grey, but with no time to wash it would have to do.

She flipped the three locks securing the door and opened it up far enough for her face to be seen, but keeping the state of the lounge hidden from their view.

Two men stood at the door. One was a policeman, his blue and white attire stating his profession. He must have been the first to knock. The other man, who was standing in front of Samara, was Trevor Delaney, a drug squad detective who had questioned her regarding Karl's drug business. He had always treated her with kindness, regardless of her inability to provide them with any new information.

"Hi, Samara. Nice to see you again." Trevor peeked around the doorway. Sam liked the way Trevor's smile crinkled his eyes. He had rugged features, a chiseled jaw line and thick black hair. She guessed he was in his early forties. The crooked curve of his nose revealed it had been broken at some stage and his above-average height gave him a commanding presence.

"Hi, Trevor. Can we talk outside please?" She whispered, sure that Layla had her ear to the door of her bedroom.

"Sure." Trevor stood aside for her to squeeze her way out of the tiny opening and into the hall. The last thing she needed was to arouse suspicion.

She closed the door behind her and looked past Trevor to his uniformed counterpart.

"Don't mind Gary here. I didn't want to blow your cover so I had him knock first. When you didn't come to the door, I thought you may have been in trouble."

His concern was genuine, but Sam knew better than to think this was a call to check on her welfare. Trevor wasn't there for a social visit—he had an agenda. "I'm fine thanks. What can I do for you?"

"We've been told Ricky Tanner is looking for you. I wondered if he had tried to make contact." He lifted his eyebrows in question.

Samara frowned. This was too coincidental. Were they following her? Keeping her under some sort of surveillance?

She decided she had nothing to hide. "He cornered me outside the club last night. Thankfully, the bouncer was able to get rid of him. I haven't seen him since. I don't know how he knew where I was."

Trevor gave her the steely-eyed look he adopted when deciding whether she was telling him the truth or not.

She repositioned her weight and met his gaze. "I told him to get lost. I can't stand the sight of the worm."

He continued to eyeball her for a few more

seconds. What an insult. She'd always co-operated with them, even to her own detriment. How could Trevor now suspect she was lying?

He looked back to the uniformed cop. "Could you give us a few moments please?"

The man nodded and turned to walk down the stairs. The heavy main door thudded closed behind him.

Trevor turned back to her. "It's important that you tell me every detail of your run-in with Ricky, Samara. We know he was involved in the assault on you." His words were soft and slow.

Sam held her breath for a second, her heart rate escalating. She could feel the fear seeping through and engulfing her. The memory of that night was still vivid. "Are you sure it was him?"

"Cell phone records place him close to the scene minutes after. We're certain he was the main assailant. Unfortunately, there's no DNA evidence supporting our suspicions, so an arrest is premature at this time."

Samara closed her eyes, taking a moment to control her increasing anxiety. She'd had two days in hospital following the assault. She'd been told she had been fortunate not to have suffered more than deep bruising and several cracked ribs

There had been a lack of evidence linking known criminals to the attack. She had been unable to identify either of the two men due to the darkness of the night, and the fact that she was hit from behind.

Samara had been lucky, or so the police had told her again and again. They didn't have to live with the all-consuming fear plaguing her since then.

She opened her eyes to look at Trevor. "He didn't tell me anything. I swear. I got away from him as fast as I could."

Trevor gave her a thin smile. "I just wanted to warn you to be on your guard where he's concerned. He's worked hard to be Karl's number one dealer, and he's as slippery as a snake. Every time it looks as though we have something on him he escapes." Trevor breathed out hard. "Don't write him off as a fool, Sam. He's learned a few things since you saw him last."

She'd known Karl had assigned Ricky to another section of his organization. After vocalizing her intense dislike for the man, Karl had kept him away from her. Last night was the first time she had seen him since Kiisay Point. It sounded as though it wasn't the first time he had seen her.

Another thought occurred to Samara. It sent chills up her spine.

"Ricky's always had a . . ." She struggled with the explanation. "A crush on me. Should I be worried?"

"It is my opinion that you should be extremely cautious in your dealings with Ricky Tanner."

Samara couldn't believe her world could be turned upside down anymore. Her instinct was to run, to find the easiest way out. But run where? She had nowhere to go, and returning home would only put her family in danger.

Besides, how could she face her father? How could she tell him all that had happened to her? If she went back home, she'd be forced to fill him in on the situation in case the Sydney detectives needed her again for questioning.

Assuming a false identity was her way of protecting herself. She had received no help from authorities. She was not considered for any witness protection, as she had been unable to give them any incriminating evidence against Karl that could be used in court.

The soft touch on her arm drew her attention. Trevor looked down at her. Deep lines furrowed his forehead. "I never thought you would get yourself into so much trouble, Sam. Stripping is a dead end. You're better than that."

She swallowed hard and fought back the tears. "I'll be okay. I know I need to make some changes."

"Well, keep yourself safe. Stay in populated areas. Don't leave yourself vulnerable."

"I'll do my best."

Trevor gave her a genuine smile and made his way down the stairs. Samara watched as the main door shut behind him.

At least she could take some comfort in the fact that the police were keeping track of her. The only way for Trevor to know about her precarious profession was if they had been watching her. But knowing the police were monitoring her movements did little to comfort her fear. Fear consumed her, controlled her, and motivated her. Fear controlled her, but she was tired of living with fear.

CHAPTER 5

God has not given us the spirit of fear, but of power, and of love, and of a sound mind.

Sam read the verse over and over again. It jumped out of the page as clear as it had last night on the train.

The afternoon light flickered through her bedroom window. After Trevor had left, she and Layla had spent hours cleaning up the flat. She had then retreated to her room to read from the little book. It was time for her to be at the club. If she didn't leave soon, she would be late. The thought of suffering Jamal's rebuke for tardiness produced a sick feeling in her gut. Being late would bring her trouble, but she couldn't move. She read the passage one more time trying to dissect the feelings it evoked in her. It made her think, gave her hope, pierced her soul.

She reread the paragraph above the passage, feeling a strange stirring within. It revealed the dangers of taking the easy road in life. The road she had taken, time and time again.

Leaving her job in the hospital to go back to her father. At the time she had told herself she was in a desperate emotional state and needed reassurance. In reality it was a convenient way to escape the truth about her failed relationship.

Running away by moving in with Flynn, using him to gain the attention of the man who had left her, instead of searching and discovering the failings she had made in the relationship.

Jumping into the situation with Ricky and Karl, looking for an easy way out of her financial trouble, and leaving with Karl instead of facing up to her mistakes with Flynn and her father.

Modelling in next to nothing in a club instead of going back to Kiisay Point or finding the courage to start nursing again.

Her entire adult life had been one easy road after another. Each decision was a lie, motivated by fear taking her further than she had wanted to go. Each easy way out had led to no way out.

The reading finished with another Bible verse in the little book.

Jesus said, 'Make every effort to enter through the narrow door, because many, I tell you, will try to enter and will not be able to'.

It spoke so clearly to her that she reread it over and over. She knew what she wanted. She wanted to be free. Free of the fear, free to have the courage to own up to her mistakes. The police weren't going to help her get there. Maybe this book held some miracle that could.

There he was. Samara had almost given up hope of finding the lanky man among the throng of people.

The afternoon street markets were now dispersing, spilling a mass of people into the area, all clamoring for space on the footpath. The cramped conditions made it almost impossible to make out an individual amongst the pedestrians.

Sam stood on tiptoe, finally spotting her target. There he was. The man who had given her the little book.

The old blue T-shirt was obviously a favorite, because it was the only one she had seen him in. She was relieved to recognize it today. It was the best way to find him in the crowd.

Samara made her way to the man, rubbing shoulders with the occasional person in her path. The sidewalks would be packed for at least another thirty minutes, and if she waited for the crowd to subside, she'd lose her nerve.

As she got closer, he looked her way, recognition registering on his face. As his grey eyes met hers, Samara froze, the familiar feeling of fear washing over her. She fought it, pushing herself the final few meters separating them.

"Can I talk to you a moment?"

"Sure." His voice was deep and soft. She hadn't expected that. He gestured to an elevated doorway behind him.

They stood together on the step. At least it was a little less crowded a few feet above the throng.

"I was wondering if you could answer some questions I have?"

"No problem. Ask away." He gave her his full attention.

Samara didn't quite know where to start. She pulled out the book he had given her and turned to the verse about fear.

"I want to know how . . ." She paused for a moment to think. "How can I get what this says? Power, love, and a sound mind?" She thrust the book in his direction, pointing to the passage.

He read it before looking up. "Your answer's right here." He indicated the verse. "It is God who has not given us the spirit of fear. It is He who has given us power. He has given us love, and He has given us a sound mind."

His answer only confused her further.

"So how am I supposed to get that from God?" She hadn't meant the words to sound as sarcastic as they had come out. *God? Really?* The implausible nature of it all made her wonder what she was doing there.

The man didn't look offended. His eyes softened and he swayed into her a tiny bit.

"By trusting in Him. By letting Him lead you. By allowing Him into your life, into your heart, giving the fear over to Him," he said. "Jesus promises to carry our burdens for us, if we let Him."

How wonderful it would be to give all the fear over to someone else to deal with. To be free of it. "I would love to do that, but God? Really?" She frowned and took a sharp breath.

"Have you got a moment?" He opened the door and stood aside for her to enter.

"Sure. Why not?" What would it hurt to hear what he had to say?

The door was an entry way to a moderately sized hall. It was filled with trestle tables and plastic chairs all lined up in rows. Several people milled around, organizing the room. Beyond the chairs, an array of old bain-marie's sat in front of an outdated kitchen. The place was shabby but clean.

"Sorry about the mess. I'm Nick." He extended a

hand.

"Samara." The second it was out of her mouth she realized she had given her real name. The error threw her introduction off and she pulled out of the handshake far too soon.

Nick smiled and gestured to the haphazard furniture. "We can feed up to a thousand homeless here each day. He led her to a little door next to a large kitchen where a gaggle of men and women were busy preparing food. "My office." He pointed to the door.

Samara felt a flash of trepidation. Was it smart to enter into the sanctum of someone she didn't know?

Nick picked up on her concern and turned to gesture towards the nearest trestle table. "Perhaps we can sit out here. If you don't mind the noise?"

"I don't mind." Samara took the chair he offered.

She spent over an hour with Nick. He started by giving her his life story which included his descent into drugs, reaching his self-proclaimed rock bottom, and ending up in hospital after an altercation with another homeless heroin addict over who scored the last hit.

He outlined his hospital stay and the impact the chaplain had had on him. The man was the acting chaplain at the hospital, a Vietnam veteran who had seen the worst crimes humanity had to offer. His life was a testimony to Nick, who wanted nothing more than to emulate the man. Nick decided to ask Jesus into his life.

"It wasn't easy. All my troubles and addiction didn't disappear overnight. But now I didn't have to do it on my own. I didn't have to draw on my own strength. I had the strength God gave me." Nick stopped to lean back in his chair. "I also had direction. I had always felt like I was just existing, not heading anywhere. Concentrating on my relationship with God brought everything into place. I don't know how it happened, but it did. I decided to trust God knew better than me."

How wonderful, how relieving it would be to know which direction to head in. Samara didn't know what to do. The few self-professed Christians she had known were people who had worked with her stepfather. They had belonged to an exclusive church group, powerful and influential within the community. Her stepfather had attempted to infiltrate the group to his own business advantage. They had rejected him because he wasn't one of them. He wasn't good enough.

If the faith had rejected him . . .

"I don't know how I feel about God. I guess I've always thought a higher being was pretty improbable. Evolution makes more sense to me."

He nodded. "Evolution is an argument that can go on and on. But I guess that's why it's still classed as a theory and not a fact. Fact is fact. Theory is an idea to be argued. The Bible says faith is believing in what we don't see. I think it's beyond theory or fact or human reason. It's about trust, decision, and most of all, relationship."

Sam could feel her frown deepen. "Alright, say God does exist—I'm not the best person in the world. I've done some stupid things. I can't imagine God would want any part of my mess."

To her horror, he laughed.

"Jesus doesn't love you for your good deeds or social standing. He sees through it all to what's in your heart. The New Testament tells us He associated with tax collectors, money lenders, and prostitutes. Some of His best friends were humble fisherman. You don't need to be a high achiever to have Him hear you. You certainly don't have to be good. In fact, nobody can be that." Nick looked at her, the intense grey of his eyes making Samara's head swim. "Asking Jesus into your life isn't about do-gooding, or church going, or even trying to fit in to some religious belief. It's about a personal relationship. He wants us to know Him like He knows us. He wants us to lean on Him, and allow Him to love us. He wants us to be free of all the stuff that keeps us from Him. And He wants us to come to Him just as we are."

It sounded too easy. Did God really want to be her friend? Sam wriggled in her chair, feeling the nervous tension of her confusion. She had always thought the theory of evolution made more sense than a creator sitting on clouds playing his harp.

She stood up. "Thanks for talking to me, Nick. But I need some time to think about it all." She retrieved her bag from its place on the back of the chair.

Nick rose to meet her. "Do you have a place to go?"

"Yes, yes… I'll be fine." Sam attempted to reassure him, but her faltering voice gave her away.

Nick saw her to the door. "I have to tell you, I'm worried. Are you sure you have somewhere to go? Somewhere safe? There are some rooms at the back.

You could stay in one a while."

Samara looked back into the hall. She considered the offer for a second.

"No. Don't worry. I'm okay." She stepped out the door. "Thanks again." She took the few steps down to the street and made her way along the uneven footpath.

"I'm here if you need me," he called.

Samara turned to give him a wave. She liked this man with the rough exterior and soft manner.

The sun had long gone down, and the pedestrian traffic had dissipated as Samara dragged herself towards the club. She searched her thoughts. What was stopping her from allowing Jesus into her life like Nick had? She knew the answer: fear. Fear she wasn't good enough. Fear she was trying to rise above her station. Fear she wouldn't be accepted by others. Fear she wasn't going to be any good at believing in God.

The irony stopped her short. The problem she needed help with was the very thing stopping her from accepting the solution.

Sam shook her head. She couldn't live another day like this. It was too much. Continuing to work at the club now was taking the easy way out.

Again. She had to make some changes to who she was.

And it had to be now.

She stopped and sighed as she neared the club, its flashing red lights symbolizing the industry, the clientele. She could make out Rocco's massive bulk framing the doorway. He looked as imposing as a rock. The all-too-familiar butterflies fluttered in the pit of her stomach. She couldn't face another night here.

She ducked into the alleyway beside the club and stood next to the industrial bin. It was the same place Ricky had grabbed her the previous night.

She pushed the memory aside and closed her eyes and whispered.

"God, Jesus, whoever you are. I'm not going to pretend I don't have doubts that you exist, because I do. I even feel like maybe I'm just talking to myself, but I've decided to believe in you, because I think nobody but you can help me. I don't want to be afraid or alone any more."

She opened her eyes for a brief moment, then closed them again.

"I know I've done wrong. Please help me."

The words felt as though they had come from the depths of her soul. The pain of them brought tears to her eyes and a ball of pure anguish formed in her throat.

"I don't want to live like this any more."

Her eyes overflowed and hot, wet trails formed down her cheeks.

"Please give me the life you have for me. Please set me free from this fear."

Samara took several deep breaths. She squeezed her eyes tight and swallowed hard. It was some time before she felt under control. She didn't feel any different from before. Every one of her fears were still there, under the surface. But then Nick had told her his problems didn't disappear in a blink of an eye. She recalled one thing he had said about his own decision to follow Jesus—that faith was a decision to trust what God said was true.

She decided to enter the club, say a quick goodbye to the girls, and collect her things. She had no idea what the future held for her, but she had to leave the life she was leading. Even though she had no idea where she was heading.

The techno beat was deafening. Even in the back rooms the walls of the club were shaking with the stress of the beat. Samara made her way along the narrow corridor and into the safety of the dressing room.

Kelsey and Mel both looked up as she entered.

"Oh girl, where have you been?" Mel was the first to address her. "You're in deep trouble. Jamal's been in, and he's fuming."

Mel was sitting at her table, meticulously applying her makeup. Samara couldn't help but notice her huge bosom struggling to break free from the constraints of the tiny halter top she was wearing. As she swung around to look at Samara one of her breasts partly spilled out of its constraint. A ripping noise indicated her problem. Mel looked horrified as she scrambled to right the wardrobe malfunction.

"Mel, I've told you time and time again you can no longer wear size eight tops." Kelsey shook her head and rolled her eyes. "Your boobs are too big to fit into anything less than a size twelve."

Samara grabbed an empty plastic bag and began collecting her things.

"But the larger sizes are baggy in the back," Mel complained.

"Well, get some tops made that fit." Kelsey offered the perfect solution before looking Samara's way. "What are you doing?"

"I'm leaving." She took a break from her task to turn and address the two women. "I can't do this anymore. You're right, it's not me."

"About time you woke up." Mel smiled at her. "Mind you, you could have done it sooner. My bet was on you not lasting one week. Your month-long stint lost me fifty bucks."

Samara was shocked. The girls had bet on how long she would last. "What did you bet?" she asked Kelsey.

The older lady smiled before answering. "Two weeks. You proved us all wrong."

Sam felt no pride at outlasting their expectations. She should never have been here in the first place.

"Hey, if you're ever looking to sell your designer bag, you know where to find me." Mel continued fixing her costume.

Samara looked down at the expensive handbag. She had allowed all the pretty things she had to define her for long enough. What a farce it felt to carry a two thousand dollar handbag when she flashed her flesh for a living. She had to let go of the idea that the things she had made her who she was.

She emptied the contents of the bag into the plastic one and handed the designer bag to Mel. "Here, have it. Consider it a parting gift."

"Are you sure?" To Mel's credit she offered the bag back to Samara.

"Positive."

"Awesome."

Kelsey stood up from her dressing table. "If I were you, I'd leave before Jamal discovers you're here. He probably already knows. He had a new security camera installed inside the door this morning."

The outdoor security camera in the alley had been broken for months. Kelsey had voiced her disgust at the security breach, as it was primarily the models who were forced to use the exit. Jamal had conceded to installing a new device inside the door, but not fixing the outside one. Kelsey had been horrified. The new security had nothing to do with protecting the models in the dark alleyway, and everything to do with keeping tabs on who came and went from the club.

Sam's heart skipped a beat. "Does that mean Rocco will also know I'm here?"

"He'll know alright. He's been watching out for you. What on earth did you say to him? I told you to let him down easy."

"I thought I did." She bit her bottom lip. "He misinterpreted every word I said. In the end I had to give it to him straight." Samara felt her stomach flip at the thought of seeing Rocco again.

"That man is an absolute moron," Mel said.

"Moron or not, he's dangerous." Kelsey crossed the small space between them and gave her a strong hug. "Get going. I'll give Jamal some vague excuse about your family needing you or something. I'll appeal to his better nature." Kelsey rolled her eyes. Jamal had no better nature.

"Thanks Kelsey." She gave her friend one last cuddle.

"See ya, kiddo. Thanks for the pretties." Mel raised her bag in salute.

Samara gave the girls one last smile and slipped out of the room.

The corridor was empty, so she made her way out the door without looking in the direction of the security camera. She opened the door into the alley, which was darker than usual. The outside light had been shattered, and there was another large industrial bin placed on the opposite side to the club, blocking any illumination from the main road. Shards of glass glistened on the concrete as the light from the hallway spilled out into the alley.

Samara weighed up her options. She couldn't use the main exit—Rocco was placed there for the night. There was no way she wanted another run-in with him. Besides, Jamal would get nasty once he knew she was leaving. Rocco would be more than happy to carry out any of his boss's orders when it came to her.

There was no choice. She stepped out onto the concrete and walked with purpose, taking large steps. She heard a clacking noise, and looked down to see her plastic supermarket bag had a hole in the bottom, and her cell phone had fallen out.

"Stupid bag." She bent down to search the ground around her. A tiny beam of light drew her attention. The phone had landed under the first industrial bin.

Samara crouched down, groping under the bin for the phone. Her hand touched it just as a huge force from behind her sent her falling to her knees. She fell hard on all fours against the concrete pavement.

Sam struggled, trying to stand, as an arm

gripped her around the waist. She managed to scream as the weight of the person behind her forced her from her knees to the ground. Pain ripped through her body as she hit the concrete. Her arms were held fast behind her back, and she was pushed to the ground, face first.

The stone chill of the cement pressed against her cheek. Before she could scream again her mouth was stuffed with cloth preventing everything but a muffled "hmmm" from escaping. She tried to kick against the weight holding her down, but to no avail.

Her attacker was too strong.

All she could do was twist and squirm.

A big hand, a hand that had to belong to a man, held her face to the ground, then released her for a second. She cranked her neck back around as far as she could. Her efforts were in vain. She was in a vice grip and unable to move more than a fraction. She could feel the free hand secure hers around her back with some kind of clip. The zipping noise of the mechanism struck fear into her as she struggled in vain against the pressure of the person holding her down.

With her hands secure, the attacker turned again to her face. In one swift movement Samara felt material against her cheeks, then the blackness of a mask covering her eyes and tied at the back of her head.

It had been only seconds, but it seemed like everything was happening in slow motion, almost as though it was happening to someone else, as though she was outside her body, looking down on the event. The shock that had first engulfed her into unconscious submission was now replaced with a very conscious fear.

Is this really happening to me?

She had to do something.

Sam felt herself being turned over. The blackness of the mask made her disorientated and she had to concentrate. A heavy pressure pushed on her stomach, hips and legs, and then a ripping noise sounded, followed by the coldness of the night on her chest.

She closed her eyes. *Dear God. Help. Help. Help.*

Her silent cry echoed in her head as she fought her assailant with all her might, wriggling as much as the constraints allowed. Her chance came as he moved forward, releasing the pressure holding her legs down.

She thrust her knee upwards, feeling it connect with the person on top of her. Her assailant let out a grunt, and a sharp pain flashed across her chest. She blew hard against the gag in her mouth in an effort to scream.

Help me, Jesus. Help. She silently pleaded as her attacker paused.

An unexpected voice sounded out of nowhere.

Be still.

The quiet, serene tone was strangely comforting. But where was it coming from?

Be still.

It was as though the world had stopped and there was nothing but the voice. It commanded her absolute attention. Sam obeyed and stopped struggling, lying as still as a corpse on the cold concrete.

Then she felt it. A feeling like nothing she had ever experienced in her life. Peace, pure peace. Like nothing could touch her. Like nothing would ever touch her again.

She was vaguely aware of the human presence still above her. The assault hadn't resumed and she lay perfectly still, basking in this unexplained feeling within her.

She was broken from her trance by a noise coming from behind her. A loud male voice was yelling from the street. The pressure suddenly released from her body. Seconds later, the beat of rapid footsteps sounded in her ears.

The face was familiar, but Samara had difficulty placing it. She blinked her eyes again and again, trying to focus. The lights inside the ambulance flickered as the vehicle hit the rough patches of road. She could hear the siren's wail.

"Don't worry. You're alright." The voice was smooth and calming, like the voice-over in television commercials. It helped Samara to place the man who held her hand.

"Nick."

"Don't try to talk. You've lost a lot of blood."

She closed her eyes and gave in to the fuzzy feeling in her head.

CHAPTER 6

The mid-morning light seeped through the blinds covering the hospital windows. The entrancing patterns flickered bright on the white walls of the room.

It had been less than twelve hours since the attack outside the club. Amazingly, the only injury she had suffered was a cut which started below her right collarbone and ran in a straight diagonal line across her chest to end on her left breast. The hospital staff had downplayed the injury, telling her it was a nasty cut but not life threatening now they had the bleeding under control. Samara had examined it when they had changed the dressing. It was shallow at the top, but became deeper on her breast. The deepest section had required a row of stitches to pull the tissue back together. The doctors were correct — it was well taken care of, but there was some nerve damage that would take time to heal. Samara knew it would be years before the scar faded.

She had suffered a considerable loss of blood due to the cut and the specialist had explained the consequences. The cut, along with shock, had forced her body into semi-consciousness and she had to be given a blood transfusion when she had arrived at the hospital. In spite of this, her progress had been positive.

The medical staff had informed her that the

police had arrived earlier to take her statement, but had been sent away. They would be back to question her when her doctor was confident she could handle the visit.

Samara searched her memory for any and every aspect of the incident, but it was a blur. The one thing she recalled was the voice and peace that enveloped her the moment she stopped fighting and started trusting the voice who told her to be still.

A soft knock sounded at the door.

"Come in."

It inched open and Nick peered around the doorway. His broad smile warmed her and she returned it with enthusiasm.

Nick had spent hours by her bedside during the night. Each time she had stirred he had been there. He had left an hour ago to get some breakfast at the hospital canteen.

He moved in to sit beside her, taking the seat next to her bed.

Samara noticed he looked a little worse for wear. His eyes were bloodshot and heavy grey rings sat underneath them. He was in need of a shave.

"I brought you a treat." He slid a chocolate bar onto her table.

"Thank you so much. I missed breakfast." She didn't hesitate, but picked the bar up, tore open the wrapper and took a huge bite.

She looked over at Nick as she chewed and marveled at how a man who barely knew her would stay by her side, sacrificing his sleep to ensure she wasn't alone. She had insisted he was free to leave, but he had stayed and comforted her. Samara was glad. There had been moments through the night where she had been distraught. Nick's calming presence had eased her distress.

She hadn't yet broached the subject of the attack with him. It had been too fresh through the night, but now she felt calm enough to discuss it. She swallowed a mouthful of chocolate.

"Nick, can you tell me anything about the attack? What did you see? I want to know."

He leaned into her. "I didn't have a good feeling after you left, so I decided to track you down. I assumed you were working at one of the clubs, so I walked the streets hoping I would run into you. I'd been looking for about ten minutes when there was a commotion from the street ahead of me. I went to investigate, and you were being wheeled out on a stretcher. I convinced them to let me ride along with you." Nick paused to shake his head. "You were pretty bloody. The ambulance man told me you were lucky."

She decided to share her most vivid memory of the attack with Nick. Her cry to God for His help, the voice, what the voice said, the feeling it evoked in her. At the end of the telling it all sounded so incredible Samara expected Nick to laugh at her. Instead he smiled and looked around the room. He opened the top drawer in the cabinet next to her bed and reached in, pulling out a Bible. He flipped through the pages, occasionally pausing.

Finally, Nick read aloud. "Be still, and know that I am God."

He handed the Bible to her, and Samara stared at the passage. "Be still." The words from her attack.

The same feeling of peace washed over her. It was the strangest, weirdest, most awesome feeling she had every experienced.

"This is it." She looked up at him. "This is what I heard."

Nick smiled. "Sometimes, when we ask for His help, God doesn't answer us quite how we expect Him to. But He always answers us, and it always works for our good. How He knows exactly what we need is a miracle."

Sam couldn't believe it. Nick was right. She had asked for peace and help and He had given it to her. "So He is real?" There was part of her that yelled, *of course He is*, and another part that said, *seriously? Isn't this just co-incidence*? Her feelings said a resounding yes, but her reasoning produced a resounding no.

"This is no coincidence." She answered her own question aloud. "I had only decided minutes before the attack that the Jesus you spoke of, and the God they talked about in the devotional book, would have a better plan than I did. I asked Him to give me peace and then help." She shook her head. "But this is certainly not how I would have expected God to be. I mean, surely He could have just flashed lightening from heaven?" She looked back at Nick. His head was cocked to one side.

"I get it! He gave me exactly what I asked for — peace. And He saved me in the process." She nodded at the realization. A second flash of revelation pulsed through her body. "God is real! I really do believe. How else could this have happened? It's so weird. But it's kinda perfect."

Nick took her hand and gave it a squeeze. "It's

pretty wild, hey? One of the first Bible verses that tripped me out said, 'For I know the plans I have for you, declares the Lord, plans to prosper you and not to harm you, plans to give you hope and a future. Then you will call upon me and come and pray to me, and I will listen to you. You will seek me and find me when you seek me with all your heart. I will be found by you.'" Nick smiled. "That's in Jeremiah. It's the verse that changed my life, because I decided to believe it was true. God did want good things for me. He did have a plan. I also realized faith is a decision, not a lightning bolt from heaven."

Sam had to giggle at his reference. God wasn't all about the lightning bolts. She thought about her revelation about peace. True peace is unexplainable stillness in her, in spite of the storm around her. God's words had changed her. Maybe they were more powerful than lightning bolts. Written words that miraculously spoke to her heart. Words that changed lives.

She couldn't explain it, but she knew He existed. And she didn't have to run away from her problems any more. She didn't have to live in fear. She had someone watching over her. "God is real! He's just not who I thought He was. Maybe He just is who He is, and I haven't taken the time to get to know Him."

Nick nodded slowly, then took the Bible and flipped through the pages. "People think this book is about religion, but it's not. It's about life, relationship. Each one of us, individually. If we open our hearts before we open this book, God can reveal some amazing things to us." He turned it back for her to view the page he had settled on. "But if we don't open our hearts, if we don't ask or expect to be shown what we need, it's just words we don't understand." He handed it to her. The top of the page had the title: Matthew.

Samara looked at the hospital room clock. "I can't believe the day's almost over."

Nick swiveled in his chair beside her hospital bed to check the clock on the wall behind him. "Four-thirty! Whoa." He got to his feet. "I need to get back to the shelter. The dinner rush is about to start."

Sam adjusted her position in her bed. "Thank you for listening to me ramble on all day." A queasy feeling surfaced over the way she had spilled her history, warts and all.

Nick touched her arm. "It was a pleasure. Anytime you want to talk, I'm here." He turned to leave as a nurse entered with the specialist.

Dr. Evans had seen to her injuries last night, and had already visited her that day.

"I'll come back tomorrow." Nick gave her a wide smile and nodded to the others before he left.

"How are we doing?" Dr. Evans lifted her chart from the bottom of the bed as the nurse went about her business.

Samara had to admit there had been times through the day she had wished she was the nurse rather than being the patient. For the first time since leaving nursing, she recognized a yearning to return. It was where she was meant to be.

"Didn't I see you a few hours ago?" She gave the specialist a grin.

Dr. Evans chuckled and raised his bushy eyebrows. "Well, that comment answers my question. Nobody that cheeky could be deteriorating."

"I'm feeling great." Sam answered seriously this time.

Dr. Evans replaced the chart and gave her his full attention. "The police want to come in to question you. I would prefer for them to wait until tomorrow morning. However, the detective has assured me you and he are acquainted and he won't put you under any undue stress. His name is Trevor Delaney." Dr. Evans looked for her reply.

"I know him." Samara bit her lip.

Dr. Evans removed the stethoscope from around his neck. "I'm happy for him to see you considering you know each other, and he will be mindful you have experienced a traumatic event. Are you okay with that?"

Samara didn't hesitate. "Sure. I'm happy to see him."

Dr. Evans pointed to the buzzer at the end of her bed. "Keep the call button in your hand if it gets too much. I'll tell the nurse to keep an eye on the switch, and someone will be by your side in seconds."

Samara smiled in appreciation.

He walked out the door and, almost immediately, Trevor Delaney entered the room.

Samara was happy to see his familiar face, even if he was a cop. She gave him the biggest smile she could. "Guess I didn't keep myself out of trouble, hey?"

"No, you didn't. It's a shame it had to come to

this, Samara. I wish you'd looked after yourself a bit better." His expression was kind, but his tone was chastising.

Samara fiddled with the bed sheet. She deserved the reprimand. "I intend to do better from now on."

Trevor took a seat next to her bed. "I hope so."

Trevor's interest in her could have been interpreted as a romantic interest, but she knew better. Trevor was a professional. He had softened towards her when he found out she was a cop's daughter. Somewhere along the path of their relationship he had developed a fatherly fondness for her that clearly drove his concern for her well-being.

"I need to ask you a few questions." He turned to the business end of his visit.

"I don't remember much." Sam shifted up in bed.

He pulled out a notepad and pen. "Just tell me every detail. Start when I left you that morning. I need to know everything. Even if it seems insignificant to you."

Samara told how she spent her day, about Rocco, the visit to the shelter, her decision to leave the club for good. She stumbled around the struggle she had with her emotions, not wanting to reveal the fear that had consumed her. She remembered the broken light, the dark alley, and the second industrial bin, recalled the pressure, having her hands tied, being gagged, the blackness of the eye mask.

He paused from his scribbling. "It's lucky you remember as much as you do. Sometimes when a victim suffers unconsciousness, they can't recall any details of the event."

"Do you know what happened? Who attacked me?"

"We don't know for sure. A street police officer saw figures moving in the alley. When he shone a torch down the street, he could see a large figure sitting on someone. He yelled out, but by the time he got down to you whoever it was had gone." Deep lines furrowed his brow. "The security camera outside the club was broken, our man didn't see the attacker's face, we didn't find the weapon, and questioning in the area came up blank." He glanced down at the heavy dressings on her chest. "Going by the smoothness of the cut, the weapon was sharp."

Samara recalled the pain of the blade as it pierced her skin. The recollection prodded her memory. "I kicked him. Hard. I think it must have been in the groin. The cut came after."

Trevor's eyebrows rose. "That explains a lot. The general consensus is that the cut wasn't planned. It was randomly placed." His bottom lip jutted out over the top one. "Your kick may have unbalanced him in some way, or he may have just lashed out in anger."

Samara rubbed her hand along the dressing covering the cut.

"The doctors assure me you weren't sexually assaulted, although we're fairly certain rape was part of the intention. Your clothes were ripped."

Sam breathed a huge sigh of relief. She was sure she hadn't been abused in that way, but it was good to have it confirmed.

"I have to admit, the fact you escaped rape was a miracle in itself. Our man on the scene told us your attacker was sitting on top of you, stone still. It's strange. Do you remember anything concerning that?"

Samara nodded. "I froze."

"Froze?" Trevor screwed up his face.

"After he cut me, I froze and stopped fighting."

Trevor shrugged his shoulders. "It must have put him off or confused him. The struggle is often part of the reason why these attacks occur."

Samara considered telling Trevor about the voice, but instinct told her he wouldn't understand.

"So what happens next?"

He put the notepad and pen back in his pocket. "We'll continue our investigation. Pursue leads. Other than that, hope you regain further memories of the assault."

The thought of being sent back into the world again was daunting, except now she didn't feel alone or unprotected.

Trevor stood up. "I'll try to visit again before you leave the hospital. Do you have any plans when they discharge you?"

"I want to go back into nursing. I suppose I'll look into the prospect of a job in a hospital." Although she knew what she had to do, she hadn't given much thought to the how.

"Ever think about going back home?"

She considered the question before answering. Was she ready to face her father and the problems she left behind? "Eventually. Just not right now." She wasn't strong enough yet.

"Well, give it some more thought." Trevor said his goodbyes and left the room.

Samara let her head sink back onto the pillow. The pain killers were wearing off and she could feel the deep cut throbbing.

She squeezed her eyes tight. How was she going to live? Where was she going to go? She couldn't go back to living with Layla.

She reached for the Bible again. *Please show me what to do.*

Nick had marked some verses about fear and she opened to one of these. *Be strong and courageous. Do not be afraid or terrified because of them, for the Lord your God goes with you; he will never leave you nor forsake you.*

She sat back and enjoyed the peace the words evoked, knowing she wasn't alone.

CHAPTER 7

Nine Months Later

Samara slumped into the chair behind her desk. It had been a busy day. Several minor incidents had escalated into emergencies, combined with the routine minor complaints—cuts to stitch, an eye to wash out, and a full-on drug overdose. Of all the patients she'd seen, the drug overdose was the routine emergency in her clinic.

Nick entered the small office and took the seat across from her. "Hard day?" His heavy eyelids and slumped posture revealed he was every bit as exhausted as she was.

"Put it this way—in the nine months I've been here, I've never seen a day like this." She smiled and kicked her shoes off.

There was little room in her office, which formed a part of a tiny clinic adjacent to the shelter. The clinic was a new venture seeking to take the pressure off the local hospital emergency ward. The homeless who frequented the area were in desperate need of medical care. The clinic couldn't offer any substantial treatments, but had become the first point of contact for many of the homeless.

Nick stretched out his lanky legs. "Well, it's good to see you're still smiling."

Sam laughed. "Watch out. I might ask for a pay rise." She gave a cheeky wink.

Nick had made the employment proposal the day before her release from hospital. He needed a temporary nurse who would work for accommodation, meals, and a reduced wage. Samara had jumped at the opportunity. It was perfect for her.

Nick shook his head and screwed up his features in mock horror. "What? The luxurious living quarters aren't enough for you?"

Sam couldn't help the giggle. The accommodation consisted of nothing more than a tiny bedroom, a shared bathroom, and the shelter's communal areas. Since she arrived, her bedroom had been a private escape where she had spent her spare time reading the Bible the hospital staff had gifted to her upon her discharge. She had also spent many months in therapy. The time had truly been an all-encompassing mental, emotional, spiritual, and physical rehabilitation for her.

"Hey, you're the saint here — not me." Sam gave him her best smile.

Nick had long ago been dubbed St Nick by the residents and homeless frequenting the charity. He deserved the affectionate accolade, but he wasn't at all impressed with the status. Sam had come to realize Nick was always the first to declare his faults and assure her of his struggles. He also led a well-attended Sunday morning service at the shelter. Everyone was made to feel welcome, including addicts, the homeless, prostitutes and ex-criminals.

He picked a paperweight rock off her small desk. "You know I'm no saint." He juggled the rock between his hands. "I know the days are hard, but the rewards are there . . ." He placed the rock back down. ". . . even if they do take time."

Samara nodded. Nick never preached fire and brimstone, but love, grace, and forgiveness. He welcomed everyone as they were, and often told her that getting them through the door provided an opportunity to love them. Some days it felt like they made a difference, while others were a struggle. But Sam knew she was where she needed to be. It was a great feeling to work at what she loved, in a place she knew was making a difference.

Nick sat leaning back on the aged office chair. It creaked as he placed his feet up on the desk. "You looked a bit frustrated when I called in to check how our new doctor was doing."

Sam rolled her eyes. Dr. Vega was a new volunteer who had recently replaced one of their retiring doctors. "I have no idea why he's here. He's a pompous, arrogant snob." She felt a pang of guilt and regretted the uncharitable judgment—after all, he was donating his time and expertise to what some would class as the dregs of society. "He's just so unpleasant. And weird." She screwed her face up and cringed.

Nick laughed. "I suspect he may be all that, but look on the bright side. He's free."

Samara shrugged. Dr. Vega was a small, balding, unattractive man in his late fifties. Today was the second time he had volunteered at the clinic. In his dealings with the patients he had been rude, obnoxious, and even discriminatory. Samara wondered why he was there. It was obvious to her, and to the patients, that he had no serious interest in them.

"And he gives me the yuckies. He asks me a lot of personal questions, and I catch him staring at me all the time. I can't shake the feeling I've seen him before, but I can't place where." The concern had plagued her all day.

Nick frowned. "I know. I get a bad feeling about him too. We need to ditch him. Every now and then we get a doctor who thinks working at a homeless shelter will boost their profile. Self-professed do-gooders. I've been told Vega is seeking promotion. Perhaps he's trying to impress the powers-that-be. He only signed up for one shift a fortnight, so I'll lobby for a replacement."

Samara breathed a sigh of relief. The rotund Dr. Vega had been the only downside to working at the clinic. Every other doctor had a genuine interest in serving the community, and Sam was impressed with the quality of care they provided.

Nick picked up a pen and twirled it in his fingers. "I had a call from Trevor Delaney today. He wanted to know how you were doing."

Samara sat up. Trevor had had gone above and beyond the call of duty, sending around a female policewoman to collect her belongings from the flat before Layla pawned them. They still hadn't caught her attacker. It could have been any number of people. Rocco, Ricky, Karl. None of them had firm alibis. The police also couldn't rule out her attacker acting on any one of these men's behalf.

In any case, regardless of the fact that she was surrounded by law-breaking individuals at the shelter, Samara had never felt safer and happier. Even so, it was comforting that Trevor was keeping a close eye on her,

"What did he say?" Sam kicked at one of her shoes under the desk.

"Reading between the lines, I think his purpose was to let me know you hadn't spoken to your family in a while. I got the strong impression he was prompting me to pressure you into contacting one of them." Nick crossed his legs at the ankles and rubbed the stubble on his chin as he spoke.

Samara frowned. Perhaps it was time to make contact again. During her time in Sydney, she had consistently let them know she was safe. She had had a brief conversation with her father after her attack, and had assured him she was safe and happy, but she had cut short any explanations as to why she had left Kiisay Point with Karl. It was too much to deal with after the attack. She also made a point of calling her brother, Mitch, every few months.

In the beginning, Mitch would do his best to convince her to call her father and come back home. Samara hadn't wanted to hear what her father had to say, so she had strategically called during the day and left messages rather than speak to him. It was another way she had managed to avoid facing up to her mistakes. Her last call had felt so wrong she'd stumbled over her words. The message must have sounded like a jumbled mess.

She sighed. "Maybe it is time to sort it all out and make peace with Dad."

Nick had been a great counsellor. She felt as though she had gained a sense of who she was again. But it was a healing process she knew wouldn't be complete until she returned to Kiisay Point.

"Did you ever hear back from Flynn?" Nick asked.

Samara shook her head. She didn't have the courage to tell Nick that she hadn't included her return address on the envelope. She had sold all her expensive designer clothes and accessories not long after she arrived at the shelter, and mailed the proceeds to Flynn. Some of the accessories had fetched a much higher price than Samara had anticipated. It was a wonderful feeling to be able to give Flynn back the cash she had stolen, along with a considerable amount of interest. She had also included a letter of apology. It had taken her ages to write the letter. She had a bin full of discarded drafts before she decided that honesty was the best policy.

In the end, she had written one draft of the letter and hadn't read it back before sealing it in an envelope. She knew if she read it, she'd either change it or not send it at all. Now she hoped her genuine regret had shone through.

Nick sat up and moved his legs back off the desk. The movement startled Samara out of her daydream.

"I had a call from Ronnie today." Nick had spoken many times about the nurse who had cared for him in the rehab facility when he was an addict. Ronnie had been instrumental in his recovery as well as a friend who had strengthened his faith. "They're finally able to replace her at the facility. She'll be free to work here permanently."

Nick gave her a smile. "I'm not pushing you out, Sam. Both Ronnie and I would like you to stay on for as long as you need to. We can juggle both of you for a while, but ultimately I don't need two nurses, and

I've always felt you would move on when you were ready. It's been a healing process and time you've needed, and we've needed you, but perhaps it's coming to an end?" Nick's piercing eyes were convincing. "We'll miss you."

Sam sighed. So much was ahead of her.

The phone rang for so long Samara was ready to hit the disconnect button. Thankfully a distinct, "Hello," sounded before she did.

"Mitch?"

"Sammy, is that you?" A sudden pang of sadness hit her at hearing her childhood nickname. Only two people ever called her Sammy. Samara was certain her brother had no idea his endearment brought back painful memories of the man who had broken her heart.

"Yes, it's me. I'm sorry we haven't spoken for such a long time." She felt a pang of regret for the stress she must have put him under.

"Oh boy, you have no idea how good it is to hear from you." Mitch sounded happy and relieved.

"How's Raelene?"

"Well…" He paused. "She's pregnant. We're having a baby."

"Mitch, that's terrific news."

Mitch was short of turning thirty. He and his wife Raelene had been trying to conceive for years. Samara knew how excited they would be.

"Unfortunately, I also have some bad news." His tone changed. "Bob's in hospital. He had an accident on the bike. It's pretty bad."

Samara and her brothers often called their father by his first name. Growing up their father had always been 'Bob, the motorcycle cop.' At times it was hard to differentiate between their father and his public persona.

Samara had often tried to convince Bob to give up the motorbike he loved. She had seen him lose control on several occasions, due to overconfidence and not concentrating on what he was doing.

"How bad?" She held her breath.

"Two broken legs—one in several places—three broken ribs, and several skin grafts on one arm. He's in hospital."

Samara shook her head then sent up a silent prayer of thanks that it hadn't been worse. "How long has he been there?"

"Just over a month. He's already giving everyone a hard time. You know how he hates to be sick."

It was a running joke in the family. Everyone avoided Bob when he was sick. He was unbearable. Samara could imagine how badly he was behaving in hospital.

"He wants to come home, but they won't let him leave without full-time professional care."

Samara could see where this was going. This was the opportunity she had been praying for. Now was the right time to go home and face her past.

"I'll be on the first plane home."

CHAPTER 8

Bob was sitting up in bed when Samara walked into his room. Both legs were plastered and one arm lay motionless on the sheets, bandages wrapped around it from the armpit all the way to the wrist. The other arm looked to be uninjured.

Samara could see her father was in dire straits. He'd aged—his hair was greyer than she remembered and the lines on his face had deepened. As he turned, the extent of his injuries became apparent. The sudden motion made him double up in an aggressive coughing fit.

Samara rushed to his side and helped him back down on the elevated bed.

"Not much of a homecoming for you, hey Sam?"

Samara gave him a tentative embrace. "No, Dad, but home just the same."

"I knew you'd find your way back eventually."

"Dad, I have a lot to tell you. I'm not . . ." She searched for the words. "I'm not the person you think I am. I've done a lot of things I'm not proud of. I've made a lot of mistakes." She had rehearsed her confessions over and over in her mind in preparation for this moment. Regardless of the mental repetition, she was a ball of nerves.

To her surprise, her father laughed a deep rolling chuckle. "Haven't we all, Sam. Haven't we all. Mistakes are not only the luxury of the young. We're all human. We're all still learning."

Samara was taken aback. She had never witnessed her father so philosophical. Was he high on painkillers?

"You don't need to tell me anything. Trevor Delaney has kept me informed from the minute you left that drug dealer and were taken in for questioning. He's a good man." Her father gave her a steely gaze that showed the painkillers weren't affecting his thinking.

The bottom dropped out of Samara's world. He knew everything?

"Everything?"

"Well, put it this way. I've suspected there's a fair bit Delaney hasn't told me. Fact is, I don't want to know. What you've done or haven't done is your business." He reached for her hand and gave it a squeeze. "Sam, regardless of any mistakes you've made, you're still my little girl. It's hard, but I have to let you live your own life. Make your own mistakes." She noticed his gruff voice hadn't changed. "I never considered you an angel. I've had plenty of time to come to terms with the failings of my children — and my own failings, for that matter."

Samara shook her head. "I don't know what to say." She had expected his explosive temper followed by severe punishment. It looked as though she wasn't the only one who had made changes.

Her father looked away. "It was probably for the best that you stayed away for so long. I wanted to throttle you when you first left. Then I feared for your safety. Delaney filled me in on the trouble and I wanted to throttle you again."

Samara smiled. This was the Bob she knew.

Her father's eyes welled with tears. "I guess that's the only good thing to come out of this accident. I got over all my anger and realized what really matters. Having you home is the best thing that's happened in a long time."

She felt her eyes well in response. She put her arms around him, resting her head cheek to cheek. Bob embraced her with his one free arm. It was good to be home.

Samara watched as the cascade of water streamed off the mountain top. It formed a series of waterfalls, inspiring visions of a magical wonderland. A dense mist accompanied the falling water and engulfed the green foliage of the steep hill.

She took a sip of her cup of tea and closed her eyes, breathing in the musty scent of wet grass mixed with the liquid antiseptic she had applied to her father's injuries.

"I wish this damn rain would ease up," Bob grumbled as he readjusted his wheelchair on the timber flooring of the patio. Despite his two plastered legs and one bandaged arm, he was getting a lot better at maneuvering himself around.

Samara rolled her eyes at his whining, and looked out at their incredible view. The area was dominated by an old volcano cone covered with luscious green foliage including giant ferns and tiny shrubs. Adorning the top of the cone was a forest of grass trees, the stalks extending so high that Samara could make out the huge individual bushes, in spite of the height of the mountain. A rising and falling mountain range extended either side of the cone as far as she could see.

Bob did have some reason to complain. The rain had fallen consistently for over a month. Sam could see the effects of the weather as she sat on the porch of the old cane-cutters cottage her father had always lived in, his childhood home. The ground was saturated, and the water that backed up in the yard had produced a quagmire.

Her father chose to live outside the seaside township of Kiisay Point where he worked at the little old police station. The one-story cottage on stilts had two bedrooms and a sleep out, and Samara remembered it as small and cramped when she and her brothers had come to stay. Now it had rot and structural problems to add to its cramped conditions.

She leaned towards the wall to examine a brownish-green patch of mold on the timber paneling. "How bad is this place? It's not going to fall apart, is it?" She could see mold was a big problem.

Her father frowned at her, his greying eyebrows heavy over his eyes. "Nah, she'll be right."

Sam resisted another eye roll and picked up a spray bottle from the table. She gave the worst-affected wood panels a squirt.

"Is that the stuff Patty gave you?"

Sam swirled the unmarked spray bottle around to mix the contents. "Yep. She dropped it off this morning. I've got no idea what's in it, but it seems to be working."

"So what did you two talk about this morning?" Bob peered at her over his teacup as he spoke.

Samara smiled. "She was catching me up on all

the local Kiisay Point gossip."

It had become obvious over the month she had been home that her father had a desire to take his friendship with Patty to another level. Considering Patty worked full-time at the local bistro but still made the trip out to deliver their supplies every few days, it was clear she had an interest in Bob as well.

Sam hoped she was doing enough to encourage the lovebirds. Patty was a wonderful woman, and exactly what her father had been missing all these years.

Bob grabbed the ruler he kept next to his chair and shoved it down one cast in an effort to relieve an itch. "What was the story she told you about McKenna and that drop kick, Ricky?"

Sam cringed at the mention of her nemesis. *I forgive him. Please bless him, Lord.* Dispelling the fear was still a work in progress.

She turned to her father. "She told me that a few weeks after I left, Ricky tried to vandalize Flynn's fishing boat to get back at him, and when Flynn found him in the act, he pulled a knife. Ricky hit his head on the pontoon as Flynn punched him overboard." Sam took a deep breath. "She said Ricky was knocked unconscious and almost drowned, but Flynn saved him." It didn't surprise her to hear that Ricky had attempted to extract revenge. A sick feeling in her stomach had grown as Patty relayed every detail of the incident. She burped. The sick feeling was back.

Bob rubbed the stubble on his chin. "Flynn McKenna's no angel, and I never liked you living with him, but I gotta feel a bit sorry for the bloke. He didn't deserve to go to jail, even if it was for only six months. Ricky swore blue murder there was no knife involved, and there was no evidence of it either, because it went over the side with him." Bob shook his head. "I wish there was something I could have done to stop the lad having to go through the justice system for assault."

Samara tried to swallow another sip of tea. She knew Ricky owned a knife. He had shown it to her many times, and boasted he was skilled with it. If she had stayed instead of running away, she could have added her testimony to the truth. Perhaps then Flynn wouldn't have been convicted.

Her father sighed heavy. "He's had a rough few years. Did Patty tell you his parents died in a car accident not long after his conviction?"

Sam nodded. She didn't know Flynn's parents well, but she had liked and respected them both. "I don't blame Flynn for retreating to Resolution. The island was almost deserted. He probably wanted to be alone. Patty said he's doing well now."

As hard as it was to have heard the tragedies in Flynn's life, it was a huge relief to know about his more recent turnaround in faith, life and romance.

"Do you know his wife?" Sam was curious as to who the daughter of Resolution Island's owner was. Patty had described Bay as a stunning beauty. Bay had been taken by her mother to America when she was four, but had arrived in search of her father — a man only ever known by his nickname, Dutch. Instead, she had found Flynn.

Bob smiled and tilted his head. "She's a sweetheart, that's for sure. He's fallen on his feet with her." He then turned and frowned at her. "Sorry, darling. I just never saw him as your type."

Sam laughed at his concern for her feelings. "Dad, you're right. Flynn isn't my type. We were a mistake. A big mistake." She watched the tea leaves swirl in the bottom of her cup.

"We all make mistakes." Her father's eyes softened with kindness. "Besides, he's in a good place these days. And busy. They've turned an old, rundown resort into a real flash eco tourist place. It's going great guns. Certainly not deserted anymore." Bob reached for a paper on the small table beside him. "Check this out." He handed it to her.

It was a full-page advertisement for the newly re-opened Resolution Island Eco Resort. The photo of the pool and main building was spectacular.

"Wow. Looks awesome. Have you been over there?"

Bob accepted the paper back from her. "Yeah. Patty and I went over for a special local's day before the reopening. It's real well done."

Sam bit her bottom lip. "You took Patty to an island resort?" She deliberately lifted one eyebrow as she glanced his way.

Bob cleared his throat. "Separate rooms, thank you very much. Patty's a decent woman with faith and morals. She deserves to be courted." His eyes sparkled.

Her father was right. Patty was a catch. In spite of a little middle-aged spread, she had a trim figure and dressed well. Her blonde hair was always piled atop her head, but she never worried when it slipped out of its constraints. Patty had a great sense of humor and Samara thoroughly enjoyed her company. And Patty had opened her arms to Samara without judgement, despite her reputation. That sort of love was rare, and Samara knew its value. She also knew Patty had spent hours talking to Bob about her faith. Sam was certain it had been her influence that had changed her father. He had softened, and gained wisdom.

Sam was enjoying getting to know him again, even if he had proven to be a difficult patient. Samara had spent the entire month convincing him that he wasn't in his twenties any more, and that he needed to slow down and stop hindering his recovery with over ambitious attempts to move around. Fortunately, he was in good health and his recovery was progressing well. Sam was relieved. As much as she loved nursing, her father was the worst patient. Patty had been a great help.

Sam grabbed the bottle and gave the panels one last squirt. "Time for your bath, Dad."

Her father groaned. "I haven't done anything all day but sit around."

Sam stepped through the doorway and into the little cottage. "I'll run the water," she called behind her.

The old timber floor boards creaked under her feet as she made her way to the kitchen. The house was overdue for some serious attention. The roof leaked in several places, and she was kept busy emptying buckets as they filled with water under the dripping ceiling. There were several broken louver windows, and the front door was so loose that the slightest gust of wind blew it wide open.

She had voiced her concerns to her father over the lack of maintenance the week she arrived. Bob admitted the repairs were beyond his handyman capabilities, and there were several things needing urgent attention. But he hadn't arranged any tradesmen to do the work. "Let's face it, who's going to bust in and steal anything from the local cop's house?"

The telephone rang as Samara reached down to swap a full bucket of water on the floor for an empty one. She moved to pick it up before Bob had a chance to yell out for her to answer it.

"Hello?"

"Hi, love." Patty's voice was clearly recognizable.

"Hey Pat, how's things?"

"Busy like a tin full of worms going fishing."

Samara smiled at the analogy.

"I've got a problem," Patty said. "I won't be able to get out to see you this arvo. Two of the restaurant staff can't make it in tonight. The creek's up and they can't get through."

That was no surprise.

"Unfortunately, I won't be able to bring out those tablets you need."

It would have been terrific if Patty had been able to bring the painkillers her father needed, but Samara was quite capable of performing the errand herself.

"No problem. I can take a run in to pick them up. There won't be any flooding between here and town."

"Do you think it's wise to leave Bob alone?"

"I can get Mr. Baker from down the road to sit

with him." Sam knew the kind old man would be willing to help.

"Good idea. I don't know if I'd trust Bob."

Samara had to laugh. "No, I can't say I trust him either."

"Well, I'd best go. Got a million things to do." Patty paused then added. "Oh, I almost forgot. When your brother calls, can you tell him I saw Jed McKenna yesterday? He's back for a bit, visiting his family over on Resolution Island. I know he and Mitch were good friends growing up. I thought they might like to meet up while he was here."

Samara felt her heart pounding and a huge lump collect in her throat. She froze, unable to move or talk. Thankfully, Patty didn't notice her stunned silence.

"I'll catch up with you when I can, love. Could be a few days before the water recedes if this rain keeps up."

Sam pulled herself together sufficiently to acknowledge her friend. "Sure, no problem, Patty. Don't worry about us. We'll be fine."

She said goodbye and pressed the disconnect button. She slumped into the nearest chair and closed her eyes. Jed was in town. What if she ran into him? What would she say? What would he say? What did he think of her? Would he even acknowledge her existence, or would he turn the other way in disgust? *Don't let me see him. Please.* Samara's heart raced. Just the thought of seeing him again evoked an emotional roller coaster within her. On one hand she ached to be near him again, and on the other the thought of having to face him terrified her.

"What's wrong?"

Sam looked up to see her father wheeling himself into the kitchen.

"Nothing," she replied.

Bob didn't buy it. "What do you mean nothing? You're as white as a ghost."

Sam stood up too quickly. The action produced a dizzy feeling in her head for a second. "I'm fine. Really."

"Is it Patty? Is she sick or something?" Bob shifted against the wall.

"No. Everyone's fine. It's all good."

"Samara Jade." Her father's voice was deep and husky.

Sam sighed. His use of her full name meant she had to spill it.

"Patty just told me Jed is in town, visiting his family."

Bob frowned. "Well, that shouldn't worry you. Or didn't you get along when you were both working at the hospital?"

Sam bit the inside of her bottom lip. She had never disclosed the full nature of her relationship with Jed. She was so far away from her father at the time, and while their relationship was full of passion, it was short. Jed had decided that.

"We kinda got along a bit too well, Dad." She held her breath and screwed up her face. "Another one of those mistakes I told you I made."

Her father let out a whistle and shook his head. "Sam, you're in more trouble than Flash Gordon."

"Not quite as much trouble, I hope. It was a short-lived relationship, and he broke up with me.

It's a long time ago now. He made it pretty clear he doesn't have any interest."

He doesn't care about me one bit. If he did, he wouldn't have left the way he did. He would have cared I was with Flynn, but he didn't. Sam could feel her heart race. At one time she thought she would never feel anything but anger for Jed McKenna. Now she knew the anger was a cover for the deep hurt she had felt when he had taken a remote posting on the other side of the country, and left without saying a word.

Bob pulled on the wheel of his chair with his one good arm. "Well, it hardly matters if you run into him now then. It's all water under the bridge. "

Sam closed her eyes.

It's been years. So why can't I let it go?

Maybe it was because of the history. She had loved Jed ever since she could remember. He was her brother's friend, Flynn's younger brother. A mainstay of her childhood. She had put him up on the pedestal of the perfect, unattainable man. He had thought of her as nothing but Mitch's little sister — until they met up in Brisbane, years later, both working in the same hospital. Samara was settled in her first nursing position, and Jed was a young doctor.

Jed hadn't changed much from when he was a boy. His rugged features had matured with his body, which was tall and toned. His blue eyes and dark hair had remained the same. Sam couldn't believe her luck.

Even though she was employed full-time at the hospital, and no longer modelled as she had at university, the profession had taught her to use her looks to their full advantage. She saw her chance to capture Jed's heart the way he always had hers. She worked overtime to gain his attention, and after they had been out on several dates she felt him falling for her.

The next three months had been the most passionate of Samara's life. They couldn't get enough of each other, spending every waking moment together. She fell into the security of knowing she was loved by the man she had always loved. Then it all fell apart. She felt Jed pulling away from her. Slowly at first, and then with force. Instead of talking to him and gauging the problem, she had pulled away from him too, choosing to gain his attention by flirting with others in an attempt to make him jealous.

She also worked hard to show him what a catch she was, that she was no longer her brothers' tomboy sister, but a high fashion sophisticate. All her attempts backfired when she came home one day to find Jed had gone. The only evidence of his withdrawal was a vague two-sentence letter.

She'd been devastated, lost and alone. She quit nursing and went straight back to the comfort of her father at Kiisay Point. Then the bitterness set in. How dare he use her! Who did he think he was? She was consumed with anger.

When Flynn noticed her, she thought it was an opportunity to get Jed's attention. To show him she was special. She had no idea of the consequences of that decision.

Samara pushed the painful memories aside and

walked into her bedroom. The small room was exactly the same as when she was a child. A single bed was pushed up against the wall, and her great-grandmother's red cedar dressing table sat opposite the bed. She looked at her reflection in the old oval mirror. How different she felt to the girl who had left Kiisay Point three years ago. She had regained the weight she had lost when she was at the club, and her subtle curves suited her far better than the skeleton form she had back then.

Sam sighed and released the top buttons of her blouse to reveal the scar slashed across her chest. She ran her fingers along it, feeing its rough, puckered edges. It was a physical reminder of the changes that had taken place within her. It had revealed to her that skin was just that—skin. Her faith had shown her it didn't matter how she looked. It was who she was inside that counted with God, and He loved her, with all her scars.

Even so, she covered the scar under high-necked shirts. She didn't want to answer questions about its origin. It was a part of her now. A reminder that she should never again get caught up in the lie the world promoted—that appearance was everything. Samara had seen the best and worst of that world. The so-called glamour of modelling, and the degrading world of stripping. Each held its own ugliness.

Sam heard her father turn on the old television in his bedroom. She refastened the buttons. So much for him having a bath.

She gave him a smile as she entered. "Patty rang to tell me she can't make it out this afternoon. A bit of flooding has stopped some staff from getting to the bistro. So I'm going to take a quick trip into town. I've only got to go to the pharmacy and I'll be back."

Bob frowned. "I don't like you driving when it's raining. Might be best to wait and see if it clears tomorrow."

"You'll be out of tablets by then. Besides, the flooding may get worse and then I won't be able to get in at all." The little bridge crossings between them and the small city of Mackay could flood if they had more rain overnight.

Bob nodded. "Okay, but be careful."

Samara could see from his expression that she was about to get a lecture on driving in bad weather. She cut him off before he could speak. "I'll call Mr. Baker to come over and sit with you while I'm gone."

A heavy pout formed on her father's mouth. "I'll be alright here by myself."

His gruffness made her smile. "I'll ask him to bring his pack of cards. You might enjoy a game or two." Samara knew her father's weakness for cards might seal the deal.

He brightened up before pulling a face at her. "If you must."

She kissed the top of his head and made her way to the phone to call their neighbor.

The road was slippery and visibility was poor as Samara made her way along the narrow road. She was grateful for the sturdiness of her ride. The tires of the four-wheel drive stuck to the bitumen and provided a sense of security.

Her father's little house was a little over ten

kilometers from Kiisay Point and almost thirty kilometers outside the city of Mackay. Some parts of the road were incredibly narrow. She had negotiated almost all of the difficult sections when she came around a nasty bend. A mass on the road ahead startled her, and she scrambled to slam on the brakes.

She peered out her windscreen and squinted in an effort to make out what it was. It looked like a small landslide had engulfed the opposite side of the road.

Sam pushed the car into gear with the thought to drive around the debris. She would be able to inform the authorities of the dangerous conditions once she reached the city. As she turned the car, an object on the side of the road caught her eye.

The rain was heavy, and the fogged-up window hindered her visibility. It looked to be a utility vehicle lodged in the drain adjacent to the road.

Sam pulled the four-wheel drive onto the narrow shoulder and hit the hazard lights, hoping anyone who rounded the corner would see her vehicle before colliding with it. She would have to get out if she was going to get a better look. The rain fell into the cab of the car as the door swung open. She was wet through in seconds. The front of the utility was submerged in water running meters deep through the drain. She looked closer and saw the skid marks in the mud trailing down the embankment. Sam ran several meters up the side of the road and peered as best she could down the steep decline into the driver's side of the vehicle. She could make out a head of long blonde hair as the driver leaned over the steering wheel. There was no movement.

She raced back to the car and picked up her father's two-way radio to call for help.

"Hello, is anyone there?" Nothing. "Hello. Hello?" Nothing but static.

Sam switched to a different channel. "Hello, is anyone out there? I have an emergency."

"This is channel five emergency. Please state your position and nature of emergency."

Sam closed her eyes tight, sending up a prayer of thanks before explaining where she was and what was happening.

"Hang on as best you can. We'll have help to you as soon as possible. Over." The voice at the other end signed off.

She sat back in her seat and breathed a sigh of relief. The constant rain increased in intensity, the severity of the deluge hindered the visibility out her window.

She opened the door and ran back down to the top of the embankment. The water had risen in the short time since she had radioed for help, and now the driver's head was inches from being engulfed by flood water.

She had to do something. Fast. She opened the back of the car, hoping her father had some rescue equipment. *Yes!* She grabbed a coil of rope from the boot. A large tree on the side of the embankment would do as an anchor and she moved to tie a rope around it. She knotted the ends as best she could, and kicked herself for not paying attention to her father when he had tried to teach her the art of knot tying.

She secured the other end of the rope to her waist and made her way down the steep, muddy embankment. The force of the water running down the hill had exposed the rock underneath the earth. It was surprisingly stable. She reached the back of the ute without too much trouble.

There was no way she was going to get the driver's side door open. It was taking the full force of the current as it washed through the drain. She'd have to use the passenger door. It took some pulling, but she got it ajar.

The driver was female, and her nose and mouth were now touching the water. Sam moved without thinking, pulling the woman's head back from the steering wheel. She felt for a pulse and was relieved not only to find one, but also to see the woman's chest rise and fall. The nasty gash on her forehead suggested the main problem.

The woman moaned as Sam fiddled with her seat belt. It had most likely saved her life. Two life vests floated in the car between her and the driver. They looked brand new. She grabbed one and moved further into the cabin, attempting to secure it as best she could around the woman, who moaned again and opened her eyes.

"What happened?" She put her hand up to rub her head as she spoke.

She was an attractive lady. "Your car ran off the road. I need you to help me get you out of here. Can you feel your legs?" Hopefully the cut on her head was her only injury.

"Yes." The woman's voice was barely audible.

"What about your back? Is it sore?" Sam hoped if there was an injury the weightlessness of the water would help with the pain.

"No," the woman answered in a sleepy voice.

Samara looked around her. The water was coming up fast.

"We need to get out of here. I want you to put your arm around me." She leaned further into the cabin to grab the woman under the arms.

The woman did as she was told. With some tugging and heaving they were out of the cabin and on the side of the vehicle. The end of the ute's tray was still out of the water. Samara stood next to the woman, holding her up as they inched their way along the length of the vehicle.

They finally reached the embankment and, holding onto the rope, made the jump from the water to the muddy side of the gradual incline.

Progress was slow up the side as they pulled on the rope. The exposed rocks helped their footing, but the strain of pulling herself, as well as another person made the going tough. They slipped and fell in the mud several times. Samara kept a strong hold on the woman and took all of her weight, mindful of the lady's injuries. It seemed like forever before they reached the top of the embankment.

They slumped to the ground next to the road as the rain continued to plummet down.

She looked over and saw that the woman had closed her eyes again, but her pulse was strong and her breathing stable. Sam ripped off the bottom of her cotton top and held it against the gash on her head. She prayed over the lady, and patted her head, trying to sooth her.

At one point the woman opened her eyes and looked up. Samara was struck by their dark green color.

"Are you . . . ?" She tried to speak.

"Shh," Sam said in a low, calming voice. "Don't try to talk. Everything's going to be okay." She didn't know that for sure. She did, however know they were being watched over.

CHAPTER 9

Jed looked out from his position on the veranda. Even through the grey haze of a rainy day he marveled at the island's transformation.

Resolution sat in the middle of a group of islands located a few kilometers off the mainland. The deep water harbor between Resolution and the southern island, Turtle Island, formed a perfect sheltered bay. It accommodated an array of pleasure boats, trawlers, and fishing tinnies. Resolution was the only privately owned island in the group. The other islands were maintained as national parks.

Resolution had been the same throughout his childhood, but now there was no sign of the weathered fibro huts that had scattered the bay. It was no longer the unkempt place he remembered. Now two floating pontoons jutted out from a landing bay, providing a comfortable disembarking point for guests. The old method of accessing the island involved swimming in to shore after anchoring the tinny.

The main building loomed largest among the landscape. It was built in the tradition of a Balinese hut, and housed the reception and restaurant areas.

There were ten individual one and two bedroom cabins, all set high on stilts to protect the natural environment. Each cabin was placed in a beachfront position. Raised walkways and a pool oasis completed the beauty of the resort.

The sheltered bay had previously been underdeveloped. Now Jed could see his sister-in-law's influence in everything from the buildings to the palm and hibiscus bushes lining the grassy area beyond the sandy white beach. Jed could even see his brother's subtle contributions in the fisherman's wash station and mud crab cooking area, as well as the fueling pontoon.

They had also been careful to leave a touch of Resolution's history. The original stone cottage still sat at the end of the bay as the island met the open sea, and the old gazebo sat high on the rocks at the opposite end of the bay. It had been patched up and a paint job had restored it to almost new.

It was certainly an attractive place, even if at one time he would have considered Resolution the last place on earth he'd ever want to go. Not that the island itself was so abhorrent—what he had found repulsive was being anywhere near his brother. Jed shook his head at his attitude. He had avoided a relationship with Flynn for years, but the minute his life plummeted into disarray, he rushed without thought to his big brother's side.

He flicked a finger onto the button to awaken his laptop, and hit the refresh on his email. It timed out without delivering anything new. No news from the medical organization he worked for could be a good or bad thing.

He had told Flynn and Bay that he was on a forced holiday. What he hadn't revealed was why he had been forced.

He opened the last correspondence from his employers. The email was from his boss at the refugee camp in Afghanistan. He read it again, just as he had done so many times in the last few weeks.

Hi Jed, I've been told the investigation into the incident involving you has begun. I have no idea how long it will take, but the good news is that you have so many holidays accrued that they won't have to suspend your employment at this time. Officially you are on leave. Unfortunately, it's a forced one. Hopefully it will all be sorted and we'll have you back soon.

Jed closed his eyes and breathed in the musty scent of rain on the wet grass. If only he had done things differently. Then he wouldn't be in this situation. Sure, the army officer he'd assaulted had it coming, but there was no doubt he'd abused his position. Now an investigation was required. He had overreacted, regardless of the provocation.

He opened his eyes to watch a series of waves pound onto the beach in heavy succession. The thunderous roll of each swell lulled his anxiety into a hypnotic calm. It felt comforting to be home, in spite of the painful history he had here. In the two weeks Jed had been on the island, the environment alone had done much to lift his spirits.

A flash from his message alert drew his attention back to the laptop. He had been sporadically involved in a live online chat with his work colleague, Cassidy. He opened the file to read her message;

So tell me more about this place. And WHY didn't you tell me your family owned a tropical island?????????

Jed smiled, and typed out a reply.

Bay (my new sister in law) and her father, Dutch only reunited a few years ago. When they came into some money they decided to turn this run-down place into an

Eco resort. Bay's mother took her to America when she was really small. You'd like her. She misses pretzels too.

Cassidy's reply came back in seconds.

Please do not mention pretzels. I wanted one so bad this morning.

Jed laughed out loud. It was a running joke in the remote Afghan camp that Cassidy would give her right arm for a pretzel. She was one patriotic American lady.

I told you my brother worked at a resort!

Yes, but you didn't tell me he OWNED the resort. I understand why you don't talk much about him, but Flynn seems like he's doing really well, and the problems between you both aren't entirely his fault. I'm praying the time you guys are spending together draws you closer, and you can forgive the past.

Jed looked up from the screen. He had been praying too. At one point he had held so much against his brother.

I know. I've been an idiot. I should have kept in touch with him. Somehow we moved in such different directions. Medicine took up my entire existence. If I had made the effort to maintain our relationship, he would have known about Samara. If he had known he would never had been with her himself.

The truth hurt. Jed had been ambitious, wanting nothing more than to pursue his professional plan. Flynn's life at sea made it easy for them to fall into a habit of rarely contacting each other. Jed hadn't shared a lot of his life after university with his family.

He had reunited with his brother briefly for their parents' funerals, but it wasn't the time or place to deal with the pain and betrayal Jed felt. It was hard enough to deal with his parents' death. Instead, he avoided his brother and left the moment he had a chance.

The screen flashed.

I sure don't want to pry, or say the wrong thing like I did last time. :-/ - but, has he said anything about Samara, or the situation? You know it's only that I care about how you're doing.

Cassidy was worried about him. She was one of the only people who knew how torn up he was about his relationship with Samara, and his brother's unintentional betrayal. Her ability to tell him the truth had led him to blow up and accept he had serious issues.

She had also encouraged him to write to his brother and fill him in on all the details. The letter had been the catalyst to forgiveness and change. But Jed had avoided any heart-to-hearts with his brother since he had arrived. Flynn had given him plenty of space, sensing his desire to be alone. He knew there would come a day when they would have to talk. Jed swallowed hard.

We haven't talked about it yet, but we will. It's been a bit hard with everyone else around.

There was a slight pause before Cassidy answered. *I'll happen when the time is right. Don't rush it. :-) ... So who else lives on this island you've barely talked about? I want details.*

Jed put aside his anguish and smiled. Cassidy was on a mission for information, and he knew from experience it would be hard to fob her off. He recalled the tenacious way she went about her work. Her perseverance was one attribute Jed had found attractive. He had even thought they would become more than friends, but time had proven God had a different plan for them. Cassidy had led him to faith. Each time the oppressive environment in which they worked had led him to question the existence of God, Cassidy had counteracted with answers that rang true in his head and heart. His decision to believe was another testimony to his friend's perseverance.

Jed also discovered his past played a big part in his inability to have any romantic connection with Cassidy. No matter how many times he had given his past mistakes over to God, the feelings of hurt, betrayal, and even longing, still sat under the surface of his prayers. All the tension was bound to erupt.

Hello?????????? Waiting!!!!!!!!!!!

Jed laughed—there was that tenacity.

I'm still here.

He moved into a more comfortable position before he typed out his reply.

I've spoken about my Dad's mate, Amos. He and his cousin, Neville live out here on the island. Remember I told you about how Amos would take us all fishing and tell us his ancestral Pacific island stories?

Cassidy replied with a smiley face, so Jed continued.

Well, he and Neville do a lot of work out here. Bay and Flynn have just built them their own huts. You'd like Neville—he's a real character. The biggest gossip you'll ever meet.

Cassidy broke in.

I'm definitely seeking him out when I visit. ;-). They assure me I'm up for leave. They're trying to organize a replacement. My family are desperate for me to go home. Mom cried when I Skyped her this morning!!!!!!!!! I've been away from them too long, so I promised them I would get there ASAP. But I reeeeeeeely want to go to a tropical island in Australia. :-). So apart from my new gossip go-to man, Neville, who else lives there?

Jed could imagine the information Cassidy would coax out of Neville.

The only other permanent resident is Yvette, Dutch's wife. She's a marine biologist. They're setting up a dugong research station on the island.

Dugongs are the same as manatees, right?

Same family… I think. You'd have to ask Yvette. She's the expert, and a lovely lady.

She took a few minutes to reply.

If you're still there when I get my leave, I'm coming over. Mom'll have to deal with it. Have you heard anything about the investigation?

Cassidy had both chastised and supported him over the incident that had forced his leaving. Her reassurance that God would work the situation for his good in spite of his mistake spoke to him.

Nothing yet. Praying. The more time I have to think about it, the more foolish I feel.

He recalled how she had told him to stop trying to be good on his own and start asking for divine guidance. Her advice had hit a nerve.

Jed looked up to see Flynn approaching. His windbreaker jacket looked soaked from the rain, and the cap on his head dripped water from the bream.

Got to go. I've got a visitor.

Jed moved to close down the other applications while he waited for Cassidy's reply.

No worries. Hang in there. Praying for you. xo

He shut down the computer as Flynn walked up onto the patio.

"Hey, mind if I join you for a few minutes?" Flynn gestured towards the spare chair.

"Sure." Jed moved the laptop on the table next to him. "I've got some cold drinks inside if you're thirsty."

"No, thanks. I'm just killing time. Bay should be back soon. It's a shame the weather's been so bad. If we can get a fine day, we can take a run out to the reef." Flynn scowled as he removed his jacket and cap.

Jed looked out at the grey sky. "It's been years since I've pulled up a decent Coral Trout. I've probably forgotten how."

Flynn chuckled. "Dad would be rolling in his grave if he heard you say that. He always said it was his life's work to teach his boys how to fish."

Jed smiled at the memory. "He also used to say his greatest achievement in life was eating an entire pumpkin fruit cake in one sitting." He laughed at the thought of his father's antics.

"And didn't we all pay later for that accomplishment." Flynn shook his head. "Mum refused to make another one for years." Both men laughed with the memory of their father and the consequences of the fruit cake consumption.

It felt good to be with his brother again, but as their laughter died down, Jed felt a great sadness at their parents' absence. "I miss them."

Flynn looked over at him. "Me too, mate."

The second he stepped foot in his hometown, Jed knew he had been avoiding returning for far too long. He had deliberately made work his life, firstly to forget Samara and then to forget his parents' deaths. Now every corner held a memory that bubbled to the surface. Getting out to Resolution with its drastic changes and new beginnings felt like a soothing therapy. He had been close enough to his memories to reflect in a healthy way, but far enough away not to get bogged down with grief.

He turned to his brother. "Thanks again for letting me stay." He was grateful for the room. Jed knew they had moved bookings to accommodate him.

"You never need an invitation to stay with us. You're welcome here anytime."

"Well, I appreciate it."

A silence fell between them as they both looked out to the ocean. White caps crested on the waves as they rose and fell in unison with the rainy squalls flowing into shore, one after the other.

Jed thought how much he had missed the North Queensland coast. There was no place like it. When he arrived on Resolution, he had felt as shriveled and sparse as the rocky, dusty terrain of Afghanistan where he had lived and worked for the last two years, the environment had drained him dry. Now the moist air, ocean spray and green masterpiece clouding his senses had revitalized him.

The sound of Flynn moving beside him brought him out of his daydream. He looked at his brother and saw him retrieve an envelope out of his pocket. He held it in his hands for a moment, turning it over and over before speaking.

"I wasn't sure whether to give this to you or not. Bay thinks I should." He smiled. "She's usually right about these things, so I'm passing it on. It's up to you whether you read it or not."

Jed frowned with intrigue as he accepted it, and

looked to his brother for further explanation.

"It's a letter from Samara."

Jed threw the envelope down on the table. It felt like a hot potato in his hand. "If she wrote it to you, why would you give it to me?" He felt himself go on the defensive. Why couldn't she have written to him instead of his brother? It confirmed how little Samara thought of him.

Flynn set his gaze on him. "I think you might be interested in some of what she had to say."

Jed crossed his arms.

"Look, we don't need to rehash this." Flynn's tone commanded his attention. "As far as I'm concerned, it's in the past. Now it's a new day. I forgave Samara a long time ago. She was a stupid kid who made stupid mistakes. We've all been down that road. Then when I found out about your history with her, I struggled to forgive her again. It was really hard until I received her letter. I know you'll get something out of reading it as well."

"She made a mess of a lot of things. Forgiveness is a pretty hard pill to swallow." Jed took a deep breath. He couldn't look at his brother without disclosing his true feelings. He'd give himself away if he said her name. Just to hear it made his pulse race.

"People change. None of us are without fault. Besides, you can't learn or grow if you think you're perfect. Look at us." Flynn slapped his shoulder, forcing him to turn his way. "Can you imagine how amazed Mum would be, looking down at us? All her prayers finally paid off."

Jed had to smile. Flynn was right. Their Mum

and Dad would be grateful.

Flynn got to his feet. "I hope you stick around for a bit longer. It's a great feeling having you back." He gave Jed's shoulder a squeeze and grabbed his wet gear.

Jed got up to see him off. "Yeah, I'll be here for a while, if that's okay?" The truth was he had no idea how long he would remain on Resolution. He had been told the investigation could take months.

Flynn smiled. "I was hoping you'd stay." He turned and walked down the few stairs to the path.

Jed picked up his laptop and turned to go inside. He retrieved the letter from the table, but couldn't bring himself to open it. A pang of self-disgust pierced his gut. Samara was so far in his past he should have been able to read the letter without a second thought. The fact was, regardless of what she had done, he couldn't shake his feelings for her. He had tried to exorcise that woman from his life so many times, and in so many ways, but time just made it harder. He hated himself for feeling the way he did.

Since the day he had left her, Samara had infiltrated every facet of his life. He thought about her, dreamed about her, and his body ached to hold her again. What frustrated Jed the most was the why? Why couldn't he get over her and move on? After all, he was the one who had ended the relationship.

He moved inside and threw the envelope in the bin.

Where you belong.

He moved to the refrigerator, opened the door and stared into its contents, unseeing. He slammed the door shut and went back to retrieve the envelope, securing it inside the top kitchen cabinet.

Samara glanced at her reflection in the mirror of the hospital bathroom. She was a mess. Mud caked her hair, and her clothes were still wet through in spite of the time she had spent under the hand dryer. She was thankful to be wearing a long shirt, even if it was now torn on the bottom.

Her cell rang, and she scrambled to tie her hair in a bun.

"Hi Dad."

"Are you alright?"

She had rung Bob from the ambulance to fill him in on what had happened. They had insisted she go with them rather than follow in her own vehicle.

"Yep. All good. It took them ages to see me, but the duty nurse has patched me up." She looked down at the gauze taped to one elbow and the huge white padding on the opposite knee. The scrapes were superficial, but still required covering. She couldn't even recall how they happened.

"You're lucky it wasn't a whole lot worse. I knew I shouldn't have let you go out on your own."

Sam looked down at her white shorts. They were now brown and green from the slow progress up the embankment. "Well, if I hadn't come along when I did, chances are that lady would have drowned."

There was a pause before Bob spoke. "Strange you don't recognize her. She must not be a local. I'm proud of you. You did what you had to in a desperate situation." A gruff throat clearing signaled her father's emotions. "Now, has anyone been up there to take your statement yet?"

"Yep, a young constable's been here. I gave him all the details. Are you going to be okay there with Mr. Baker for a bit longer?"

"Don't worry about us. We're fine. I'm giving Baker a hiding at poker. We're using dried beans instead of money, and I reckon I've got enough in my pile for a decent pot of soup."

Sam laughed. Now the event was over and the woman she rescued was receiving medical treatment, she felt her adrenaline levels fall away to exhaustion. She had the potential to fall in a big heap any second. It felt good to talk to her father. His calm demeanor brought her back down to earth.

"Don't worry about the car," he said. "I've organized for a couple of blokes from the station to come and pick you up. They can take you to it. Are you sure you're alright to drive? I can get one of them to bring you back if you want."

Sam was grateful again for her father's foresight. The police had told her the mudslide had been cleared, and she was fine to drive as long as she received medical clearance.

"Thanks, Dad. They gave me the all clear, and the duty nurse took your prescription to fill, so I can come home straight away."

"Well, it'll be a little while until they get there to pick up you. Can you stand having to wait a bit on your own?"

Sam smiled again at her father's concern. It was a nice feeling to be back home. "Actually, the delay will be good. I want to see how the lady I rescued is doing before I leave."

"Righto, love. Try and stay out of trouble, will ya?"

Sam laughed. "No problem. I've had enough trouble today."

She pressed the disconnect on the cell phone and checked her appearance once more, it hadn't magically improved. *Still disgusting. At least I'm only going home.*

She pushed the door to the toilet open and stepped back into the waiting room as a nurse came in from the corridor opposite. Samara recognized her as one of the nurses on duty when they had arrived in the ambulance. The young woman made a beeline for her.

"Here you are. I came in here a few moments ago but you weren't here."

Sam looked down at her clothing. "I've been in the bathroom, trying to clean up."

"Oh, that explains it." The nurse gave her a kind smile. "The lady you saved is conscious and asking to see you. She's through all the scans and her head trauma isn't dangerous." She turned and walked several paces across the room. "We usually don't let anyone but family in at this stage, but considering the circumstances we thought it would be okay. Her family's due to arrive any minute, but she's alone right now."

Samara felt a wave of relief as she followed her through the doorway. "I'd love to see her."

"Follow me." The nurse led the way down the hallway.

Sam knocked on the hospital door and peeked in to make sure she wasn't intruding.

The woman she rescued was sitting up in bed sipping on a glass of water. She looked up as Samara entered.

She was beautiful. Her long golden hair splayed across the pillow and her dark green eyes sparkled as she greeted Sam with a broad smile. Sam returned the smile as she moved to her bedside. The white plaster patch on her forehead covering the gash did nothing to detract from her beauty.

"Hi."

Sam walked into the room and stood at her bedside. "Hi back. You gave me a bit of a scare. How are you feeling?" Sam remembered the anxiety she had felt when the woman had fallen back into unconsciousness.

"My scan says I'm fine." She touched the spot on her forehead. "A bit of a headache, but it's fading." The woman had a distinct American accent. "I can't thank you enough for what you did for me. The ambulance men told me the ute was completely underwater by the time they arrived." Her eyes softened with genuine appreciation. "I never would have made it out of there on my own."

Sam touched her arm. "I was in the right place at the right time."

She felt empowered at having done the saving this time. To be of service to another when so many others had served her was a welcome change. It gave her an opportunity to give back.

A commotion of raised voices in the hallway, and the abrupt swinging open of the door drew their attention. The door slammed into the wall with such force that Samara jumped. The muscular frame of a man filled the doorway. His red-tinged brown hair and rugged handsome features made her stomach drop and eyes widen. *Flynn McKenna.*

"Bay, are you alright? Are you hurt? Do you have any injuries? Is anything broken?" He fired the questions one after another as he entered the room and covered the distance to her bedside, scooping her out of the bed and holding her tight.

Samara froze.

Bay?

The name went over and over in her mind. She wanted to kick herself—she should have realized who this woman was. Her appearance alone should have been enough to reveal her identity, but the American accent had been a dead giveaway. Why hadn't she recognized the woman Patty had described? Now Sam was stuck in an awkward situation.

Not that Flynn had noticed.

For all he cared Samara could have been invisible. She looked towards the door and felt her fight-or-flight kick in.

"I'm fine now." Bay pulled away from the encompassing embrace. She grabbed Samara's hand as she spoke.

Sam held her breath. *Looks like it's going to be fight. Or freeze. Maybe a bit of both.*

"But if it wasn't for this wonderful woman, I wouldn't be here right now." Bay acknowledged her with a bright smile.

Flynn looked her way.

Samara took short breaths. She deliberately darted her eyes everywhere but at him. The silence seemed to go on forever.

"Samara?" He broke the tension.

She took a chance and glanced at him. He was frowning in a strange way, like she was some strange specimen of plankton that had washed up on the beach. Her stomach began to heave and her chest hurt. She had to get out of there.

"Hi." She managed to find her voice. "This is awkward for all of us. I should just go." She pulled her body towards the door as she spoke, but Bay still had her hand and was holding on tight.

"Samara? You mean, *the* Samara?" Bay asked Flynn, eyes wide with shock.

Oh no, save me from this. Please.

"Yep, *the* Samara." Flynn and Bay stared at each other. Their faces mirrored disbelief.

She felt a pang of anger replace the panic. This was ridiculous. They were talking like she wasn't even in the room. They could at least let her go.

Bay looked back at her. Samara thought her hand was going to fall off it was being squeezed so hard. "You saved my life." Her green eyes were like saucers and her lips parted in shock. She turned to Flynn. "She saved my life. She dragged me from the ute and pulled me up an embankment. I wouldn't be here if it wasn't for her."

Flynn's expression changed. The look he gave her now was less plankton specimen and more stunned mullet. Sam didn't know which was worse.

The silence went on and on without anyone saying a word.

She forced the shallow breathing to stop and took a deep intake of air. The oxygen did her good.

She used her free hand to release Bay's grasp, softening the action by giving her hand a pat as she placed it back on the hospital bed.

"I'm thankful I was there to help you. I know you'll recover quickly. Now you two must have a lot to talk about, so I'm going to go." The intensity of their stares was borderline creepy. She turned towards the door with relief.

She got three steps towards freedom when the door swung open again. A familiar chiseled face peered into the room.

Jed McKenna.

Samara froze. The foundations of her world felt like they had collapsed. How could this happen to her all at once? *This is crazy. Just crazy.*

As Jed's blue eyes met hers, her heart was beating so violently, she thought her chest might explode. She shifted her weight to check if she was still on earth and hadn't entered some alternative universe of pain.

Jed's eyes widened and his mouth dropped as he looked past her to Flynn and Bay.

Samara also glanced back at them. She felt moisture building up behind her eyes. She was going to lose it. She had to get out of there.

The flight kicked in. "I . . . I was just going." She didn't know what to do. He was blocking the doorway. She shifted her weight from one foot to the other and scanned the room for an escape route. She must have looked like a deer in the headlights because he moved a little to the side. Samara saw her chance and rushed the door, brushing his shoulder as she sped past him. She ran as fast as she could down the hallway.

"Was that who I think it was?" Jed looked to Bay and Flynn for confirmation.

Flynn was the first to speak. "Sure was. I wasn't sure at first. She certainly isn't the sophisticated chick I remember." His eyes were wide and he had a distinctly bamboozled look on his face.

Bay frowned, clearly affronted by his comment. "Hey, you'd be in a bit of a mess if you'd just dragged someone up a huge mud hill."

Jed moved into the room and closed the door behind him. "What, Samara?"

"She saved me from drowning." Bay giggled. "Do you want to hear something funny?" She glanced at them both. "When she had pulled me up the hill, I opened my eyes and I thought she was an angel." Bay grinned at her husband who shook his head and grinned back.

It was way too much for Jed. "How could you possibly confuse that woman with a celestial being?"

Bay gave him her death stare. "Regardless of how you feel about her, she saved my life today." She then turned to her husband. "And, Flynn, she prayed. I heard her. The entire time we were waiting for the ambulance. She didn't know who I was, and she prayed for me."

Flynn leaned down and gave her a kiss on the forehead. "Then we have a lot to thank her for." He gave her a lopsided smile. "Now can you please stop having near-death experiences? This is taking years off my life." He reached down again to kiss his smiling wife.

Jed couldn't believe his ears. Samara? Praying? Bay must have imagined it. It seemed implausible for the woman he had known.

He took the chart from the bottom of Bay's bed. His hands were shaking so hard he needed to do something. He read the chart in an effort to gain some composure, but no matter how hard he concentrated, he could still feel his shoulder burn from her touch.

Samara had a hard time keeping her emotions in check during the lift to her car. Once she was alone she sobbed the rest of the drive home, like a toddler who had passed the stage of reason and couldn't regain control. It was only when she thought about how red her eyes would be, and the explanation she would have to give her father, that she pulled herself together.

Patty had warned her there was a chance she could run into Jed, but she had wanted to be prepared. She had wanted to be ready. Not how she was today. Not looking like a drowned, dirty rat.

She didn't regret her actions, didn't regret stopping, didn't regret saving Bay. She'd do it again in a second. But that didn't stop her wishing her first meeting with Jed had been under different circumstances.

She pulled up at the house and drew a sharp breath. There were three four-wheel drives parked out front, and several men milling around the front and side of the house.

What on earth? Samara shut off the engine and was out the door in seconds.

"Dad!" She ran to the porch, recognizing her father's fishing partner.

"Bob's okay, Sam," he said. "The ceiling had a little cave in."

"What?" A little cave in?

"Seems the old place finally gave out. The ceiling was saturated. Came down in a big heap. Just as well Bob wasn't in his bed. The whole mess would have fallen on top of him."

Sam rushed inside to find her father sitting up in the lounge chair. The remnants of the card game were still laid out on the table beside him.

"Here she is!" he exclaimed as she walked in the room. "The house is a mess."

"Dad . . . What? How?" Samara looked around. There was a massive hole in the wall and pieces of plaster were scattered from one end of the floor to the other.

"The whole lot came down. We've gotta get out." Bob said. "They reckon it's full of asbestos."

Samara covered her face with her hands and shook her head. *Not today.*

"No good worrying about it." Bob tried to reassure her. "We'll have to get out for a bit so they can fix it."

Samara sighed. Her father was right. It wouldn't do her any good to fall in a heap, even though it was exactly what she wanted to do. "How long will it take to fix?" She was almost afraid to ask.

"About eight weeks, if they can get all the approvals through fast enough."

Where are we going to live until then?

Her father must have read her mind. "I've already called Patty and she's arranged for us to stay at the motel. It's a bit inconvenient though, because all the units are upstairs, which is no good for me." He looked down at his two plastered legs as he spoke. "She's got us in adjoining rooms. It's all they had."

"I guess it'll have to do for now. In the meantime, I'll look into a holiday rental that might be suitable and available." Anything she rented would have to be appropriate for her father in his condition. At least the cottage already had wheelchair access—it had been put in years ago, for her grandfather.

Her father looked her up and down. "You look pretty bad, Sam," he said, as if he had only now noticed the state she was in.

"Thanks for pointing that out, Dad. It's been a big day." She sighed as she walked down the hallway and into her room to pack. Samara knew her father didn't mean the comment as an insult. It was his way of opening up the conversation about what had happened, but she was in no mood to talk about it. She was afraid she would burst back into tears at any moment.

Living in the motel was the pits. The only two adjoining rooms available were on the sheltered side of the motel. The view from the room was nothing but mangrove and swamp. It was hot, reeked of stale cigarette smoke, and the mosquitoes and sand flies were unbearable.

To make matters worse, Bob did nothing but complain. It was too hot, too stuffy, too smelly, and they didn't have any of his sporting channels. She couldn't blame him. Her father also had trouble using the bathroom, as the room with disabled facilities was unavailable. Maneuvering him around the small space was difficult. As a consequence, he was stuck in bed most of the time.

She'd escaped this morning, insisting they needed provisions. With the shopping done, she now took reluctant steps back along the pathway to their rooms.

Patty was babysitting her father in her absence. The older lady was the only positive aspect about living at the motel. Patty occupied her father and didn't put up with his bad moods. She also gave Samara a break each day, a break she desperately needed.

As she neared her father's doorway, she heard voices and laughter. It looked as though Patty had been able to lift Bob's spirits.

She walked in the door without a thought. Samara had expected to see Patty, but the lady was nowhere in sight. Instead, sitting on the chair next to her father's bed was Bay. She and Bob were laughing uproariously.

Samara stopped short, dropping her shopping bags on the ground. She scanned the room for signs of additional visitors, but it looked as though Bay was alone. She breathed a sigh of relief and gave them both a smile.

"Sam, come on over and hear this story about Neville."

She moved to take the chair on the opposite side of the bed from Bay.

"He was in the bush, camping on one of the islands and got chased by a scrub turkey. He climbed up onto a ledge to get away from it. A full day later Amos went to find him, and he was still up on the ledge. The turkey was long gone but Neville was still scared. Amos had to do a full search of the surrounding bush and assure him it was safe before he would get back down." Bob gave another loud laugh.

Sam smiled at her father's hilarity.

"Bay told it much better." He wiped his eyes where tears had formed from laughter. It was good to see him in a lighter mood.

Bay gave him a big smile. "That's Neville. He'll be relaying the story of his brush with death to anyone who will listen for the next month."

Samara laughed along with them then turned to Bay. "Good to see you up and about. How long did they keep you in hospital?"

"Just one night."

"Bay's offered us a cabin on Resolution," Bob said.

Samara could feel her eyes widening. She didn't have time to think the comment through before her father continued.

"They've got a purpose-built disabled access cabin complete with ocean views." Bob's tone revealed he was completely sold.

Samara opened her mouth to squash the idea.

"They also have my sports channels." He finished with the clincher. It was going to be hard to discourage her father with that carrot dangled in front of him.

Samara looked over at Bay who smiled back. "I told Bob it would be our pleasure to have you both stay. It's the least we can do considering what you did for me. We want you there as long as you need accommodation. Everything's on the house. You'll be our guests."

Samara could see where this was heading, and it was nowhere she wanted to be. Stuck on an island with Jed McKenna was the equivalent to emotional suicide.

"It's so good of you, Bay, but we can't possibly accept."

Bob looked at her like she was crazy. "Why not?"

She stopped short. What was she going to do? Go into details about the emotional dynamics of her past relationship?

"Because . . ." She stalled for a plausible excuse. "We don't want to be a burden to anyone."

Bay looked between them. "You wouldn't be a burden. We'd love to have you out there. It was actually Flynn's idea. When he heard about the problems with your house, he suggested it right away."

The look of glee on Bob's face said it all. He didn't need any further convincing.

She thought of another barrier. "It would be far too difficult getting you out there, Dad. It's way too rough in a tinny." Sam sighed. Finally a legitimate negative that would squash the idea, but Bay countered again.

"No problem. We can wheel you straight down

the new pontoon at the boat ramp and onto our boat. We've just bought it. It's a fifty-five-foot cruising cat. You'll be nothing but comfortable on the trip over."

Samara sat in silence and racked her brain in desperation. She had to find another excuse.

"Sounds perfect. And I can fund a part of my stay. This was a workplace injury and the department is meeting some recuperation costs, so thank you for the offer and we'll take it." She heard her father say the words, but couldn't believe what had just happened.

"You don't have to worry about any lack of medical attention while you're over there, Bob," Bay said. "We've got Flynn's brother, Jed, staying with us at the moment and he's a very good doctor. He can help if necessary."

"Oh, I've known Jed since he was a kid. He and Mitch used to knock around together. It'll be no problem. Right, Sam?"

They looked at her for a reply. Samara wished they had both gone on talking between themselves, now she had to agree with the plan without stuttering.

"Sure." She tried to smile.

Bay got to her feet. "It's all settled then. We can pick you up tomorrow morning."

Sam sat in stunned silence as Bay said her goodbyes to her father, then turned to her. "Samara, would you see me to the door?"

Sam stood up and walked her out, allowing Bay to take the lead.

Bay turned to her when they were out of her father's earshot. "Samara, please let us do this for you. I know it's not ideal, but it's a small way we can repay you." Her eyes conveyed the gratitude of her words.

Sam put her hands up. "You don't need to do anything. Honestly. There's no repayment necessary." Maybe she could still talk her way out of this.

"I know that too, but we can do it, so we will." Bay gave a firm nod. "And don't worry about the history with Flynn. He wanted me to tell you it's all in the past as far as he's concerned. He forgave you long ago. I'm also not worried by it. It was all long before I came into the picture, and I know the two of you never loved each other. We've all made mistakes."

Samara felt herself liking this woman more and more, but there was one other, bigger, problem.

"What about . . .?" She stopped short of saying his name. Bay came to her rescue.

"Jed knows about the arrangement." Bay bit her lip, as though she didn't quite know what to say. "He understands why we've asked you and he has given us his support."

The subtext was obvious. Jed wasn't overjoyed at the idea of having her in such close proximity. Samara could second the feeling. She would like nothing more than to avoid seeing him altogether.

Bay must have seen her falter because she grabbed her hands and held them tight. "I have a good feeling about this, Sam. I can't explain it, but it's the right thing to do. Bob needs help, and we have the means to give it to him. Please come." Bay's eyes pleaded.

Her stomach swirled with the thought of it, but there wasn't much she could do. She would have to grin and bear it as best she could. Perhaps she could arrange things so she could avoid running into Jed. She took a deep breath.

"Okay. I guess we'll see you in the morning." She managed a tense smile.

Bay threw her arms around her. "We'll be here around ten."

Samara closed the door behind her. The sick feeling in her stomach stopped her from going further into the room. She felt the fear she had all but eradicated from her life hit her with full force.

Oh God, please help me through this time on Resolution. Help us all to heal. In her heart she knew, like Bay did, that it was the right thing to do. Now she had to trust.

CHAPTER 10

Jed studied the 'to let' section one more time in the hope he had missed something. There wasn't a single viable option amongst the advertisements. Everything was either too expensive or unsuitable. Volunteer doctoring paid, but only a fraction of what he'd earn in a hospital role, and he didn't want to get a job only to leave it the instant he was cleared and sent back overseas. Besides, why should he put himself out? It was his extended family who owned the island.

Jed could understand Flynn and Bay's desire to give back. Samara did, after all, save Bay's life. What he didn't need was to be forced to share the island with her.

He put the paper and his thoughts aside to take another sip of his coffee. His cabin veranda had become his favorite spot. The blue water of the bay shone in the early morning light, and resort guests were already taking advantage of the beautiful day. The rain had cleared.

Flynn rounded the corner of his cabin, and Jed stood as he approached.

"Finally, some decent weather." Flynn indicated the clear sky as he walked up the steps.

"Maybe we can take a trip out to the reef?" Jed had been itching to get out since his brother had suggested it.

Flynn screwed up his nose. "Can't today. I have

to take the new boat into Kiisay and collect Bob."

Jed felt a flare of anger. "Do they have to come here?"

"We have the means and they have the need. It's as simple as that, Jed. Mate, you've got to find a way of putting all this behind you. I have, long ago. I don't understand why you would want to hold onto it. People change. Sam's changed."

Jed huffed.

His brother shook his head. "She was a young girl and she hurt you. She made stupid mistakes. I did when I was young. I'm still making mistakes. It's called growth. We can't learn or grow if we think we're perfect. If you expect forgiveness, you have to give it."

Jed turned away from his brother to look out past the coconut trees dotting the shoreline. Forgiveness itself wasn't the problem. Forgetting was a different matter. As hard as he tried, he couldn't let go. His heart wouldn't let him. The intensity of his feelings made him angry at her, angry at himself, and the incident in Afghanistan confirmed the anger and frustration was destroying him.

Cassidy said part of the problem was that he had to admit he needed God's help. It all started there, but how could he? Admitting he was a failure was too hard. It would go against everything he thought he was.

He turned back to his brother. "It's not as though I don't appreciate what she did for Bay. I'd just prefer not to be around her." He didn't tell his brother that avoiding contact with Samara was pure self-preservation.

Flynn frowned. "I don't expect you to go out of your way to see them, or even have anything to do with them."

"Well, you don't have to worry about that."

"Just don't go out of your way to do anything . . . Well, un-nice."

Jed laughed at the expression. It broke the tension between them. "Okay, okay." He nodded. "I promise not to be deliberately un-nice."

Flynn gave a lopsided grin. "Hey, you're the one with the university education. I'm only a humble fisherman."

Jed shook his head at Flynn's self-description. He knew his brother had used the pathetic English to get a laugh from him. "You have my word I won't cause any trouble."

"Good." Flynn walked back down the stairs. He gave a wave over his shoulder as he left.

Jed considered how much he had missed his brother. Despite their five-year difference in age, they had been close growing up. Flynn had always taken the time to spend with his little brother, always been there for him. It had been good to spend time getting to know each other again, but now it felt as though this peaceful escape was turning into his worst nightmare.

Samara sat on her patio and watched the sunset. She was still captivated by the changes on Resolution Island. The last time she had visited, the island had been nothing but a few weatherboard cabins and an old bar. Now it was a modern eco-resort.

She sipped her iced tea, feeling instant refreshment from the cold liquid.

Patty lolled in the seat next to her, sipping her own cup. "This is a step up from the motel."

Sam closed her eyes and took a deep breath of the fresh sea air. "Certainly makes a change from the stench of mangrove mud."

"I can't believe Bob's already found all the sports channels." Patty turned to look in the front door where the television blared football commentary. Her blonde hair bounced in its bun as she moved.

Samara thought how attractive her new friend was. Her face was marked with the fine lines of life and age, but the softness of her eyes, and bright demeanor always had the ability to lift her spirits. "Thanks for coming over with us. I know it's a bit of a pain having to get back to Kiisay Point this afternoon."

Patty let out a loud, "Ha, are you kidding? I've been on an ocean cruise and enjoyed a day at a resort. I feel like I've been treated like a holidaying millionaire."

Sam smiled. The welcome, comfort and ease of the journey to the island had done much to calm her nerves. "Bay and Flynn have really rolled out the welcome mat." Sam thought about the way Flynn had helped her father onto his new boat, and the magnificent morning tea Bay had served on the short voyage over.

Patty reached over and gave the top of her hand a pat. "Flynn certainly seems like he's forgiven you. At least you have one less thing to worry about."

Sam sighed deep and long. She hadn't been sure

how to act around him, but she had taken Bay at her word when she said Flynn had put it all behind him long ago. She had decided she should be herself. It had proven to be the best plan of attack, and Flynn's attitude towards her was nothing but gracious.

She looked over to smile at Patty. "He thanked me so many times for helping Bay. He clearly treasures her. I'm so grateful I finally got to do something good for him, and for Bay."

Patty raised her eyebrows. "It was a real act of heroism, and I'm certain the Lord put you in the right place at the right time to do more than save Bay. He's already used that event to mend a few broken bridges."

Sam thought of the way her father and Flynn had talked on the boat. It was obvious that they had come to some sort of unspoken truce. She nodded in agreement. "You're right about that. Dad's always seen Flynn as some sort of nemesis. Did he ever tell you about the marijuana growing incident when we were kids?"

Patty's eyes were wide. "No. What happened?"

"My eldest brother, Andy and Flynn made a dangerous team. One school holidays they decided to make a garden. For a lark they included a marijuana plant. It grew too well and they got caught. They weren't delinquents or anything. Just stupid kids, but Bob decided Flynn was a bad influence."

Patty groaned. "I suppose Bob kept the flames of that grudge burning for most of Flynn's life."

"Yeah, but times have changed. I'm sure Bay's had a lot to do with it. Dad adores her."

Patty stood up and collected their cups. "She's certainly changed a lot around here. The place is thriving. I suppose I'd better get a move on or I'll miss my ride back."

While Patty moved inside, Sam sat up to get a better vantage point over the verandah rails. The ocean view stretched out to the horizon. Blue and green water, as far as the eye could see, glistened in the sun. Samara smiled as a white sea eagle plunged into the water of the bay. It emerged triumphant - its fish dinner hanging from its claws. The sweet fragrance of a frangipani tree in flower wafted in on a slight breeze.

She couldn't imagine a better place for her father to recuperate. Every building on the island was joined by a raised walkway or concrete path. It would be easy to get around.

The two-bedroom disabled cabin was spacious and spotlessly clean. Both bedrooms were of generous size with queen beds, sitting areas, wardrobe space and ensuites. The furniture was an eclectic mix of timber and cane. The bedrooms adjoined a large, combined kitchen-living-dining area that opened out onto a veranda overlooking the bay.

Samara recalled her earlier phone call to Nick in Sydney. It felt good to talk to him. His praise for her brave decision to go to the island had spurred her confidence. He had ended the conversation with the promise to pray for her.

Samara closed her eyes and leaned back into the comfort of the outdoor chair. She knew she would run into Jed at some stage, but for now she had determined not to let fear enter into her mind. Her Bible reading that morning had confirmed her mindset.

Therefore, do not worry about tomorrow, for tomorrow will worry about itself.

She had determined to do it.

Jed tipped the contents of the first aid kit onto the bench and sighed. It was well stocked with a variety of bandages and dressings, but no antiseptic strong enough for the wound in front of him.

"I'll do the best I can to patch you up, but I'm afraid you're going to have to go back to the mainland," he told his patient.

The fisherman gave him a pained look. "Is it seriously bad, Doc? Can't you pull it out and stick a bandage on it? I'm leaving tomorrow anyway."

Jed turned on the light of the magnifying glasses and had another look at the small gash. A piece of pink coral stuck out of the congealed red mess.

"Cuts made by coral get infected quickly. If I can't get my hands on some strong antiseptic, you'll have to go back immediately." He made a mental note to get some decent medication for the first aid kit the next time he was in town.

"Come on, Doc. I've got one more night left. If I go back now, it'll be after midnight before I get home. The missus doesn't drive, so I'd have to, and the kids are already exhausted from the day. The trip'll be a nightmare for us all."

Jed could see his predicament. Three small children and a long drive after a busy day was a stressful situation. A thought occurred to him. "Hang in there. I may have a solution." He picked up the phone before he had a chance to change his mind.

The phone rang so long Jed was about to hang up and go over to the reception himself, when his call was picked up.

Dutch's wife answered the phone.

"Hey Yvette, it's Jed. Is Bay or Flynn there?"

"Sorry, they've gone over to the research station. I'm holding down the fort."

Jed smiled. Yvette was always willing to help, but she lacked proficiency at office work. Bay didn't leave her in charge often.

"I'm down at the first aid station. I've got a man here with a piece of coral stuck in his foot."

"Oh my! Is it bad?"

"No, it's small, but we don't have anything strong enough to treat it with. I was wondering if you could go down to Bob's room and ask if they have any antiseptic liquid I could use. They're bound to have something there considering Bob's injuries." Jed knew it was the best chance he had of seeing to the cut.

"I have strict orders not to leave reception, but perhaps I can find someone to fill in for me while I go."

"That would be great, Yvette."

"I'll see what I can do." The phone went dead.

Jed hung up and turned to the patient. "If I can get my hands on something appropriate we can see you through until morning, but you have to promise to go to the doctor as soon as you get home. Coral cuts are dangerous, especially on your foot."

The man nodded. "Sure thing, Doc."

Jed prodded the injury. "Now, you'll have to be still while I pull this out coral out and rinse it."

As the minutes ticked away, Jed started to wonder if Yvette had forgotten his request. He was about to pick up the phone again when the door opened. He looked up to find Samara in the doorway. His heart raced into a speeding pace, and cold sweat washed over his skin. He cringed at his own body's betrayal, and mentally steeled himself. He hated that seeing her inspired this reaction in him.

She didn't look good. Her hair had escaped its ponytail and trailed in long wisps around her face. Her high-necked blouse was buttoned unevenly, and her dowdy skirt fell well below her knees. She wasn't wearing a scrap of make-up, her eyes were bloodshot, and her face was deathly pale.

What had happened to the perfectly manicured Samara he had known years ago? That woman wouldn't have stepped foot outside without her 'face' having been done, not to mention the designer wardrobe and coiffed hair. Toning down the materialism was a positive, but it seemed she had adopted an opposite bag lady style. The stunned look on her face gave away her surprise in seeing him there.

He recalled his promise to Flynn to be civil. One of them had to talk. Might as well be him. "Did you have the antiseptic?"

"Yes." She produced the bottle, holding it at arm's length for him to take.

Jed grabbed it, careful to avoid physical contact

with her.

He undid the bottle and proceeded to tip the majority of the liquid into a bowl.

Samara remained in the doorway. He could feel her eyes trailing his every move. It was so unnerving his hand started to shake. He looked up to see her huge brown eyes fixed on him.

Jed felt his pulse race and frustration take hold as he threw the empty container in the bin. *Why does she still do this to me?* It was a question he had asked a million times before. The absence of an answer fired his temper. He could feel the cold sweat of frustration taking hold again.

He turned to her. "If you're going to loiter, you may as well make yourself useful. Have a dig around in those bandages and find me a waterproof one." He indicated to the pile of medical supplies he had tipped out of the first aid kit. There was no way he was going to let her see him rattled. If she wouldn't leave, the next best thing was to give her something to do.

"Where's Yvette? I asked her to bring this to me, not you." Jed could hear the insult in his voice. His promise to Flynn was waning and the anger was back, but he couldn't stop. Anger was a coping mechanism he had employed every time he thought of Samara. It was hard to extinguish now she was standing right next to him.

"I don't know. She told Bob she needed some antiseptic urgently. I volunteered to bring it because she couldn't leave the office."

"Lucky me!" He had meant to say it under his breath, but the sarcastic comment came out much louder than he expected. Jed licked his lips, trying to force down the truth that he did feel lucky.

He put the antiseptic in a bowl and diluted it with saline solution, then looked at his patient, who was squirming on the bed. It was obvious he had picked up on the tension in the room. "I'll run this over the cut. It should clean it out and kill any of the coral left in the wound. It's going to sting."

The man nodded. "Whatever you say, Doc."

Jed could hear Samara going through the box. The loud rustling of plastic suddenly stopped. "I'm sorry. I can't find any waterproof dressings."

He paused before tipping the liquid onto the foot, and turned and gave her a withering glance. "There should be one there. Did you bother to have a decent look?"

Samara raised one eyebrow and stared at him. "I'll look again. Doctor." Her pursed lips gave away her frustration.

Her look did strange things to Jed's insides. The increasing pressure to acknowledge his attraction only mounted his frustration with her.

Remember what she did. The pep talk reminder of her betrayal satisfied his confused state. She was the enemy — plain and simple.

Jed positioned the bowl of antiseptic and took hold of his patient's foot. "You have to keep still while I do this. Like I said, it's going to sting."

It didn't take long to wash the wound out. The man winced a few times, but remained still enough. Jed could hear Samara scrounging around again on the bench behind him.

"Found a dressing yet?" He hoped he was wrong

and there wasn't one there, just so he could continue taunting her.

"Yes, in fact I did." She held it out to him. "It had fallen on the floor. Some idiot had tipped the contents of the medical cabinet onto the bench and it must have fallen down."

Jed seethed. She would have known it was him. *Some idiot hey? Yeah. An idiot for once taking up with you.*

He snatched the dressing from her and ripped open the plastic.

"You can put it all back now you've found it," he snapped at her as he dressed the foot.

Jed heard her let out a sharp breath.

"Last time I looked this was not a hospital, and I am not the nurse on duty."

He turned to her. One eyebrow was raised and she was as red as a beetroot.

Jed felt the anger he had suppressed for years bubble up to explosion. "Listen here—"

"Whoa." The patient waved his hands between them. "If you guys are going to kill each other I'd rather not be around." He looked at Jed. "Doc, if this foot is okay, I'm going to split."

Jed took a deep breath. "You'll be fine. But make sure you see a doctor when you get home."

"No problem." He was out the door in seconds despite the injured foot.

Jed stared back at Samara. The interruption had broken their momentum and neither spoke. They stared each other down, like two boxers in the ring.

He tried to think of the most effective insult, settling on a comment he knew would have wounded the woman he had known. "The years sure haven't been kind, Sammy. You look horrible. Couldn't you have fixed yourself up a bit before coming down here?"

Jed was pleased with himself. Attacking her physical appearance was the worst thing he could have done. It astounded him to see her unfazed. She stood there, staring at him and tapping her foot.

"Is that all you've got? All these years, and you throw me a pathetic line about how I look? I'll have you know that the first time you saw me I had just pulled a lady up a mountain of mud. This time, despite being sick, I dragged myself out of bed to bring you something you could have gotten yourself." Her eyes pierced right through him.

"You were sick and you came down to a first aid station? Real smart! Some professional you are."

Samara shifted her weight from one foot to the other, changing her stature and placing one hand on her hip. "Oh, that's right. I'm so sorry. I forgot I was speaking to the perfect Doctor McKenna. I guess attacking me in front of a patient, the way you just did, doesn't fall into your definition of unprofessional behavior." She shook her head. "You never did see your own imperfections, did you?"

Sam didn't know how close to the truth she was. Jed felt his one remaining speck of control disintegrate. He had pushed aside his feelings for so long the force of all that bottling was going to erupt. Now there was no stopping it.

"You slept with my brother." His voice was way louder than he had planned. The echoed force of his words reverberated off the walls.

Samara's eyes widened and she reeled back. "You left me without even a goodbye," she shouted, breaking eye contact for a second to throw a nonchalant glance at the ceiling. "Oh, that's right, there was a note 'It's not working'. Well, there's something else you're not perfect at, Jed. You suck at ending relationships."

"I didn't think you'd notice I'd gone. There were plenty of men lining up to take my place."

She closed her eyes for a second and shook her head. "I came home one day and you were gone. No conversation about what had gone wrong. Not even a goodbye. You just up and moved to the other end of the country without warning."

Jed could see pain in her eyes. Could he believe she had been sorry to see him leave? "It's pretty obvious I didn't mean that much to you, considering you had a relationship with my brother." He had thought he had forgiven her but it angered him to think of her with anyone else, let alone Flynn.

Samara was silent for a moment. Jed said nothing, letting the accusation hang in the air. She pulled away from him and looked out the one little window in the room. Jed could see her chest rise and fall. She finally looked back, tears brimming under the surface of her eyes.

"Taking up with Flynn was a mistake, a horrible mistake. I felt you'd used me, and it hurt so much." She dropped her head. "I was so mad at you I couldn't handle how I felt. I wanted you to acknowledge my existence, so I did the most extreme and destructive thing I could. Haven't you ever done that, Jed? Haven't you ever made a really big mistake? Haven't you ever needed forgiveness?"

Her deep brown eyes locked with his. He took a breath.

Extreme and destructive—the exact words used in the report regarding his actions in Afghanistan. Jed had read and re-read the document so many times he knew it by heart. He had pondered for hours over those two words, wondering how the description could apply to him. Was he judging her when he was guilty of the same thing? He couldn't look at her. What to do? He looked at his shoes and shook his head for what seemed like ages.

"Oh, that's right. Jed McKenna's perfect." Her comment should have been sarcastic, but there was so much sadness in her voice. He looked up at her, racking his brain for something to say. He was too late. She was walking out the door.

"Wait," he called to her retreating back.

Samara set a stunning pace down the pathway. "I don't want to argue with you anymore, Jed."

He followed her. "Stop."

She kept on walking.

They were half way down the path leading back to the cabins when Jed stopped. "Sammy."

To his surprise she turned to face him.

Now he had her attention, he had no idea what to say. He stared at her, and she stared back. Her eyes had been red before, but now they were on fire as tears streamed down her face. His stomach dropped. Her eyes had always captivated him, dark brown and deeper than he could ever fathom. But there was something different about them, an honesty he hadn't seen before. It drew him in, and he realized he believed her. He felt her sadness. It made him want to reach out to her. He forgot how much he hated harboring the feelings he still had for her. All he wanted to do was wrap his arms around her, to feel her again, to be with her.

She tilted her head. "What? What do you have to say?" Her voice cracked under the emotion.

Jed opened his mouth to speak but no words came out. It seemed like eternity went by while he waited for his brain to give him something to say, anything to say, but his mind was blank.

Samara shook her head and looked out to the beach before locking eyes with him once more. She reached up to wipe a tear trailing her cheek, then turned and walked away.

Jed watched her go. He felt like such a fool. He closed his eyes as though the darkness would jot out the emotions raging inside him.

First I attack her with everything I have, and then I run after her and have nothing to say. What is wrong with me?

He looked out to the beach. Several guests lay sunbathing on the sand, next to crystal clear water which stretched as far as the eye could see. The ocean's flat surface reflected mirror images of the surrounding islands and produced a lazy lapping noise on the shoreline. A perfect day.

Perfection, that's what she accused me of. Do I think I'm perfect?

Maybe. Somewhere in his childhood, the drive to be the perfect son, to make up for Flynn's shortcomings, had motivated many aspects of his life. His university grades, his career goals, even his relationship with Samara.

Jed had loved her so much, she had consumed his every thought. He wanted to spend every second of the day with her. It was like an obsession, and the time he devoted to Sam had an impact on his career. His goal was to work with a charity overseas. How could he do that with an intense, high-maintenance relationship hindering him?

Then there was the confusing way she acted when she was around others. It was as though she had a split personality. When they were alone, she was the girl he had fallen for—fun, playful, beautiful—but when she was in company, she played the role of the fashion model. Fake. Without substance. Men had been all over her, and it drove him crazy, convinced him she didn't love him the way he loved her. It scared him, and he left instead of facing the fear. Left without even saying goodbye.

But it wasn't only her behavior that had justified his leaving. The relationship didn't fit his perfect plan. Samara didn't fit his ideal of the perfect partner. How would she survive working in a war-ravaged country?

Standing here, now, it all felt ridiculous. Who had ever asked him to be perfect? His parents had only ever wanted him to be happy. Flynn had never asked or expected him to be anything other than himself. It was a standard he had set for himself.

What was it Flynn said? You can't learn or grow if you think you're perfect.

Jed could see his pursuit of perfection, both in himself and in Samara, had been fuel for his anger.

I understand what you're trying to tell me, God. I'm

not perfect. I never have been and I never will be. I've made some horrible mistakes. If I want forgiveness, I have to forgive. Jed felt the anger he had harbored for so long subside. How could he judge her when his own guilt was so clear?

Samara was sick. Not just stuffy-nose-and-cough sick. Laid-up-in-bed-unable-to-move sick. The hot and cold flushes pointed to an infection of some sort. It had hung on to her for over three days, starting the day she had fought with Jed.

Samara sat in bed, cold compress on her head and water within reach. The paracetamol she had taken at regular intervals through the night had done its job to ward off the temperature, but the fire in her throat was not so easily extinguished and was getting worse. She should get a doctor's appointment in town, but she didn't want to put anyone out. She also didn't relish the ocean trip in a tinny. Not in her condition.

At least Bob was recovering. He only had one leg in a cast now, but the injuries to his left arm would need complete rest to heal. He could get around on crutches, which had led to greater mobility and a happier man. Samara could hear him laughing at something he was watching on the television in his room.

She tried to sit up and reach for one of the magazines Bay had delivered that morning. Since finding out about her flu, Bay had made regular visits to monitor her condition. Sam had tried her best to discourage her, not wanting her to catch the dreaded virus, but Bay had swept aside her concerns. Last night she had brought yummy chicken soup and, despite having next to no appetite, Samara had managed to eat a decent amount of it.

A knock on the door drew her attention. She wanted to yell for her father to answer it, but didn't have enough voice left. The knock got louder and louder. Samara shook her head as she heard her father laugh. He had the television so loud it was impossible for him to hear anything.

She was about to put her feet on the floor when a head peeked around the frame of her opened doorway.

"Hi, Amos." Her voice was hoarse.

"Hey. I've got something for you. Bay told me you're sick." He walked in the door with an old worn flask in his hand.

She sat up a little.

"I got some good medicine here for you. Fix you right up." Amos flashed a wide smile.

Samara couldn't help but smile back as he poured a good helping into the cup from the top of the flask.

Bob hobbled through the door. "Amos! I thought I heard someone."

"Hey, Bob." Amos nodded to him in acknowledgment. "I got something here that I made up traditional way."

Amos handed the cup to Samara. It emitted a distinct pungent odor. Amos was of Pacific Islander heritage and she wondered what traditional ingredients he had used.

"What is it?" She held the cup away and screwed

up her face.

Amos smiled. "It's a good brew. Bit of apple cider vinegar, some garlic and some fresh ingredients. Don't worry. Lots of doctors have looked at it and there's nothing bad in there. It's all good stuff. Go on, get it into ya."

Samara stared at him for a full five seconds. He wasn't going to leave without her having at least a sip of the gruesome liquid.

"Go on, Sam. Toughen up." Her father wasn't helping.

She held her nose and hoped for the best. *At least I have limited taste.* She took a huge swig. It tasted like rotten eggs. She forced herself to swallow and reached for a glass of water from her bedside table.

Her father laughed as she gulped down the water, trying to rid her mouth of the foul taste.

"You'll feel better tomorrow. You'll wake up and that flu will be gone." Amos re-filled the cup. "Your turn now, Bob." He handed the cup over to her father.

"No way. You're not getting me to drink that stuff."

Sam smiled as he tried to back away, a hard task considering he was on crutches.

Amos shook his head and smiled. "You need a teaspoon of cement first, to toughen you up?"

Sam grinned. Her father prided himself on his toughness. He reluctantly took the cup from Amos. "Are you sure this stuff is going to do me good?"

"You ever seen me sick?" Amos raised his eyebrows.

"No, as a matter of fact I don't recall ever seeing

you crook." Bob frowned.

"That's because of this stuff." Amos pointed to the cup.

Bob lifted his shoulders in defeat before gulping the contents of the cup. He screwed up his face and grabbed the bottom of his shirt, holding it up to his mouth and rubbing the fabric over and over on his tongue. "That's the worst stuff I've ever tasted, Amos. What have you got in there? It isn't going to kill me, is it?"

Amos laughed as he replaced the cup back on top of the flask. "Don't taste good, but do you good."

Samara smiled. "Thank you." Even though the medicine was disgusting, she appreciated the sentiment and the effort. Amos wanted to help—it wasn't his fault the 'cure' was unpalatable.

"No problem. Trust me, tomorrow you feel better." He turned to leave.

"Hey, what about me? Am I going to wake up and kick off this other cast?" Bob asked.

"Nah. It won't do anything for you. I just wanted to see you drink some." Amos's mischievous grin said it all.

Samara tried to laugh at the horrified look on Bob's face but her throat was too painful.

Amos turned to leave.

"It better do me some good, Amos, or I'll lock you up for unlawful doctoring." Bob called after him, hobbling out the room as fast as he could.

Samara lay back down and fell fast asleep.

Samara felt detached from her body. She

couldn't move, couldn't even shake her big toe. Not even a tiny wiggle. The struggle was too much for her. It would have to stay where it was.

She turned to look at the clock. Midday. She had slept for three hours but felt exhausted. The infection had been viral to begin with, because she ached from the top of her head to the tip of her non-functioning toes. But telltale symptoms suggested it had turned into a bacterial infection. To add to her trouble, her voice had now disappeared altogether. She couldn't even manage a squeak.

She looked up as her door creaked open and Bay peeked inside. Sam mustered up a small smile.

"How are you feeling?" Bay entered the room and took a seat next to the bed.

Samara turned to look at her. It felt as though her entire skull was stuffed with cotton wool. She opened her mouth to talk, but only a slight squeak came out.

"Oh, no. You've lost your voice." Bay picked up her hand off the bed and gave it a firm squeeze. "This is ridiculous. I can't see you suffering when we have a doctor right here."

Loud warning bells rang in Samara's head. *Doctor. Right here.* She could see where this was heading. She tried to protest, waving her hands in a theatrical way and shaking her head so hard her vision blurred.

Bay's eyebrows dipped low and she pursed her lips. "Very dramatic, Sam but you're just going to get worse if you don't see a doctor. It's Jed or town. I don't want to have to call the rescue helicopter for a medical evacuation, and there's no way you're travelling in a tinny in this condition." She stood, placed her hands on her hips and stared down at Sam.

Samara rolled her eyes and reached for the pencil and notebook her father had given her. She wrote in bold letters: *Now who's being dramatic?* She turned it around to show Bay, who read it and grinned.

"You two may have a painful history, but he's a good doctor. It'll make me feel much better knowing he's checked you out. I'm sure he'll be professional. I'm going straight away to ask him." Bay left before Sam could answer.

She and Jed having a painful history was the understatement of the year. She dreaded the thought of having to see him again, considering their last encounter. Hours in bed reliving the gruesome event over and over in her mind hadn't helped. After analyzing and dissecting every second of their fight, Samara had come to the conclusion that Jed didn't just dislike her—he despised her, and it hurt.

Yes, it was all in the past. She had forgiven him and moved on, and was a different person. But one conversation with Jed and she found herself back in the skin of her younger self, hurt and desperately in love with him

How can I still love him? It's been years. I've changed. I don't want the same things now. We don't even know each other anymore. There was no sense to it.

And he hates me. The pain was more than emotional. It cramped her stomach and made her head throb, heaping more physical stress on her flu-ravaged body.

Samara settled back onto her pillow. Maybe he

would refuse to come. It wasn't necessary. She felt horrible, but the virus had peaked and she was in no danger. If she stayed in bed and didn't overexert herself, she'd recover soon. And the fever was probably fighting any infection she had.

She forced her mind to quiet and closed her eyes, falling asleep in minutes.

Jed sat on the veranda of his cabin, cursing himself again for agreeing to something that made his stomach churn. Bay had visited him earlier, concerned about Samara. She wasn't getting any better—in fact, Bay said she'd deteriorated. Bay was so concerned for her she had come straight over and asked if he would see her. Jed had baulked at the idea of another encounter.

Bay had picked up on his reluctance. "I know you don't want to see her, Jed. But I wouldn't ask if she wasn't so sick. Samara and Bob are our guests. I want them to have the best attention. Can't you put your feelings aside for a few minutes and be a doctor?"

Jed cringed. It was exactly the problem. He wished he could put his feeling aside. Way aside.

"For me, if not for her?"

Jed rolled his eyes. How could he say no? Bay had been so accommodating where he was concerned. Not only had she made room for him at the resort, she had accepted him as family and had incorporated him into her world like a brother. To say 'no' would be unthinkable.

"I'll go over there as soon as possible," he had

said.

Now he regretted the promise. He had steeled himself twice to go over to Samara's cabin, telling himself not to be so pathetic. He'd faced ongoing physical danger in Afghanistan, yet here he was, reluctant to face an ex-girlfriend. But it wasn't just any ex-girlfriend. She was the woman he'd never forgotten, the woman he still had feelings for, the woman who had him so wound up he couldn't string two words together.

Jed shook his head again when he recalled their last encounter. He'd felt like such a fool standing there with nothing to say. The last thing he wanted was a repeat of that idiocy. Twice during the day he had made it as far as the path, only to stop and retrace his steps back to the safety of his cabin. Now it was late afternoon, and as the sun moved off the veranda he knew it was now or never. If he didn't go, Bay would be back for an explanation.

Why did you say yes? Why? He picked up his bag and dragged his feet over to the steps leading down to the path.

And then decided to take the long way around.

Samara fought to focus in the soft light of the room. She recognized the huge palm fronds outside her window, swaying in the breeze, casting wild shadows on the timber blinds. She must have slept for hours. Movement in the corner of the room caught her attention. Somebody was in the room. She reeled back as she recognized Jed. There was a heavy bang as her head hit the timber bed head.

Jed jumped to his feet, and they stared at each other for a second. Samara rubbed the back of her throbbing scalp.

He opened his mouth as if to say something, then closed it again before looking towards the open doorway, then back at her. "Sorry. I didn't mean to scare you. I was just . . ." He gestured towards the door. "Bob told me to come in. You were stirring, so I thought it best to wait."

Samara looked around the room, then at the clock. Five. How long had he been there?

Jed must have read her mind. "I've only been here a few minutes." He shuffled his feet and fidgeted with the handle of the medical bag he was holding. "Bay asked me to come by. She told me you've been ill."

Sam nodded. There wasn't much use trying to speak. The thick, tight feeling in her throat confirmed she still had no voice.

"So, is it OK if I take a look? Bay seems to think it's necessary."

She nodded again.

He picked up a bag at the side of the chair. Samara's stomach did a flip-flop as a shock of hair fell over his forehead, longer than she'd ever seen it. Her hand itched to reach out and smooth it back. He was more muscular than she remembered. He'd always had an attractive physique, but complained about medical school and hospital life making him soft. Any softness had disappeared and she could see his muscular form under his t-shirt and board shorts. He looked up at her, catching her staring at him. Samara pretended to be captivated by a moth on the ceiling.

He took a seat on the edge of her bed. Having him in such close proximity was agony. *Don't think about him. Don't think about him. Don't think about him.* He opened the bag and pulled out a stethoscope.

"Can you tell me your symptoms?"

Samara looked to the bedside table for her notebook and pen. The notebook was there, but the pen was gone. She looked back at Jed and shook her head.

He sighed. "I'm here on a purely professional basis, Sam. I'm not going to jump down your throat or yell at you. Just tell me what you've got, let me take a look, and I'll leave."

She felt a pang of hurt at his bluntness. What did she expect? That he was there out of concern for her wellbeing? Bay had asked him to come, so he had.

"Well?"

Samara pointed to her throat, then cut the air with her hands and mouthed 'no voice'. Her explanation was met with a confused expression. She patted around the bed covers, then leaned over and looked down beside the bed. The pen had rolled off the table. She could see the tip under the timber frame. As she reached down to retrieve it her hand rubbed against Jed's knee. He shuffled back down the bed. She pretended she hadn't noticed, and turned to scribble on her note book: *I have a throat infection. Sorry. No voice.* She turned it around to show him.

"Nothing at all?" His eyebrows raised.

She shook her head.

"This might turn out better than I expected." He

gave her a lopsided grin. Samara felt the warmth of his cheeky smile. Jed had always been good-looking, but he had matured in the last few years. The boyishness had gone, and his rugged features and wide smile made her heart skip a beat.

"Let me get this right. You're telling me you can't speak a word? Nothing? You're truly a captive audience?" His blue eyes teased her.

Samara rolled her eyes and wrote on her notebook: *I still have very fast penmanship.* She turned it around to him, offering up a grin and one raised eyebrow.

"I should have known better." He shook his head and grinned back.

He put the stethoscope in his ears and placed the round end on her chest. Samara was grateful he hadn't asked her to open her high-necked t-shirt. The last thing she needed was questions about her scar—especially when she had no voice to explain.

"Take a few deep breaths."

Samara did as she was told.

"Sit forward." He placed the stethoscope on her back. "Deep breaths."

Samara was far too aware of his close proximity, and hoped he didn't notice her heart beating faster as he leaned further into her.

"You can sit back down." He placed the stethoscope back in the bag.

"Open your mouth, please." He checked her throat. He also checked her eyes and ears. He paused and gave her an apologetic look. "I have to check your glands. Okay?"

She nodded. His hands rested behind her ears

and his fingers probed in slow movement down her neck. Samara tried not to look at him, finding the moth again and fixing on its motley brown wings. His hands were warm and sure, gliding smoothly over her skin. It felt so good to be touched by him that Samara couldn't help but swallow hard, then hoped he hadn't noticed her nervous reaction. His fingers probed back up behind her ears, and settled under her ear lobes.

She expected him to drop his hands and say her glands were swollen, but instead he kept a firm hold on her. Her gaze moved from the moth to his face. His eyes were as deep blue as she remembered, like a winter sky.

Their eyes locked. It felt as though the world had stopped. Complete silence surrounded them, and Samara was vaguely aware of the pulsing in her neck, below his touch. He tilted his hands, allowing his palms to touch her jaw line and cup her face. Samara felt her torso sway towards him. His gaze dropped to her lips as his body mirrored her movement. Their faces were inches apart.

"How's my girl? Is she going to survive?" Her father's booming voice sounded from the doorway.

Jed dropped his hands. "She'll be fine." He retrieved his bag and got to his feet. "You're right. It's a throat infection. A bad one. I'd say it started as a viral infection, but from the sound of your chest it's turned bacterial, so I suggest a course of antibiotics. It'll be the best way to effectively clear it up." He looked to Bob. "Lots of bed rest. Lots of fluids. Amos is in town now. I'll email the prescription to the pharmacy and get him to pick it up. That way you can start taking them tonight."

"That's a relief. Finally a decent doctor, and not some weird concoction Amos forced down your throat." Bob grunted.

Jed laughed." Don't tell me Amos mixed you up some of his cure-all."

"He did." Bob said. "And it almost killed me."

Jed picked up his bag and looked at Samara. "I had that stuff forced on me when I was a kid. Does it still taste like rotten eggs?"

Samara nodded and rolled her eyes. She penned her answer: *I think it's what took my voice.*

Jed laughed when she turned it around to show him. "Maybe I should get Amos to mix me up some and I'll keep it handy for our next meeting."

Samara saw her father frown, confused. Not much got past him. She didn't care. Jed wanted to see her again. Even if she couldn't talk. There was hope. Maybe he could forgive her.

He turned to make his way to the door. "As horrible as it is, his concoction works incredibly well." He looked back. "Even if you're feeling better, stay in bed and rest. You'll be fine."

The two men left the room. Sam heard Jed ask her father how he had been. Bob went about describing his injuries in great detail.

She propped the pillows up behind her back and touched her neck where his hands had been. Then closed her eyes and visualized the way he had looked at her. She could feel the tightness of the scar on her chest as she took a deep breath. She certainly wasn't the same girl he had known. How could he want her now, after all she had done?

He doesn't really care about you. It's just physical chemistry.

Maybe physical attraction was all it ever was.

Sam felt tears well. She had to let these feelings go or they would hurt her again.

CHAPTER 11

Jed could see the tinny containing Amos and a female passenger pound into a rogue wave as it came to rest beside the floating pontoon. He made his way down to the jetty to check Amos had collected the right medicine for Samara.

Bay skipped down the office steps to join him on the path. "I can take the tablets over to her if you like." She placed a hand on his shoulder. "You've sacrificed enough for one day." Her smile was kind, and Jed could see how grateful she was.

"Thanks. The dosage will be on the packet, so there's no need for me to visit." They walked down the path to the water.

Yet visiting Sam was exactly what he wanted to do. *Get a grip. Don't be an idiot. She wasn't a good choice the first time, so why go back?*

The internal pep talk didn't stop a vision of Samara's long dark hair covering her pillow like a halo as she slept. She was beautiful even without makeup. The puffy redness under her closed eyelids didn't distract from her attractiveness. He had smiled when he saw how she was sleeping—one long leg outside the covers and wrapped around the sheet. It was how she had slept when they were together.

He reached up to rub the back of his neck. The emotional tension he was under was taking a physical toll.

Bay stopped short of the pontoon walkway. "Was it horrible?" Her deep frown and downturned mouth showed her concern.

Jed shoved both hands in his pockets. "No. It was fine." He shrugged his shoulders in an effort to look nonchalant. "She was asleep when I got there, so I waited for her to wake up. And she's lost her voice, so that was kinda fun." He hoped his grin was enough to satisfy his sister-in-law.

It was. Bay laughed.

Jed took a deep breath. In reality, it was no laughing matter.

As they strolled up to Amos and his passenger, he recalled how Samara's one long leg and exposed thigh had affected him. In an effort to counteract the physical stirring within, he had tried to recall how different she was in company, how jealous he had been at the attention she had enjoyed from other men.

Bay welcomed the lady passenger with a hug and kiss while Jed helped Amos with the luggage. The new arrival was of Pacific Islander heritage, the same as Amos. Her tight curls were pulled back on one side and clasped with a flower hairclip, and her tropical print shirt sat in bright contrast with her navy shorts. She smiled at him, her face as bright as her dark brown eyes.

Bay did the introductions. "Esther, this is my brother-in-law, Jed. Jed this is Amos's sister, Esther."

Jed reached out to shake the lady's hand. "Nice to meet you."

"Actually, we've met a few times, but you would have been around sixteen the last time I got down from Cairns to visit."

Jed glanced at Amos as he joined them on the pontoon. "I'm sorry, I don't remember. That's a long time in between visits."

Esther picked up her handbag from the offloaded goods. "I know. It's too long. Of course, we've all been together many times over the years, but I don't get down here often. I'm only visiting now because I can't get out and do the job I came here to do."

Amos picked up a satchel from the goods. "Esther's a nurse. She works in Indigenous health. She's supposed to be out at Bonalah, but the doctor couldn't get here. So she come to see us instead." He opened the satchel and rummaged around in it.

"What were you doing out there?" Jed had never visited the township of Bonalah, seventy-five kilometers west of Kiisay Point.

"Immunizations. They had me booked in there for a week. It's a real shame. We don't get out there enough." Esther swung her bag on her shoulder. "I look after everything including the outlying areas, but I need a doctor to be there. Most of the time it's a technicality, but still necessary. They'd organized a local GP, but he had an emergency. Now I've got to wait to see if the department can organize a replacement." She sighed. "Oh well, at least I get to see my brother." She gave Amos a squeeze around his shoulders.

Jed accepted Samara's medication from Amos. He racked his brain for an excuse to give Bay that would justify him delivering the medicine.

What are you doing? He pulled himself up. He

needed a distraction. A plan formed.

"If they don't find you a replacement, I'll attend the clinic with you, Esther. I've got nothing to do all day."

Esther's eyes widened. "That's generous Jed, but I couldn't let you. Amos told me this is your first break in years." She waved her hands in the air. "No. No. We'll be fine. You enjoy your time here with your family."

Jed could see his escape slipping away. "Esther, please. It would be a pleasure to help you out. I spent some time out at a remote community before going overseas. I'd love to get back out in that environment." Not only would the short project be convenient, he would enjoy the opportunity.

Esther looked from Amos to Bay, then back to him. The others remained silent. Esther nodded. "Okay. If they don't find a replacement tomorrow, I'll tell them I've found my own. Are you sure now?"

Jed rubbed the back of his neck. It was still seized with tension. "I'm positive. It would be a gift to me." He focused on Esther to assure him of his sincerity.

The road to the remote township of Bonalah was old and poorly maintained. What were once narrow bitumen roads were now holed tracks through the bush. Heavy weather had battered the region over the last few months and further deteriorated the access. Progress was slow.

Regardless of the time and effort it took to get there, Jed had enjoyed the two days he had spent servicing a clinic in the township. The chance to get away from Resolution and use his skills was a welcome diversion. The hours spent travelling back and forth from Resolution to the isolated settlement was a welcome distraction. It had given him an escape from the island and had taken his mind off Samara.

It was five days since he had seen her, and his absence meant he had successfully avoided another encounter with her. The less time he spent in her presence, the less confusion he had to battle within himself. It was a great theory, but unfortunately, the long drives had given him hours to think about her, remember their time together.

He couldn't stop thinking about the girl he had fallen in love with, the captivating side of Samara he had never forgotten. She had a magnetic tomboyishness about her. Growing up, she had only been Mitch's little sister, attempting to impress them and trying to tag along on their childhood adventures. When he had seen her again in the city hospital, he couldn't believe how she had changed. The annoying little girl he once knew became the object of his desire.

He hit the steering wheel of the four-wheel drive. *What is wrong with you? Get over it.*

Jed tried to replace the desire with anger, telling himself again how she had taken up with his brother. How much that had hurt him. Regardless of how hard he tried to conjure it up, the anger wouldn't come. Jed rubbed his face in an attempt to alleviate some of his frustration. He had always been able to replace his feelings for Samara with anger. He was sure the anger had driven him to make a stupid mistake in Afghanistan, and with that event the pressure of it had lifted so now he couldn't retrieve it as a coping mechanism.

Then there was the feeling that had resurfaced after seeing her so sick she couldn't talk. He'd wanted to kiss her. Thankfully, Bob's sudden presence pulled him into line.

The four-wheel drive lurched sideways as it hit another pothole. Jed's head thumped the back of his seat as the car pulled to the right. The road was so narrow it was impossible to dodge every hole. He was thankful the huge four-wheel drive vehicle was more than capable of negotiating the off-road conditions.

Jed swerved to miss another pothole and wondered how he could remain on Resolution. It was impossible to live in close proximity to Samara and not think about her.

How will I ever leave her again? The thought made him stop the car with a sudden jerk.

Jed stared out his windscreen. He was gripping the steering wheel so hard his knuckles had turned white.

Why would he entertain the thought of a relationship with her? He knew Cassidy's influence had set him on the path of forgiveness, not just for Samara and Flynn, but for himself. Over time Jed had felt the weight of bitterness diminish, but he had also prayed he would be free of his love for Samara, which he believed had continued to poison his life. He was confused and frustrated. Those feelings never lessened.

Now here he was, exhausted from anger and

struggling yet again to admit he needed help. He recognized the problem: he was trying to deal with this on his own. He prayed aloud.

"OK, I've admitted I'm not perfect. I've tried to be, but I'm not even good; my own actions have proven that. But your love for me is perfect, and I need your help. I've tried every way I know how to overcome these feelings, and each time I've failed. Please give me your direction. Only you have the perfect plan for me."

Jed felt an instant peace. This wasn't something he had to overcome by his own efforts or understanding. He had to trust God had a plan for him, and it was perfect.

Samara felt the advantage of good health as she prepared lunch in the kitchen. The chicken pieces she was frying smelled so good her mouth watered. Amos's remedy had been remarkable. She had woken up feeling significantly better days after taking the dreadful liquid. The week-long course of antibiotics had seen an end to the remnants of her infection.

She turned the pieces in the pan, inspiring another burst of sizzle. It was over a week since Jed had paid her a visit. She had spent the time trying to stop him from creeping into her thoughts. It was almost impossible, and she found herself constantly reminiscing about their time together.

Visions of the fun they had on dates filled her mind as she watched her lunch cooking. The shrill ring of the cabin's landline telephone broke through her daydream, and she scrambled to take the pan off the heat in order to answer it.

It was strange to hear it ringing. The only calls they received were from in-house reception, or Bay asking if she was home for a visit.

She picked up the mobile receiver. "Hello?"

"Samara?"

She was sure she knew the voice. "Trevor?"

"Great, I was hoping to get you at home. You really need to keep your cell phone on. I've been trying to reach you." He sounded a little gruff, put out.

Sam took a seat on one of the stools adjacent to the kitchen bench. "Sorry. I don't have any need to monitor it out here." She looked out to the ocean beyond.

"I have some disturbing news, and I wanted to speak to you myself."

Sam picked up a pen and fiddled with the clicker on the top. "Have you found my attacker?" She had been praying hard for Trevor to have a breakthrough in the case.

"No. I wish that was the reason for my call. We've had a homicide and we believe it may be linked to your attack."

Sam could feel a thick ball in her throat. She swallowed hard. "What kind of link?"

"Well." Trevor paused for a moment. "The victim was a club worker, like you. She had similar cuts to her body, and a gag and blindfold were both used. We believe the weapon was the same."

Sam closed her eyes. "Would I have known her?"

"No. She was new to the area. I wanted to see

how you are doing. You haven't had any further recollections about that night?"

Samara went back to clicking the pen. "No. I'm sorry. If I had I would have told you straight away."

"I know you would have." Sam heard Trevor sigh. "Just watch out for anything unusual, and call me if you think of anything, no matter how insignificant it may seem."

"No worries." Sam put down the pen.

"And stay safe. I've filled your father in on the new development."

Sam didn't know whether to feel relieved or concerned that Trevor had kept Bob in the loop. He couldn't give her much protection with his injuries, and she didn't want to stress him out while he was still in recovery.

"When did you speak to him?" She didn't want to sound angry with the detective, but she needed to know exactly what she was dealing with.

"About fifteen minutes ago. I had to call him on his cell phone because I couldn't reach you. He was the one to suggest I try contacting you thorough the resort reception line."

Sam picked up the pen again and made square doodles on the notepad by the phone. "I promise I'll keep my cell phone on in future." She couldn't blame Trevor for contacting Bob when she hadn't been available.

"Good. We don't believe you're in any danger, so you don't need to go into hiding. Just be on your guard."

They said their goodbyes and Sam replaced the phone back on its cradle. She placed the frypan in the oven to keep it warm. The chicken didn't seem appetizing any more.

She looked out the window to see her father expertly negotiating the wheelchair ramp in spite of the awkwardness of his crutches. There had been a significant improvement in his mobility in the last week. With her laid up in bed, Bob was forced to do a lot for himself, and the activity had proven to be a boost for his self-confidence. In the last few days he had been visiting the main building to sit at the restaurant and order coffee, talking to guests and staff wandering around the area.

Sam checked the time. He had left at nine and was now returning at twelve-thirty. He'd been gone so long Samara had phoned down an hour ago to check he was alright.

He hobbled into the living area, balancing his crutches at the door, and sinking onto the cane sofa.

"I've had a great morning, Sam."

"I gathered you found plenty of people to talk to at the restaurant."

"Yep." Her father stretched his free leg out in front of him. "Did Trevor Delaney get hold of you?"

Sam nodded.

"I wish he had a more positive report." Bob reached over for the television remote and turned on the sporting channel. "It is what it is, I guess. We have to deal with it as best we can." He looked over and gave her a smile before turning down the television volume. "Amos was in for a while. He got a call from his sister, Esther. She's a nurse, working up at Bonalah for a few weeks doing immunizations in the community there."

"I'm pleased the authorities are finally getting some services up there." She was well aware of the disadvantages the isolated community faced. Many of the residents didn't have the means to make the journey into the city for care.

Her father frowned. "The organization pulled her out unexpectedly and sent her back up to Cairns. She was upset because she doesn't know when she'll get back down again."

Samara took a seat next to him. "What a shame they'd start the job and not let her finish. It's about time those people got some decent medical care. What about the children who didn't get immunized?"

Samara felt the government didn't put enough resources into the needs of its remote population. The biggest hurdle was getting qualified professionals to service the isolated areas. Most doctors and nurses preferred city life and city salaries to working in remote areas, despite the dire need.

"It's nothing but a disgrace." She sank back onto the cushion.

"I thought you'd feel that way, so I volunteered your services to finish the job."

"Excuse me?" Samara raised her eyebrows.

"I'm going fine here, Sam. I can do most things for myself, and I feel like you're stuck here with me. It's about time you got out a bit. Take your mind off things. Patty agrees with me. She's going to come over for a few days and give me some company while you have a break." He put his leg up to rest on the coffee table as he spoke.

Samara looked at him and smiled. It was obvious

what was going on. "Are you trying to get rid of me, Dad?"

Her father feigned astonishment. "Who? Me? What gives you that idea? I reckon it would be good for you to be busy." His sly smile gave him away. This wasn't all about her.

Samara shook her head and rolled her eyes. She wasn't about to discourage her father. She had seen Patty's good influence on him. And the change of scene would do her good. It would be blissful to get away from Resolution for a few days, and a relief to use her skills for more than dressing wounds.

"Okay, I'll get out of your way so you can romance Patty." She couldn't help but tease him.

"Who said anything about romance? We're just good friends."

"Whatever you say, Bob." Samara patted his hand as she got up and walked back to the kitchen. "So what arrangements did you make for me?" She needed particulars.

"Esther jumped at the chance to get you into the job. She has to leave tomorrow, but she's going to wait until you get out there to fill you in on what needs to be done. You can get a lift out to Bonalah with Jed McKenna in the morning."

Samara choked on the water, coughing up the liquid that went down the wrong way as her father spoke. She tried to catch her breath.

"Ease up, Sam. It doesn't have bones in it!"

"What do you mean, a lift with Jed McKenna?" Her voice came out squeaky and high-pitched.

"He's been out there the last few days giving her a hand. She needed a doctor, and he was available.

You said the history between you and him wasn't a problem. You seemed to get on the other day." Her father jutted out his bottom lip and gave a nod of approval. "In any case, she'll organize it with him. You need to be ready to go at six in the morning." Bob reached for the television remote control.

"But I can't possibly go." Samara could feel the tightening in her chest. It was hard enough spending ten minutes alone with Jed. There was no way she would survive all day with him.

Her father turned to her, his eyebrows slanted. "Why not?"

"Because." She busied herself wiping the kitchen counter in an attempt to hide her nervous energy. The explanation was pitiful. *He's never going to accept that.*

"I don't get it. What's the problem? Don't you want to help out?"

Sam was stuck. She either had to tell her father about her feelings for Jed, or steel herself to spend hours with him. She tossed up the least painful option and decided to come clean.

"Dad, I was in love with Jed. Like completely and utterly in love. He broke my heart and I tried to get back at him by having a relationship with his brother." She took a quick breath. "Except it didn't work. He didn't love me, and he didn't care about me and Flynn."

Her father flipped the off button on the television and turned to give her his full attention. "Why didn't you tell me about this?" Now Bob was in fully-fledged Dad mode. His eyes were wide and he sat up a bit straighter while he waited for her answer.

"It hurt. I never told you because it's painful, and I didn't want you to worry about me. This is the first time I've seen him since then, and I'm finding it hard to deal with." It was the understatement of the year.

She could see the wheels turning in her father's mind as he processed the information. She said nothing, waiting to see if she was off the hook.

"Did all this happen with him before you left the hospital and came back home?" He stared at her with what her brothers liked to call the interrogation eye.

Sam looked away before answering. "Yes."

Her father let out a resounding "Humph." He repositioned his remaining leg cast with a plunk before continuing. "You were pretty unhappy back then. If you have unresolved issues concerning your past then you're better off facing up to them than running away. You don't want to make the same mistake twice. Fear can drive you into many corners. Trust me, I've been there. Why do you think I never remarried? I never dealt properly with the break up with your mother. It's not healthy to stick your head in the sand."

His poignant words struck home. She'd allowed fear to control her life. Running away from her problems was her specialty, but her faith had shown her a different way. Now she was in danger of making the same mistake. Her father was right. She had to face up to Jed, and deal with what had happened between them, as well as the feelings she knew she still had for him. But she didn't have to do it alone.

Samara sighed. "You're right, Dad. I have to face it."

"Mind you, I wouldn't mind a few words with the boy first. Sort him out, so to speak." Bob's gruff, protective tones were a strange comfort.

Samara smiled, Jed was thirty, not a boy any more. Even so, it was nice to have a champion.

Sam closed her eyes. Her resolve to trust had given her the courage to face whatever came her way.

She recalled one of her favorite verses. *I waited patiently for the Lord; he turned to me and heard my cry. He lifted me out of the slimy pit, out of the mud and mire; he set my feet on a rock and gave me a firm place to stand.*

Jed didn't have a choice. He had to pull himself together and rely on the strength of his faith, and the security of his professionalism to see him through the next week.

Just don't make an idiot of yourself.

He had resolved not to fight or question Esther's decision to hand her job over to Samara. Resolution Island wasn't a big enough place to avoid her forever—further contact with her would be inevitable.

Jed sat on the end of the floating pontoon. He had already prepared a boat to take them over to the mainland. He looked out to sea. It was another exceptionally beautiful day. The ocean was glassed out, with nothing but a gentle ripple lapping the shoreline of Resolution Bay, and the sun shone in a blue sky. A flock of white cockatoos had arrived to ravage the shoreline. Their presence produced the occasional chorus of squawks as they moved from place to place along the beachfront.

He closed his eyes and took in the scent of the day. The early morning air was pleasantly warm, and there was a whiff of disinfectant coming from one of the boats tied to the pontoon.

The resort was already a hive of activity. Jed waved to Amos's cousin, Neville, busy at his job of cleaning the pathways. Neville waved back.

Jed checked his watch. Five minutes to six. He considered getting into the boat and starting the engine when he spotted Samara coming up the path towards him. She was wearing three-quarter length pants and a cotton blouse buttoned all the way to the top. Her long ponytail swung behind her, and a large bag moved back and forth on her shoulder as she walked. Jed recalled how he would often give her ponytail a tug. He had playfully done it when they were children and she was trying to join in the boys' games, then he did it to get her attention when they were dating. It was part of their history, an unspoken communication.

She was curvier than he remembered, but it was hard to tell under the nondescript outfit. She certainly didn't dress like the Samara he used to know. That girl would be horrified at what this one was wearing, but these clothes still suited her. Somehow they made her look more like herself. It was impossible not to look at her.

She stopped to smile at Neville, who gave her a massive grin. Neville pointed to something beyond his vision then ducked away. He returned with a fully bloomed red hibiscus flower. They spoke as Neville passed it to her, but Jed was too far away to hear their words. Samara took it and smiled. Her delight at his gift lit up her face.

The exchange was harmless, but Jed felt a stirring in his gut. He wished it was him, not Neville, who had been the recipient of her smile.

He stood as she approached. She gave him a smaller, more cautious version of the smile she had given Neville.

"Good morning. Isn't it a beautiful day?" Her greeting held overtones of nervous energy.

He casually placed his hands in his pockets. "Best since I've been here."

Samara twirled the stem of the flower around in her hand as they stood in awkward silence. Jed had run out of small talk, and he could tell Sam didn't know how to proceed beyond the formalities either.

Jed rolled his eyes. *Great!* "We should get going." He gestured towards the pontoon.

The noise of the boat's engine prevented any conversation as they made their way to the mooring at Kiisay Point. After securing the boat, they set off in the four-wheel drive parked in a holding yard at the top of the boat ramp.

Jed breathed a sigh of relief for the massive width of the center console separating their seats. Having Samara all the way over the other side of the wide car was a blessing.

Yet the silence between them made him squirm. He frowned at the stereo as the warbling tones of a love song trilled out from the radio. Jed reached over to flip through the channels in an effort to find something less affronting. He settled on a national talkback station. The subject under discussion was the state of psychiatric facilities for the homeless. The banter was intense as one guest—a psychologist who worked in a homeless shelter—did battle with a government representative from the health department. The psychologist highlighted the lack of support for the mentally disabled, while the representative stressed the government's commitment to funding support for the homeless.

Jed heard Samara let out an exasperated snort as the representative attempted to account for his department's pathetic decision-making process. He glanced across and saw her shaking her head as the debate heated. When the claim arose that government funding was entirely adequate for the homeless in Australia, Samara exploded.

"Can you believe this guy? Talk about blind bureaucracy. He hasn't got a clue about what facilities exist for the homeless, let alone the pathetic funding. Why doesn't he shut up and listen to the people on the ground? He might learn something."

What? The Samara Jed knew wasn't passionate about anything but designer clothes and the latest look. He glanced sideways at her and couldn't help but smile at the sight of her red face. The last time he had seen her so frustrated was in a discussion about the eighties fashion revival. The contrast was amusing. She looked over, catching his smirk.

"What?" Her exasperated tone made him glance at her before turning his attention back to the road. He could feel her stare boring into the side of his face. He shrugged and glanced sideways at her again.

She was pursing her lips and squinting at him. "It's nothing to smile about. People are dying because they have nowhere to go to get help, and there are certain factions in the government who won't listen or take advice from those in the know. They stick their heads in the sand and ignore the problem." She lifted a bottle of water from the console as she spoke, then slammed it back into its slot.

A mental picture of her disgust over the revival of florescent yellow socks flashed into his head. He couldn't help it—he smiled again.

"Is there something wrong with you?" The potency of her words squashed his amusement.

Jed shook his head and tried to inject some control. "No. I totally agree with you. It's just . . ." He paused and contemplated whether it was wise to reveal his thoughts. "I don't ever recall you having such intense feelings about this kind of subject."

He glanced at her several times to gauge her reaction to his comment.

Samara sighed and looked out her window for a moment before answering him. "Experiences change people, Jed." Her voice was soft and reflective. "I guess you could say I've grown up a lot. I worked in a homeless shelter in Sydney, and I've been witness to the red tape and lack of support in the system. It's disgusting and frustrating."

Her revelation caught his attention. Samara and homeless shelters didn't go together in his mind. "What sort of work were you doing there? If you don't mind my asking."

"No, I don't mind." She went into a detailed explanation of her position at the shelter, her day-to-day-tasks, and the people she treated.

Jed listened with interest. It was apparent she

had loved her time in the role, and the fact she was paid so little for her work astounded him. There was more to this new Samara than a change of clothes.

"How did you come to be there?" The instant he asked the question, Jed regretted it. It was too personal—her silence confirmed his gut feel. "Sorry, you don't have to answer."

She ignored his lifeline. "I made mistakes that changed my perspective." She sighed as she pulled her hair out of its tie, letting it hang loose.

Jed waited for her to continue.

"I've told you a little about my life. What about you? Bay told me you're here on a forced vacation. What's it like in Afghanistan?"

The change of subject disappointed him. It was an obvious attempt to sway the conversation away from herself. What mistakes had changed her? He wanted to know. He forced his curiosity aside to answer her. "It's hot, dirty and hard work."

"Sounds like a challenge."

"It is. I've enjoyed the experience, but if I had to be honest I'm happy to be home." Jed surprised himself with his revelation for two reasons—working overseas had always been his goal, but he was finding it a relief to be back in Australia. It also surprised him that he could be so open about his feelings with Samara.

"Well, they say home is where the heart is." It was flippant conversation filler, but the throwaway comment disturbed Jed. *Is my heart here?*

The tension in the air was thick as they both allowed the comment to sit between them. Jed racked his brain for an appropriate impersonal response.

Samara wriggled in her seat, uncrossing then recrossing her legs.

She spoke first. "How long were you over there?"

Jed talked about his time overseas as Samara showed genuine interest in his experiences. They spent the rest of the journey talking about the various medical challenges in developing countries. It surprised Jed that, although Samara wasn't educated on the subject, she had a great desire to hear his opinion, asking many poignant and relative questions. Jed let his guard down and indulged her interest.

The scenery changed as the dense bush they had been travelling through gave way to luscious green rolling mountains.

"Wow. This is spectacular. I've heard about this area, but I've never been here." Samara sat up higher in her seat as they negotiated a one-lane bridge spanning a rapidly running creek.

"It's not well known. We used to come camping up this way. Not as far as the township though." He concentrated on the last section of the drive. "The valley's camouflaged by the bush. Most people don't go to the effort of negotiating the rough road to get here."

"It's so green."

"Thanks to the recent rain. Unfortunately it's normally in drought with the rest of the country, but when it's like this you can see why it's called Bonalah. The local indigenous word means 'place of green grass.'"

As they rounded another mountain, the outskirts

of a community began to appear. Little old cottages dotted the roadway, and the locals stopped to turn and wave.

They passed the local school, and some children playing in the field stopped their game to wave. Jed wound down the window to wave back.

"I only came out here three times last week, but they all seem to know my name."

Samara laughed. "It does look like you're a bit of a celebrity."

They drove up to the two-room clinic. It wasn't much more than a little shack set atop a green hillside. The larger front room was used as the clinic, and the room at the back served as the living quarters for the visiting nurse. At the back of the structure the ground slowly declined to the edge of a creek running through the township. The water was deep and cool, and a popular destination for the local children to swim on a hot day.

Jed pulled into the driveway. As he parked the car under a huge rain tree, Esther appeared at the door and walked down the three steps at the front of the clinic to greet them. Her bright red glasses complemented her multi-colored blouse and long skirt.

"Hello there," she called.

Jed was met with a hug. He did the introductions and they all moved inside.

"I can't tell what a relief it is to see you. Some of these people haven't seen a doctor for years. I came out here specifically for immunizations, and we've ended up seeing to all sorts." Esther took a seat behind the tiny, ancient desk. "I feel so blessed that you both would volunteer your time. I don't want to keep you any longer than necessary so I've organized for it all to be done today and tomorrow."

She stopped to hand them both a schedule. "As you can see, I've divided the clinic times into three sections: morning immunizations, general health checks and a few hours in the afternoon for elderly patients." Esther pointed out the various sections indicating each available timeslot.

"Did you happen to bring a change of clothes?" Samara nodded in confirmation. "Great. Because it would be best if you both could stay here tonight rather than having to come all the way back out in the morning."

Jed felt a slight panic at the thought of the one bedroom.

"Samara, you can take the room and Jed can sleep out here in the clinic. I've organized a trundle bed." Esther indicated the folded mattress tucked away in one of the corners.

Jed considered the arrangement. It was either a return drive and sea trip back to Resolution or a comfortable forty-eight hours at the clinic. Clearly it was best to stay.

"Well, that's about it." Esther got to her feet. "I'll give you a tour of the clinic, and then I'll have to go. I've got a long drive and a flight to catch. They need me back in Cairns by this afternoon. I'm sure you're both going to do fine." She gave them a warm smile.

Samara looked up, surprised to find late afternoon light filtering through the room, and black clouds looming on the horizon. The day had gone by fast, and now rain was on its way.

The residents of Bonalah were wonderful people, though most were shy and Samara had to work hard to gain their confidence. Jed had been accepted by them all. His casual, joking manner put every patient at ease, from the youngest to the eldest. Samara was impressed with his skills, both medically and personally. He was a terrific doctor.

She had enjoyed her day so much that as they saw to the last patient she wished it didn't have to end.

"Here you go." Jed smiled and handed a bandage to a young teen who had been in during the morning with a cut on his hand. It wasn't a nasty one, and a regular Band–Aid would have been sufficient, but this was his third visit to the clinic.

He was no more than sixteen. He glanced her way several times, giving her shy smiles as a light blush filled his cheeks. Samara grinned at his teenage antics and continued with her job of sorting the supplies. The small room severely lacked storage. The only available space was a high, long cabinet that stretched the entire length of one wall. She found the stepladder Esther must have used to reach the highest shelf, and hopped onto it in order to gain access to the area.

"Thanks, Doc." The young man slipped the dressing into his shorts pocket. "How long you staying? I might have to come back in."

"We leave tomorrow afternoon." Jed lifted one corner of his mouth and looked over at her from under his eyebrows. He had picked up on the young man's innocent crush.

The boy nodded and inched his way out the door, sneaking looks at her as he went. He gave her one last shy smile and closed the door behind him.

Samara shook her head and raised her eyebrows. She resumed her job, reaching up onto the shelf to replace a bottle of antiseptic. The room was small, but the ceilings were high and the shelves reached all the way to the top. She rose onto tiptoe, and was working out her unsteady balance when she felt a firm tug on her ponytail. She scrambled to grip the top of the ladder, then swung around to see Jed leaning on the counter behind her. His smile was wide, as he winked at her.

"I think you may have won a heart, Sammy."

She rolled her eyes and shrugged. "Always nice to win one, I guess."

Her heart gave a skip at his teasing action. He used to tug her pony tail all the time, especially when he wanted her attention. She turned back to the task of securing the bottle, taking her time fiddling with the other objects on the shelf. When she turned back Jed hadn't moved. He was a few feet away, leaning back on the counter. She stopped short, not realizing he had been watching her so intently.

Samara felt dizziness creep in and she took a deep breath. Self-conscious, clammy moisture prickled her palms, and she wiped her hands on her pants before making her way down the ladder. As her foot sought the step, a piece of loose tread caught the side of her shoe, tipping the ladder to its side.

She repositioned her weight to correct her balance, but overcompensated. She was falling.

It was as though it happened in slow motion—the ladder, the fall, the landing in Jed's arms.

She could feel the strength of his hands close in around her waist as she tried to right herself. When she regained her balance, he was still holding her. Her hands splayed across his chest in an unconscious attempt to cushion her fall.

Samara became aware of his body, warm and strong against hers as she leaned into him. He was taller than her, and she looked up into his face. His eyes were fixed on her, and her pulse quickened at the blatant desire they conveyed. She shifted her hands on his chest feeling the rise and fall of his muscles under her palms. Samara blinked hard in an effort to pull herself together. She broke away from his eyes to stare at her own hands. A hard lump formed in her throat.

Push away. Her mind screamed self-preservation, while her body remained firm against his. Jed moved his hands around to settle on her lower back, pulling her closer to him. Their bodies fit back together as though they had a memory all of their own.

Samara could hear her heart beat in her ears and her body ached for him the way it always had. She swallowed the hard lump and looked back up. Their faces were inches apart. Jed's blue eyes were so intense Samara held her breath. She knew her emotions were betraying her, and he could see her desire for him, but she didn't care. He was holding her again. She could feel him, see him, touch him.

He released her with one arm and reached up to run a hand down the side of her face. His eyes trailed his fingers as he lingered at the high neckline of her blouse. Tingles pricked her skin, carving a pathway where he touched.

Samara opened her mouth to say something, but nothing came out. Jed saw the action as an invitation and closed the gap between them. His lips were warm and soft at first, then as she reached up to encircle his neck he tightened his embrace, crushing her with a desperate grip. His lips became hard and commanding, forcing her compliance.

Samara surrendered, knowing it was everything she had wanted and dreamed in the years that had parted them. She moaned and pushed her body further into his. His grip softened again as his hands explored the contours of her back. Samara stretched out her fingers to entangle the hair at the back of his head.

Jed slowed the kiss. As his lips left hers Sam opened her eyes. They simultaneously pulled back from each other. Their eyes locked as the reality of what had occurred set in. Jed continued to hold her.

He blinked hard. "Sam. I—" He didn't get to finish as a rasping knock on the door drew their attention.

"Doc. Doc. Are you in there?" a young male voice yelled. Jed dropped his arms from around her and turned to open the door.

A boy of about ten stood outside.

"Doc, it's me Mum. The baby's coming. She's screaming heaps." He gasped for breath.

"Okay, we'll need to take a few things." Jed turned back to her. "Can you get some towels from the back? I'll get the medical supplies."

Samara gathered up as many towels as she could

find in the back room, as well as cotton sheets and a few extra pillows.

They made their way behind the boy, who had assured them the house was close and there was no need to drive. He was right. It was a few meters down the road and across the trail of a horse paddock. As they neared the house, they could hear the screams of a woman in labor.

Samara followed as Jed raced up the front steps and into the house, dumped his bag and made his way to the woman. She was doubled up and leaning over a lounge chair. Another woman stood rubbing her back as she wailed.

"How far along is she?" he asked the woman supporting the pregnant mother.

"Six hours. She's fully dilated. The baby wants to come out but it's breach. I act as midwife out here. This labor is proving to be a bit of trouble."

Jed turned to the woman in labor, who had settled down as the contraction passed. "You need to lie down so I can examine you." The woman did as she was asked.

"You're right. Baby's certainly breach." The midwife gave him a satisfied nod. "I don't believe either baby or mother is in serious danger. They just need a bit of help. I could call for an emergency evacuation, but I think she's going to deliver before it gets here."

They set about making the environment as comfortable as possible for the delivery. After a short thirty minutes that included a lot of effort from everyone, a healthy baby boy was born. His wails heralded his entry into the world.

Samara began the cleanup while Jed and the midwife saw to the afterbirth procedure. It didn't matter how often she was a spectator in the birthing process, it never failed to amaze her. In no time the little newborn was sucking strong on his mother's breast.

Samara gathered the soiled towels together, placing them in a plastic garbage bag. Jed made his way over to her. "They're going to be fine." He looked over to mother and baby.

She smiled and reached up to touch his arm. "You did a great job."

He returned her smile. "This one was a joint effort. I'm going to stay a few hours and make sure there aren't any complications or hemorrhaging. You go back and get some sleep. No sense in both of us having a late night. I'll get Billy here to take you back." He gestured to the boy who had retrieved them earlier.

Samara was pleased to comply. She'd had little sleep the night before, and she relished the time alone to think about what had happened between them.

"No worries." She picked up the bag of towels to take with her.

"Sammy?" Jed stopped her as she turned to go. She looked back at him. He frowned and shuffled from side to side before placing his hands in the pockets of his shorts and looked up at her. "About before." He paused to shuffle some more, removing one hand from the pocket and running it through his hair. "Seeing you again has brought back a lot of memories. I lost control and I'm sorry. It won't happen again." His eyes flashed dark blue in the light.

Samara felt her stomach drop. The kiss had meant nothing to him. It was just a trip down memory lane. The set of his jaw told her he was as good as his word — it wouldn't happen again.

Samara didn't know what to do. She wanted to scream at him to take it back. It had to happen again. Even after all this time she still loved him. She still wanted him. She felt tears prickle behind her eyes.

You don't have the right to make demands from him. How could he love you?

"Sure." It was the only word she could get out before turning to leave.

The night air was thick with moisture as she made her way behind Billy. The heavy atmosphere reflected her mood, and the soft raindrops that trickled down her face camouflaged her tears. She said a brief thanks to her guide before letting herself into the clinic.

The heavy timber door thudded closed behind her. She turned to lean back against it, relying on its bulk to hold her up. She was soaking wet and looked down to see a puddle collecting on the floor where she stood. She slid down the door and pulled her knees up to her body, wrapping her arms around her legs and cuddling herself.

Sam rested her forehead on the top of her knees. How had she ended up here again?

What am I going to do?

CHAPTER 12

Jed slumped down onto the bottom step outside the clinic. He was still in love with her. It was hard to admit the very thing Cassidy had pointed out to him months earlier. At the time her bluntness had made him angry, and he'd denied the accusation. He had sulked for days, but then it all exploded in one drastic event.

Now he knew in his heart what Cassidy had said was true, regardless of how absurd it seemed. *How can I still be in love with her? It's been over three years and we've both changed so much. I don't even know her anymore.*

It was clear Samara had changed, and he liked what he saw. The Samara he had known had a façade of sophistication, displaying to the world the person she thought she should be. He had fallen for the girl she was when they were alone. The one who loved being a nurse, who would sit and laugh at the most ridiculous things, who wore her hair loose, and slopped around in nothing but his t-shirts. It was the façade he had run away from. That he couldn't live with. This Samara didn't have a hint of that fake persona. The façade had disappeared altogether.

Her manner had fascinated him over the last two days as they worked together. She attended to each patient as if they were her most important, winning over everyone who stepped foot in the clinic.

Now their second day at Bonalah was drawing

to a close, and Jed was relieved to retreat to his spot on the steps outside the back door of the clinic. It was his first break of the day. That morning he had commented to a patient that he was surprised such a small community had so many people attending the clinic. He was told word had spread about the clinic, and many people from outlying settlements had made the journey in to take advantage of the free medical care. Some had travelled from an outback station over two hundred kilometers away to see them. As a consequence they had worked without stopping.

He sipped a cup of coffee and watched the local children play in the murky brown creek below. It wasn't a huge expanse of water, although it looked swollen from the heavy overnight rainfall. The river bank was muddy and thick with overgrown grass. The children had hooked a rope around one of the branches of a huge eucalypt tree lining the creek. They were swinging off it, then dropping at height into the water below. Jed envied their ability to cool down.

He could hear Samara tidying up inside. There was little to do and he suspected that she was procrastinating in an attempt to avoid him. He wasn't surprised considering how he had mauled her the day before.

Jed shook his head at his own indulgence. When she had fallen against him he couldn't help himself. He'd imagined kissing her again since the day he had visited her when she was sick. When the opportunity had literally fallen into his lap, he had given into the desire.

Samara had erected the trundle bed for him in the clinic when he had returned last night, and the door to her room was shut. Jed considered what had happened. His first reaction was disgust with himself. How could he be so stupid as to lose all self-control? She must be appalled. But when he replayed the kiss in his mind, Jed realized Samara had been as much a party to the event as he had. Did she still have feelings for him? Or was she reliving part of history? She'd been strictly professional today, keeping any personal interaction with him to a minimum. It was clear their encounter wasn't something Samara wished to pursue.

He couldn't help but think he was heading for another disaster with her. Now he had held her again he wanted nothing else, but this time he didn't have to run away.

His morning reading had spoken to him. *Seek the Lord and he will give you the desires of your heart.*

Yes, there was a reason his prayers to eradicate Samara from his heart had gone unanswered. God had a plan. He was waiting for Jed to get it too.

You know the desire of my heart. I don't have the answer to this problem, but you do. Please give us both your direction. Your way or no way, Father. My way didn't work.

Bay had told him Sam had found strength in her new faith, just as he had. Bay hadn't shared Samara's story with him, but she'd told him she and Sam had conversed extensively about the wonderful things God had done in their lives. Jed could see how much faith had changed her.

"Hey, Doc, come for a swim." One of the boys

called from the river bank below. He waved and shook his head. The children all stopped their raucous behavior and looked his way.

A chorus of encouragement broke out as they all yelled for him to join them. The water looked cool and refreshing. Jed could see he wasn't going to deter them with his protests, so he gave in and ran down the bank. He pulled off his shirt on the way and jumped for the rope, swinging several times over the water before dropping with a massive splash into the creek below.

The children cheered as he surfaced. Their laughter was contagious and he joined in. The coolness of the water was a great relief after the heat of the day.

"Hey, Miss Nurse. You come in too!" one of the girls yelled up the hill.

Jed swam to the edge and pulled himself up on the muddy bank. Samara stood at the back door of the clinic. Spurred on by their success with Jed, the children all yelled a second chorus for her to join the fun. She shook her head and called back. "No way. These are the only dry clothes I have, and I am not going back soaking wet."

She laughed as each child continued to call to her, rejecting her reasoning.

"Absolutely not," she called back down to them.

Her downfall was the huge smile accompanying her protest. In spite of her words, some of the children raced up to drag her down the bank, resistant, but laughing.

When they got to the creek Samara planted her heels. "No, seriously guys. I really can't get wet."

The children continued their persuasion, pulling at her arms and tugging on the bottom of her navy blue polo shirt. It had to be hot, buttoned all the way to the top.

"Throw her in," some of them yelled from the creek.

Samara grabbed a tree branch to stop her descent. Despite her protests, Jed could see she wanted to join in the fun.

"Help us, Doc," one little boy called to him when their efforts proved in vain. Jed got to his feet. The muddy bank was caked thick on his arms and legs.

Samara was still holding onto the branch, but she couldn't stifle her grin as he approached.

"Don't you even think about it, Jed McKenna." She tried to wave a finger at him, but was thwarted by one of the children who saw the opportunity to grab her hand.

Jed laughed. "Come on, Sammy, get in and cool down. We'll borrow some dry clothes." He reached out for her hand.

Samara looked at the faces of the children, then rolled her eyes. "OK, OK. I'll get in." She let go of the branch.

"Throw her in, Doc," one of the boys called from the creek.

Jed moved to grab her.

She pulled away just in time, holding her arms out to create a defensive barrier. "Don't you dare!"

He took a step closer, noticing how her smile reached her eyes. "Did you just dare me?"

She backed away, keeping one hand in a stop position. "Ok, I'm getting in."

He took her outreached hand and led her down the muddy bank to the water's edge, the children clapped and cheered them every step. Then in a playful move he motioned to push her in, but she had the same intention and grabbed him at the last moment. They both tumbled unceremoniously into the creek.

Jed laughed as their heads surfaced.

Samara feigned disgust. "You're a dead man." She swam over and dunked his head under the water like they had done back in childhood days.

When he surfaced for a second time she was swimming towards the bank. Jed jumped to encircle her waist, pulling her back again. The children squealed with delight at their antics.

"You're not getting out yet," he said as she surfaced in front of him.

Samara looked up. Long wet strands of hair framed her face where they had escaped from her messy pony tail. Her smile was broad, reaching dark brown eyes as they glistened with the droplets of water sitting on her eyelashes.

A smile for me. Jed reached for her, his hands closing around her waist before the noise surrounding him served as a reminder of where they were. He released her, pushing his body back in the water and turning so she couldn't see his face.

He took off at speed, swimming down the creek in a conscious attempt to put some distance between them. *Don't kiss her again.* When he turned back, there was a gathering at the water's edge. Samara sat in the mud with children on either side. One of the boys was showing her a small animal he had caught on the bank. Jed recognized it as a Yabby, a creature similar to a prawn, but much larger.

Samara picked it up without hesitation. She turned it over while she listened to the story the boy was telling her. The other children milled around. Two of the girls came up behind and gently pulled her hair from its constraint and began to plait it. Samara sat in the middle, covered in mud. Her animated face showing how much she was enjoying the interaction.

Jed treaded water while he watched her. This woman had so much more substance than the one he had fallen in love with years ago.

Samara sorted through the borrowed clothing, tossing up her options. A fitting singlet top with a low neckline, or an old stained blue polo shirt that was way too big, but could be buttoned up to cover her scar. The shirt had been meant for Jed, but as his was still clean she had grabbed this shirt for herself, knowing she might need the coverage. She didn't have much choice. The day had been long and she was keen to get home. Now wasn't the time to be revealing her scar.

She looked down at it. The water had made the skin pucker, and the usually reddish areas looked a murky purple.

He's hardly going to miss it.

She rolled her eyes, and thought about the trip home. Being a doctor, he would want to know how it had happened.

I can't deal with that. Not today, anyway.

She pulled on the shirt and gathered up the rest of the garments, making her way out the door of the clinic. The bottom of the shirt almost rested as low as the hemline of the skirt she was wearing, and the sleeves ended well below her elbows. It was huge, and Samara knew she looked like a crazy person, but it would have to do.

The reaction she received when she stepped out of the door was confirmation of her concerns. The lady who had acted as midwife the night before gave her appearance an undisguised cringe. Jed did a double take, and not in a good way.

"Sammy, what on earth?" His eyebrows raised high as she approached them.

"Didn't the top fit, love?" the older lady asked as Sam handed over the unused clothes.

She shrugged and tried to look nonchalant. "I like the extra space."

"Extra space! You could fit a whole other person in there." Jed grinned, clearly amused at her appearance.

She ignored the comment, choosing instead to say her goodbyes to the crowd of locals who had gathered to see them off.

It was after dusk by the time the car pulled away. She felt Jed sneaking glances at her as he drove. After a few kilometers, it got so unnerving that she turned to him. "Is something wrong?"

Jed kept his eyes on the road. "I can't work you out. You seem to have gone from being a fashion model to a bag lady."

His comment was more curious than insulting. Samara considered her reply and decided to play it cool. "Can't a girl change her look? Besides, you just spent the last few years in a foreign country where women are covered from head to toe. How do you know what's in style?"

Jed's loud laugh showed his amusement. "Alright, Sammy. I give up. I even have to admit you make that shirt look good."

Samara enjoyed the compliment, but it only highlighted the difference in her appearance now from before. Would Jed think she was beautiful after seeing the piecing red gash ripping across the front of her chest? She pushed the thought from her mind. He wasn't going to see it.

A comfortable silence fell between them as Jed negotiated the rough road. Soft music played on the radio, and Samara sat back to enjoy the long, bumpy ride.

On the outskirts of Kiisay Point Jed finally broke the quiet. '"I'm sorry I left the way I did."

His voice was so faint she wondered for a second if she had imagined his words. She looked over at him. His profile was softened by the vehicle's dash lights. He was so handsome she wanted to reach over and touch him. She turned back ahead and concentrated on an answer.

"I didn't understand why you left. I thought you loved me." A sharp emotional pain pierced her chest.

"I did love you. But you were two different people. I got confused as to which one was real."

Samara couldn't argue—she had been two people. "I was trying to be something I wasn't. I know that now. I've changed a lot since then."

Jed glanced over at her. "I can see that." He

stopped to turn onto the road leading to the township. "What you said that day at the first aid station was right. I did want to be perfect. I've recently been reminded of how imperfect I am, and it's forced me to own up to a lot of mistakes."

Samara bit her lip hard.

Is he serious?

This was a first. She racked her brain to think of a time past when Jed had admitted to being imperfect. Nothing. There was a great satisfaction in hearing him say it. His honesty about his failings reminded her about her own.

She took a deep breath before launching into her confession. "Jed, I can't tell you how sorry I am about what happened with Flynn. In some warped part of my mind, I convinced myself you'd pay attention to me if I was with him." She mentally cringed. It was hard to be so honest. "It sounds crazy now, and maybe I was a little crazy. I was so hurt. That was the first horrible mistake in a long line of horrible mistakes. I feel partly responsible for all that happened to Flynn, and then your parents died. I didn't know about it until recently." She stopped to gauge his reaction.

He tapped the steering wheel several times. His agitation was clear, even in the poor light of the cab. "I'm not going to pretend that you being with my brother didn't hurt me. It did. It broke my heart. But how were you to know? I was so preoccupied with chasing my ideal that I forgot my happiness. And yours. I hurt you and I'm sorry I did that. So very sorry." Jed glanced at her before continuing. "As far as Flynn goes, he's told me that although he would never have wanted any of it to happen, God can turn it around for our good. I don't know how. But It's amazing that He can."

Samara smiled. "Yeah, it is."

"And Sammy, I like the changes in you. I like them a lot."

Samara felt the warmth of his words flow through her as the lights of the township came into view.

It was well past nine o'clock by the time they drove into Kiisay Point. Jed suggested they stay at the hotel for the night rather than make the trip over to Resolution in the dark. Samara was grateful. She was exhausted.

They settled into their rooms and planned to meet down at the bistro to gauge what was available for a late supper.

Samara looked down at her dowdy attire. She was pleased the busy dining hours would be over. Patty was on Resolution with her father. Perhaps she could slip in and grab a bite without being noticed by anyone.

She arrived at the entry to the bistro before Jed, and peeked around the doorway to check on the number of diners remaining. There was an elderly couple having coffee at one of the tables, and a young woman at another. She was attacking the biggest steak Samara had ever seen. The size of the meal was in complete contrast to the eater. The lady was a petite woman with fine features and a blonde pixie haircut framing her face to perfection. Samara watched her as she cut a huge chunk of meat and stuffed it into her mouth, chewing with great gusto.

"Is the food still on?" Samara jumped at Jed's voice next to her.

"Looks like it." They both opened the door and entered the dining room.

Samara grabbed a chair at the first available table.

"Cass?" Jed's voice echoed through the room.

He bolted past her to the blonde woman, who stood, smiling as well as she could with a chunk of steak in her mouth.

Jed grabbed her in a hug, lifting her up off the floor.

Sam stood back and watched the dramatic embrace, feeling her heart drop. Who was this woman?

"What are you doing here?" Jed put her feet back on the floor.

The woman took a moment, holding her hand up to him and swallowed her mouthful before answering. "My father was coming over here for a conference in Sydney, so I decided to travel with him and come up to see you." Her American accent was pure Gone with the Wind.

"I have to admit this was a little further from Sydney than I expected." She smiled and playfully slapped his arm. "But y'all have ruined my surprise. Your brother was going to pick me up and take me out to Resolution tomorrow." She faked a pout.

Samara pushed her chair back in and moved to stand next to the pair.

Jed turned to acknowledge her. "We've been volunteering the last few days at a remote community inland from here. We're back later than planned, so we decided to stop here for the night."

The woman looked past him to her and then back to Jed.

"Sorry," he said, realizing introductions were in order. "Samara, this is Cassidy. She's my partner in Afghanistan. We've been stationed there together since I went over."

Cassidy lifted her eyebrows at Jed, who gave her a sheepish look in return. She turned back and extended her dainty hand. "It's a pleasure to meet you." Her smile made her face light up.

Samara stepped forward and shook her hand, offering a forced smile in greeting.

"Please, won't you join me?" Cassidy gestured to the spare chairs at her table.

Jed didn't hesitate, taking the seat closest to Cassidy and leaving the one across the table for her.

"You've got half a cow there, Cass."

His playful teasing sent Samara's stomach plummeting.

Why are you here? Sam wished she could ask the question aloud, but she knew it would come out every bit as aggressive as she felt.

"And you can watch me eat every last bite." Cassidy cut off another huge chunk.

Jed laughed. "I can't believe you're here."

Cassidy shrugged her shoulders and screwed up her button nose. "When I saw my father's schedule, I knew it was right." She turned to Samara. "He's a minister. He's speaking at a conference in Sydney. It runs for a little over a week." She stopped to cut another piece of steak and offered it to Jed, who popped it into his mouth.

Sam could feel her jaw tighten to the point of seizing.

Cassidy turned the steak and cut the other side. "I told you I'd get here."

"Yeah, but I didn't think you were serious. I thought you wouldn't take a break, or if you did get away you'd go back home and not want to move," Jed mumbled between chews.

"Are you kidding?" Cassidy indicated her meal, offering to share with Sam.

Sam managed to give her a tight-lipped smile and shook her head.

Cassidy looked back to Jed. "I pushed hard for leave. The camp wasn't the same without you there."

Samara pushed her seat back a bit. The spoon sitting on the table in front of her was starting to look very attractive as a weapon.

Cassidy didn't pick up on her battle vibes. "I went back home, but all my friends were busy with their lives. My family was happy to see me. My mother had a million social engagements lined up for me, but it all got boring fast. I needed a purpose." She touched Jed's arm. "Besides, I missed you."

Oh boy, are you in trouble lady. Samara wanted to rip her pretty blonde head off. A mental picture of the T-bone connecting with her face flashed before her.

"I've missed you, too." Jed patted her hand.

Now she wanted to rip both their heads off, and the T-bone was a weapon of mass destruction.

Samara sank in her chair, looked down at her lap and saw her mud-caked fingernails. It was a sudden reminder of how horrible she looked. She was an oversize giraffe wearing a tent, cowering next to this beautiful pixie-like princess. *Get out. Leave. Now.* She leaped to her feet.

"I'm going to bed." Her announcement drew their immediate attention.

They both had the decency to give her questioning looks.

Cassidy got up. "No, don't go. You haven't even eaten yet."

Sam wished the pixie would sit back down. She was drawing more attention to the differences between them.

She scrunched up one bottom edge of her enormous shirt in an effort to give it some shape around her body. "I'm so exhausted that I couldn't eat, and I'm sure you both have a lot to catch up on." She hoped her excuse sounded convincing.

Jed frowned. "But when we checked in you said you were famished?"

She gave him a death stare. *Thanks for pointing that out.*

"What I need is some sleep. It's been a long day." She pushed her chair back under the table and mustered up a smile for them both as a means to sweeten her exit. Cassidy looked concerned as she glanced back and forth between her and Jed.

"It was nice to meet you. I hope you enjoy your time here." She couldn't bring herself to extend her hand.

"It was an absolute pleasure to meet you, too. I hope we get to see more of each other while I'm here." Cassidy's voice was as smooth as honey.

Sam grabbed her bag from the floor next to her

chair and took off as fast as she could out the door. Relief took hold as she reached her room.

She sat on the bed and felt tears of frustration prick her eyes. *What is she to him?*

Samara knew the answer didn't matter. Jed had determined to never kiss her again. But she thought about the way he had reached for her when they were in the creek, and the conversation they had in the car on the way back. Could he still have feelings for her?

Regardless, any chance she may have had was now squashed with the entry of the lovely Cassidy, the woman Jed had lived in close confines with for years. It was obvious they had a deep relationship.

Samara got up and showered. She rinsed the creek water out of her shirt and hung it on the back of a chair outside her room. Hopefully it would dry overnight, and she wouldn't have to put the tent back on tomorrow.

She turned the television on and did her best distract herself.

Sam stared out the window of her cabin. The day was picture-perfect-tropical-island-paradise. She sighed at her self-exile and tried to watch the brainless sitcom on the television. It was hard to concentrate on the senseless storyline when so much had happened in the few days since they had been back from Bonalah.

This was Cassidy's fourth day on Resolution. As much as Samara had tried to keep her feelings for her neutral, the lady was making it hard. Very hard. Her outgoing, friendly manner had won her hearts all over the island. She was honest without being unkind, and her slightly overbearing zealousness was softened by her humor.

Cassidy had managed to endear herself to everyone, including Samara. Bay and Flynn threw a welcome dinner in Cassidy's honor the night she arrived on the island, and all the locals attended. Cassidy fit right into the scene, discussing American politics with Bay and relaying stories about Jed in a playful attempt to embarrass him. It was obvious from their banter they knew each other well. Samara had to swallow several times to push down the pain she felt at seeing another woman so familiar with Jed.

In spite of her jealousy, Sam had to admit she liked Cassidy. If it weren't for the fact that she was in love with Jed, she would have been happy to seek out the company of the down-to-earth young woman. But Samara knew any contact she had with Cassidy and Jed would only serve to further flare the green-eyed monster lurking under the surface.

It also didn't help that they were both determined to include her in their activities. They had attempted numerous times to get her to join them. Firstly, in the pool when she had accompanied her father to the restaurant for his daily cup of coffee. Cassidy and Jed had both called for her to join them for a swim. There was no way she was having anything to do with water. It meant having to wear a bathing suit, and keeping her attack to herself felt like a good idea. She had managed to avoid swimming by faking a headache and retreating to the cabin.

Then Cassidy had dropped by to visit one

morning. Samara had finished making morning tea for her and Bob when Cassidy had arrived, declaring she was at a loose end. Bob had invited her in to take a seat across from him.

Samara made her a coffee and retreated to the kitchen to wipe over the benches several times in an effort to look busy. She knew she was being inhospitable. She had determined not to get to know the woman who was so close to the man she loved but couldn't be with.

Thankfully, Bob had been more than happy to monopolize their visitor. Her father had been restless since she had arrived back on Resolution. Patty had stayed in the cabin next to theirs and had looked after Bob for the two nights Sam was away. Her return from Bonalah meant Patty had no excuse to stay, and Sam could tell Bob missed his companion. Patty had promised to visit again soon.

Then, that morning Jed had turned up at their cabin, asking her to go with them on a boating trip out to the reef.

She had been ecstatic to see him, her stomach doing strange things at the sight of his handsome face and bright blue eyes. She reveled in his company until he explained the purpose of his visit.

"Come on, Sammy, you haven't been out for years. It'll be fun. I've got all the snorkeling equipment and I'll find us a nice patch of reef to dive. Bay's packed us a gourmet hamper, and Neville's decided to come as well, so we're taking the new cat." His enthusiasm for the trip was overwhelming.

Samara frowned. *More swimming.* If she went, how would she explain not getting into the water?

She hesitated, coming up with the perfect excuse.

"I'm sorry. I can't leave Bob."

He had squinted at her. "Are you seriously going to use that as an excuse? As a doctor, I can assure you your father will be fine on his own for a morning."

Jed gave her a smile of encouragement. His eyes had held a glint of adventure that promised an exciting day. "Come on, Sammy, come out with us."

Samara wished for a moment that it was possible for her to go. She knew she'd have to reveal her injury at some stage. She just didn't want it to be in front of a boat full of people.

She turned to walk in behind the kitchen bench, firmly stating her intention to stay put. "Sorry. I can't."

Jed had run his hand through his hair. His frustration was evident. He stared at her before throwing his arms up. "Fine." He turned on his heels and left.

Samara spent the morning hours in boring, menial tasks, wishing for every second she was with him instead.

Now the afternoon had brought a whole new set of worries. She had missed a call from Bay, who had left a message explaining that Jed had asked her to extend an invitation for dinner that night. It was to be a group affair—Bay, Flynn, Cassidy, Jed, and herself. Samara felt like the fifth wheel in a romantic foursome. There was no way she was going to put herself through that.

She knew she was chickening out of the encounter, and it was plain rude to decline so many invitations, but she couldn't stand by and watch Jed and Cassidy's playful banter, even if by some unlikely chance they were nothing but friends. She also knew Jed assumed she wouldn't be able to say no if Bay was doing the asking. He was using Bay as a ploy to get her to agree.

Instead of waiting to see Jed when he got back from the reef to personally decline the invitation, she had written him a note to be delivered by her father. He had left to go down to the restaurant for his habitual coffee and chat.

Bob had given her a look when she had asked him to slip the note under the door of Jed's cabin as he walked past. "What's going on here, Sam? Are you and he in some sort of relationship again?" His bushy eyebrows met in the middle.

"There's nothing going on, Dad. I'm just declining a dinner invitation. You can read it if you like" Her openness seemed to satisfy Bob, who went on his way.

Samara was pulled out of her thoughts by a firm and commanding knock. She made her way over to the sliding glass door. Her heart raced when she saw who it was.

Trevor Delaney

He peered through the glass, hands on hips, while his reflective sunglasses shone off the door.

Samara felt prickles on the back of her neck. What would bring the Sydney detective all the way to North Queensland, let alone Resolution Island? She opened the door.

"Samara." He nodded his greeting and gave her a smile.

She held onto the door handle. "Trevor. What are

you doing here?"

"Can I come in? I'll be able to explain everything."

Samara stepped aside for him to enter.

After she had made him a drink and explained that Bob was out for his daily sojourn, they sat down to discuss his visit.

"The local drugs squad's called me up here to help them with an investigation, so I decided to come out and see you rather than talk by telephone. I wanted to warn you that Ricky's moved back into this area. To be honest, it's the reason I'm here."

Samara felt her pulse race. She made fists with her hands placed in her lap. "What does that mean?"

"We still haven't found the person who attacked you. We're certain your attack and the recent Sydney murder are related. Ricky is a suspect in the murder case, as well as yours. The victim was a stripper and a user, with connections to him."

Samara's stomach did flip-flops.

"The good news is that we've been able to rule out Rocco in the assault on you. In fact, you have nothing to fear from him. He's in custody awaiting trial for king-hitting a patron at the club."

Samara didn't know whether to be relieved or not. Rocco was the lesser evil among the suspects. If he had been her attacker, his aim would have most likely been to scare and beat her, but she didn't see him as a premeditated murderer.

"Samara, I have some other bad news. We found your former flatmate dead last week. Drug overdose. We know Ricky had made her acquaintance, probably while he was looking for you. He moved in with Layla and was supplying her with drugs."

Sam felt a wave of sadness fall over her like a blanket. *Poor Layla.* She put her head in her hands and thought of the woman who never found the strength to rise above her upbringing. Layla chose to use drugs to numb the pain that wouldn't go away. She wished she had gone back to talk to her flatmate. If only she had tried to get through to her, it might have bought her some time.

Trevor said nothing for a while, giving her some space, letting her come to terms with the news. When he did speak, his quiet, firm tone made her look up and give him her attention.

"Samara, I know you're upset but you have to listen to me. We believe Ricky is obsessed with you. After Layla was found dead we raided the flat and found a mass of photographs of you. Most of them were from your time with Karl. We assume he had either given them to Ricky, or Ricky had stolen them. There were also many taken when it was obvious you weren't aware there was a camera pointed at you."

She felt a chill run up her spine.

"None of the pictures were taken here, so you don't need to worry about him stalking you since you've been back. We do know Ricky's been the driving force in their move back into this area. There's no sign of Karl. He is in on the action, but as you know, we don't have enough on him yet." Trevor sat forward a little in his chair. "I don't need to remind you of how dangerous these men are. Together they've moved a mountain of meth in the last few months. They're both cunning so we still don't have any evidence that will stick. Our only hope is that they trip up somewhere, and I think I know where it will be."

Trevor's forehead wrinkled and his eyes fixed on her. "If Ricky contacts you in any way, call me immediately. Stay on the island. You're safe here, and there's far less chance of him getting around unseen. We don't have the resources or the excuse to position a man out here, but we're watching him like a hawk."

Samara closed her eyes for a moment.

"Sam, we suspect Ricky's obsession with you has brought him back here. You need to be vigilant, but don't let it run your life. If you give into the fear, he's winning."

He was right. The love and protection her faith in God gave her was stronger than the fear Trevor's words evoked. God wouldn't desert her.

"I won't let Ricky do that."

Trevor leaned over to pat her hand. "Good girl." He got to his feet. "I'm going down to introduce myself to Bob. I never told him about your job at the club, but I think he may have guessed after I confirmed you weren't into drugs or prostitution. I hope there wasn't trouble for you when you arrived back. I know how much your father loves you."

She conjured up a smile. "No, there wasn't any trouble. Thanks for coming out to see me." It was easier to hear the bad news with the strength of his presence.

"You're welcome. You can repay me by calling if you hear from Ricky."

Samara smiled at his request. Once a cop, always

a cop.

Trevor moved to the door. "I'm going to be here for a few hours. Why don't you take a moment to get yourself together then meet me down at the restaurant? My shout for lunch. You can tell me what you've been up to since you've been back."

"Sure. I'll be down in a while." As he turned and moved to the steps, a thought occurred to her. "Trevor, first I have to go and tell Flynn McKenna that Ricky's back. He's the man who went to jail for assaulting Ricky years ago. I'm sure it was a setup. Ricky hates Flynn and lied about the assault."

Trevor paused to place his sunglasses back on his head. "Okay. Let him know, but stress the importance of keeping it under wraps. I don't want Ricky to know we're onto him."

Sam nodded and waved goodbye as Trevor left.

She went into her room, closing the door and taking some time to cry and pray for the loss of Layla.

CHAPTER 13

Jed was past frustration. He was now feeling the full force of the McKenna temper envelop him.

He'd tried every way possible to include Samara in his activities during the last few days, but she had remained aloof in spite of his persistence.

Cassidy was convinced it was due to her presence, and that alone made Jed's blood boil. Cassidy was his friend. She was working hard to get to know Samara, and the constant refusals were insulting.

They had arrived back from the reef earlier than planned, and he had stepped off the boat to see Sam in the restaurant having coffee alone with some random bloke. He stood now and watched them from a distance as their heads bent together over the table. The man gave her his undivided attention. She spoke, stopping occasionally to take a sip of her water. The man threw his head back and laughed at something she said. Jed felt his blood heat to boiling point. He wanted to storm up there and demand an explanation. Why did she continue to reject him only to bestow her company on a complete stranger? Or was he a stranger? For all he knew, the man could be her boyfriend.

The sudden appearance of his sister-in-law stopped him from making a complete and utter fool of himself.

"How was the trip?" Bay asked as she walked up

from the boat mooring.

"Fine." Jed picked up the bags he had dropped when he had seen Sam. Cassidy had already gone ahead of him to her cabin.

"Just fine?" Bay sounded disappointed.

"It got a bit rough so we decided to head back early." His tone was more abrupt than he had planned. He checked himself. It wasn't Bay's fault he couldn't convince Sam to spend her time with him.

Bay dropped the bags she had been carrying. "What's wrong, Jed?"

He gestured up to the restaurant. "I don't know what I've got to do. She's knocked me back for days. Now she's up there flirting with some random guy."

Bay looked up towards the direction of his sweeping hand before answering him. "I wouldn't read too much into it. Flynn said he was a policeman, a friend of Bob's." Deep creases furrowed her brow. "I've asked Sam to dinner tonight."

Jed felt some of his anguish dissipate. "Thanks for doing that for me."

Bay reached out to touch him on the arm. "You haven't read the letter she wrote to Flynn, have you?"

Jed had picked up the letter several times to read its contents, but had put it back each time, afraid of what it might say. "Not yet."

Bay gave him a smile. "You will. When you're ready. Now could you please help me with these supplies? I've spent all day running around picking them up, and there are far too many bags for me to carry."

Jed followed her back to help Bay offload the goods.

When he arrived back at his cabin there was a piece of paper stuck under his door. It was a message from Samara declining his dinner invitation. He felt the pang of rejection before the anger set in.

He was going to sort this out.

Sam looked at her reflection in the full length mirror. The night slip had a delicate flower pattern, and it still fitted her perfectly. The silk felt so good against her skin she could almost forget about the redness of the scar showing above the low neckline of the garment. The shallow sections of the cut had faded, but the deep end of the gash was still purple.

The slip was modest enough, covering her breasts and finishing above her knees. The lace trim was beautiful but did nothing to camouflage the puckering of the scar pulling through her breast tissue.

Samara stared at her reflection. She had taken the time to wash and dry her hair, and it fell down her back, long and shining. It looked beautiful as a contrast against the cream silk of the night gown, a special gift that had travelled everywhere with her, wrapped in its box. This was the first time she had taken it out in years. It was the only truly attractive garment she now owned. She was tired of wearing high-necked cotton shirts. She wanted to feel something special against her skin.

She had tracked down Flynn before meeting Trevor and her father at the restaurant, and had relayed the news that Ricky was in town. Sam felt horrible to be the bearer of such disturbing news when Bay and Flynn had been so good to her, but it was vital they be forewarned.

Patty had also arrived, as promised, and she and Bob were having dinner together at the restaurant. They had just left when Patty arrived back in search of Bob's wallet. She had left for the second time when Samara noticed his mobile phone on the kitchen table. They hadn't come back for it, and she had promised her father she wouldn't leave the cabin. After speaking to Trevor, Bob had been reluctant to leave her, but Samara convinced him she would be fine for the few hours they would be gone. It was a wonderful feeling to be alone.

She had showered and decided to try on the night slip on a whim. The cut of the garment was beautiful. She pulled on the matching wrap, securing it at the waist so it hid the scar. She sat looking at her reflection, recalling how thrilled she had been when Jed had given it to her years ago.

A heavy rapping on the door made her jump. Bob or Patty.

Samara moved into the lounge, grabbing the mobile phone he would be looking for. "I'm coming."

She got to the door and opened it without bothering to pull back the curtain. "Here it is." She held out the phone, but it wasn't either of them who stood in the door way.

Samara recognized the expression on Jed's face. The redness in his neck and the clench of his jaw was testimony to the fact he was there for a confrontation.

"Mind if I come in?" He didn't wait for her reply, but pushed past her into the cabin.

She took her time shutting the door.

He stood in the lounge and glared at her. "What's with you? You've either got a big problem or you're just plain rude."

He stood tall and squared his shoulders, as if poised for a fight. She threw the mobile phone onto the nearest chair and tried to answer honestly. "I've had a very bad day, Jed. Trust me, I would be bad company tonight."

She wrapped her arms around her torso, pulling the wrap to ensure it was secured.

"That's a sudden change from the wonderful company you were this afternoon. Looks like you were having a great time when you were with your boyfriend."

Samara frowned. "What boyfriend?"

Jed snorted. "The one at the restaurant."

He had seen her with Trevor. "That was Trevor Delaney. He's a detective from Sydney."

"I don't care what he does. I just think it's strange you failed to mention him."

Samara felt indignation rise up inside her at the suggestion she had been less than honest. "What exactly are you implying, Jed McKenna?"

"You tell me." His spoke through clenched teeth.

"Trevor is not my boyfriend, nor has he ever been. Who do you think you are, throwing around accusations about secret loves? Never in any of our conversations did you ever mention Cassidy but I've had to spend the last four days watching you with her. How do you think that's made me feel?" Samara pulled her lips tight and squinted at him. Who did he think he was, accusing her of not being forthcoming about relationships when his girlfriend showed up all the way from Afghanistan?

Jed's blue eyes that had flashed with anger a second ago switched to confusion. "Did you think Cass and me. . .?"

She felt an instant pang of regret. Her attempt to throw Jed's accusation back in his face had landed her squarely on the defensive. She had given herself away.

Jed took a step towards her. "Cassidy and I are just friends. We think of each other as brother and sister. There's nothing even remotely romantic between us, nor has there ever been. If you had spent any time with us, you'd have seen that for yourself."

Samara stood her ground, not replying, not knowing what to say. Everything she could think of would make her sound jealous. She could feel her frustration mounting. Trevor's visit had already exhausted her emotions, and now to be caught out by Jed was the final straw.

"I think you'd better go." She stood aside so he could get past her. At least if he left she would have time to think it all through.

She looked out the glass door, but the light gave her a full view of Jed's reflection. He wasn't moving.

He shook his head. "I'm not leaving."

Sam became aware of a very large, very high lump in her throat. *Stop. Stop.* She willed it to subside, but it was to no avail. She knew she had to do something. If he wouldn't leave, then she would.

She turned back around to face him. "Fine. Stay as long as you like. I'm going to bed." Her voice was shaky and disjointed as she made her way to her room.

"Sammy?" Jed called from behind her.

"What?" She got to the doorway of her room when she felt him behind her. He swung her around, and pulling her to him. He held her tight as his arms encircled her waist.

"Jed, this is no good for either of us. You should let me go." She held his forearms, trying to lessen his grip.

"I will if you want me to." His voice was soft, but firm. She could feel his breath warm against her ear.

She made one more half-hearted attempt to break free, but he wasn't letting her go unless she told him to. She sighed, submitted to his embrace, and allowed her body to relax. The agony of being exactly where she wanted to be set in, and she felt her willpower for self-preservation crumble.

Jed relaxed his grip, continuing to hold her to him, his breathing heavy as his chest rose and fell with hers.

If she had wanted to leave his arms she could have, but her body betrayed her. It remained rooted to the spot. She closed her eyes, feeling the strength in his arms as they encircled her.

He said he had resolved not to kiss her again.

But she had made no such promise.

She decided to surrender, to give in to her compulsion for him. She let go of his arms and reached up to cup his face in her hands, pulling his head down and tilting her head up to touch his jawline to her lips. She trailed soft kisses along his jaw. Each time her lips touched his skin she felt a shiver down her spine. When she reached his chin, she leant back to look at him. His eyes snapped open to lock with hers.

Samara wasted no time pulling him to her. She touched her lips to his, taking the lead. As she wrapped her arms around his neck Jed moved to take over the kiss, his lips driving into hers.

Jed relaxed his grip, keeping her close and rubbing his hands on her back in gentle movements. It felt so good to be held by him. She leant against him, running her hands up the back of his neck. She was lost in his arms, not wanting him to ever let her go.

His lips left hers and he trailed soft kisses down her neck starting at the back of her ear. Samara moaned and closed her eyes, tilting her head back as he made his way down her neck. She could feel his warm hands through the silk slip. The wrap fell open as he moved his hands to tighten his grip around her waist. She felt paralyzed, unable and unwilling to move. A voice in the back of her mind screamed at her to pull away and cover herself, but she couldn't. He was everything she wanted.

When Jed reached the base of her neck he stopped. She felt his head snap up. She opened her eyes to see him staring at her. His eyes were wide and creases formed on his forehead.

Samara pushed herself away, and his arms dropped to his side.

"Sammy, what happened to you?" His face revealed his horror at the sight of the injury.

She pulled the wrap closed and crossed her arms around her body.

His mouth fell open and his eyes searched hers

for answers. Samara didn't know how to proceed. *This is your chance. Tell him.* She took a deep breath before explaining.

"I was attacked when I was living in Sydney. I was on my way home from work and I was grabbed from behind." She didn't have the courage to tell him what the 'work' had been.

Jed frowned. "Who attacked you?"

"The police haven't found him yet. I got this injury when I fought back." She reached up to touch the scar under the wrap.

Samara could see Jed's chest rise and fall with the depth of the breaths he was taking. "Were you raped?"

"No. Just this. Trevor Delaney was the detective in charge of the case. He already knew me. He's questioned me several times before regarding my ex-boyfriend, who was also a well-known drug dealer."

Jed's mouth dropped open and he paused to run a hand though his hair.

"I told you I made some very bad choices."

Confusion covered every inch of his face. "You were a drug addict as well?"

Samara shook her head violently. "No, I never did drugs. Karl was a way out. I was running away from the situation I had created here in Kiisay Point. I spent a lot of time running away from my mistakes."

"So what was the detective doing here today?"

Samara took a deep breath before relaying all she had been through in the last three years. Karl and Ricky. The first attack. The second. Layla. Her death. It was hard, but she forced herself to continue. She kept her club job private. It was the thing she was most ashamed of, and she wasn't ready to reveal it. She told him about her encounter with Jesus and the peace He had brought her. What a wonderful influence Nick had been. And the reasons for Trevor's visit. When she was finished Jed looked baffled.

"This is crazy." He rubbed his face in his hands.

"After Trevor left, I found Flynn and told him that Ricky was back in the area."

His eyes flashed angry. "You're saying Flynn knows all about this, but you're only telling me now?"

"No, not everything. Just about Ricky. I had to warn Flynn he was back. I haven't told anyone about the attack. Why do you think I wear high-necked shirts?"

He stood silent for a long time, looking at his feet. Samara waited for him to collect his thoughts. He was clearly blindsided, and she could understand why. She had only ever confided in Nick, and he had such a calming presence that her story had come easily. She could see Jed was struggling, and she felt for him.

"I think . . ." He looked for the right words. "I think I need some time to absorb all of this."

Samara could see his confusion. "I know it's a lot." It was too much information.

He looked up at her. "I'm sorry. I... I just need to go for a walk or something."

She dropped her head and nodded. "I understand."

He turned to go, but then stopped and moved

back to take her in his arms, holding her close. "I'm so sorry that such a horrible thing happened to you, and about your friend's death." He pulled away to place a soft kiss on her temple. "I'm not abandoning you. Not one bit. I just need some time to process everything you've told me, ok?" She nodded. He then turned and left.

Samara stood in the same spot long after he was gone. She didn't feel either relief or anguish. She felt numb and emotionally drained.

Jed trudged along the beach, trying to digest Samara's story. Her chest injury had been a huge shock, but it seemed almost insignificant compared to the account of her time in Sydney.

He felt shell-shocked. His thoughts were jumping all over the place. The drug dealer, the attack, Ricky's obsession, Flynn, the detective . . . it read like some sort of soap opera.

To add to the confusion, there was the way she felt in his arms. The kiss, the softness of her skin, the way she held him back.

Her scar didn't mean a thing to him. It was a shock to see, but he had viewed much worse in his career. It didn't change who she was, or the way he felt about her.

Jed stopped short and turned back for the sanctuary of his cabin. What he couldn't make sense of, God could. He walked with purpose through the door and opened the top kitchen cabinet, feeling around for Samara's letter. It fell to the ground as his hand swept the shelf.

It was time to read the letter. Perhaps it would help make sense of everything. He sat down.

Dear Flynn,

I have tried many times to write to you. I want to tell you how sorry I am about what happened between us. I used you for a purpose you weren't even aware of, and I am so desperately sorry.

You may know by now that Jed and I had a brief relationship. I was very much in love with him, but he didn't feel the same for me and he left me. I was angry and hurt and I thought I could get his attention by being with you. I was wrong.

I have made some horrible mistakes. For a while I was with a known drug dealer. When the relationship ended I was all alone. I found myself questioning my choices, and I realized I had spent much of my adult life fearful and running away from my problems. The easy way always looked the best way — but it wasn't.

I was also trying to be someone I was not. The model persona wasn't really who I was. Am. It took a great hardship, and a miraculous encounter with Jesus to show me the way. I don't expect you to understand my faith, and I want you to know I'm not using it as an excuse for how I behaved. I take full responsibility for the hurt I have caused you.

I hope and pray you and Jed will be able to forgive me one day. Even though I still hurt, I still love your brother, even more so now that I know what real love is. I know I will carry my feelings for him for the rest of my life. The difference is, now I take heart in the fact I don't have to go through this world alone. My faith has given me strength and purpose. I am a work in progress. I want you to know I pray every day that God will help me to love others the way Jesus loves me, and to give the same way He has.

It is my constant prayer that your life holds many wonderful blessings.

Samara.

PS: Please accept this money as material restitution for what I took from you. I hope one day you will be able to forgive me for the emotional toll.

Jed sat for a long time reading the same words over and over. *I still love your brother.*

Samara could see Cassidy on her verandah. She had spent a restless night thinking and praying about the situation, and had come to the conclusion Cassidy was someone she had to see.

Now she was certain Cassidy and Jed were nothing more than good friends, Samara felt horrible about not trying harder to get to know the lady.

Cassidy gave her a huge smile as Samara approached. "Good morning." Her voice was as sweet and thick as honey.

She returned her smile. "I hope I'm not too early for a visit."

"Never. I'm an early riser. Besides, I still haven't adjusted to the time difference. I was up at four this morning." Cassidy screwed up her face. "Come on up and join me. Can I get you a coffee?"

Samara took a seat on one of the outdoor chairs. "That would be great."

After they were both settled back down with fresh cups Samara looked to address the reason for her visit. "Cassidy, I'm sorry I haven't made myself more available to you. I wanted to assure you that my hesitation is no reflection on you personally."

Cassidy looked relieved. "Phew." She wiped her forehead in a comic gesture. "I thought for sure you had taken an instant dislike to me. I know I'm not the most unassuming of people. My Papa calls me his little canary because I'm loud and never stop talking."

Samara laughed at the analogy. "No, that wasn't the problem.'

Cassidy bit her bottom lip and glanced in her direction. Her fine features were frozen in a worried frown. "Samara, you do understand Jed and I are just good friends, don't you?"

She sighed. "I do now. I'm sorry. It's hard for me to be open about my feelings." She wasn't about to launch into an explanation of how much she loved Jed and the pain she felt at seeing him with another woman.

"I understand completely. We are close. I think being in the type of situation we're in every day breeds a familiarity you wouldn't otherwise develop." Cassidy took a sip of her coffee. "Right from meeting Jed, I knew his heart was somewhere else." She looked down into her cup. "And to be honest, so is mine. My recent trip home showed me that." She sighed deep and long, then pulled her head back. "So let's change the subject. I love your country."

Samara smiled at her enthusiasm. She wondered for a second if she should ask Cassidy more about her trip home, but decided her new friend had changed the topic for a reason.

They sat for some time chatting about Australia—the landscape, the people, the colorful history. Cassidy relayed how much she had loved hearing the stories of the island that Amos had shared one night, and Samara detailed their days in Bonalah.

Sam was surprised to look at her watch to see over an hour had passed. "I'd better get back. Bob'll be wondering where I am." She got to her feet.

Cassidy got up with her. "It's been lovely talking to you. Thank you so much for coming by."

"I hope we can see each other again before you go." Sam meant the request.

"Unfortunately, I leave this afternoon. I'm flying back down to Sydney to meet my father. We're travelling back to New Orleans together. Then I guess they'll want me back in Afghanistan. I must admit, even before Jed left, I was starting to feel as though it wasn't the place for me anymore. His decision not to go back has given me a push in the right direction. I'm seriously considering other options."

Sam felt her heart skip. "He's not going back?"

Cassidy looked a little shocked. "Sorry, I thought you knew. He gave his notice yesterday. Even though the investigation gave him the all clear, I think he realized his heart lies elsewhere."

"Investigation?" Samara felt her forehead furrow.

Cassidy bit her lip. "Oh no. Me and my big mouth. I'm going to get into so much trouble." She put her hands up to her face. "Oh, well. I'm in it this far, I may as well go all the way. Jed loves you so much. You have to know that. He's put up a good job of fighting it, and his anger made him do something very unwise. He needs to be the one to tell you the full story." She paused to let out a heavy breath and roll her eyes. "But I've got to tell you I'm in agony watching you two. Will you get it together already?" She waved her little arms around in exasperation as she spoke.

Sam couldn't help but laugh. She was so blunt, yet so comical, it was easy to forgive her interference. "Unfortunately, it's a bit more complicated than that." She thought about last night.

"Well, I can assure you it's nothing God can't deal with. Take whatever it is back to Him. He can sort it out."

Cassidy's statement was the confirmation she needed. Taking it all back to Him was exactly what she had done. She knew He would have a plan, not only for her and Jed, but also for the situation with Ricky. She just needed to wait and trust.

Jed felt as though he hadn't slept a second all night. He had risen several times with the sole purpose of going back to Samara's cabin. Each time he made it to the door he turned back around. It wasn't the ideal situation—turning up on her doorstep at eleven o'clock at night. It didn't get any more ideal at one-fifteen or three-thirty either.

By four in the morning he was so exhausted he had fallen asleep on the couch with the television blaring. It was nine before he woke again to sun shining through the window.

He'd felt as though his life was on hold until he saw Samara again, and every second of his future depended upon him getting this right. Now that he was sure of her feelings for him, there was nothing left standing in their way. All the problems they faced, they could face together.

Jed could see how the love he had for her had taught him so many things: patience, forgiveness, seeing past skin and into the heart. He had been forced to acknowledge his own imperfections and accept the imperfection in others. Without that lesson, he knew he would never discover the life God planned for him. Samara had stayed in his heart to teach him so many things, and she remained in his heart for a reason too.

He scrambled to get out the door, then remembered he hadn't showered or changed his clothes and was most likely in need of a shave. He turned back around to do all these tasks, leaving fifteen minutes later.

Bob was sitting on his veranda when he arrived at the cabin.

"Morning," he called as he approached.

Bob squinted. "Jed. How are you?" His voice was gruff and very policeman-like.

"I'm well." He came to the bottom of the stairs. "Is Samara around? I thought perhaps she might like to take a walk?" He couldn't say what he needed to with her father present.

Bob squinted further, jutting his chin out and pursing his lips at the same time. "She's not here. Gone visiting. Why don't you come on in and wait a while. I wouldn't mind a chat with you."

Jed could tell from his tone that Bob had an ulterior motive for getting him alone. He didn't know which plan of attack was best—face it with a smile, or run a mile. He decided he was no chicken.

"Sure." He walked up the stairs.

He and Bob retired to the lounge. They took seats opposite from one another.

"I think it's time you and I had a serious discussion." Bob gave him a steely-eyed glare.

Jed sat back a bit. He had the strange sensation of being back in the school principal's office being interrogated over one of his many childhood misdemeanors. It wasn't a pleasant feeling.

Bob plunked his plastered leg up onto the coffee table. "I guess I should just get to the point. No sense beating around the bush. What is going on between you and my daughter?"

Jed knew Bob wasn't going to be happy with any of his answers. At this point, he wasn't certain he knew himself. He knew where he wanted it to go, but he wasn't going to get into a discussion about it with Bob.

A noise from the doorway interrupted them. They turned to see Patty walk through the glass door. "Don't feel as though you have to answer that, Jed."

She turned to Bob, hands on her hips and a stern look on her face. "What do you think you're doing? Leave the poor man alone."

Jed breathed a sigh of relief.

Now Bob looked like the naughty schoolboy. "I was just talking to the lad."

Patty didn't budge. "It's none of your business.' She turned to Jed. "Can I get you a coffee, love?" Her voice sweetened when addressing him.

Jed didn't have a chance to respond before Bob

cut in. "I'd like one."

"I'll sort you out in a minute.' Patty dismissed him.

Jed smiled at the exchange. They were like an old married couple. "Thanks for the offer, Patty, but I just stopped by on my way for a walk." He gave his excuse in the hope they would release him from the cabin.

Patty got the hint. "No worries. It's a lovely day. Sam shouldn't be too long if you want to wait outside."

Jed nodded his thanks and stood to leave. He turned back to Bob who was giving him the squinty eye behind Patty's back. Jed couldn't leave without saying something. As inappropriate as it was to discuss his relationship with Samara at this stage, he was no wimp. He decided to be honest and let the chips fall where they may.

"I love your daughter, Bob. You don't have anything to fear from me." Jed met his gaze with a determined one of his own. Bob sat back a little.

"I'd better not." He huffed under his breath.

Jed held out his hand for Bob to shake. To his credit, Bob didn't hesitate.

He turned to acknowledge Patty on his way out. She was cuddling a coffee cup to her chest and smiling broadly. Her eyes twinkled as she let go of the cup to give him a wave goodbye.

Jed shook his head and smiled as he walked down the steps of the cabin. He sent up silent thanks for his lucky escape.

Samara's visit with Cassidy had lifted her spirit. Hearing Jed loved her was marvelous. She wondered about the details of the investigation Cassidy had spoken about, and felt a little hurt Jed hadn't confided in her. Then Samara remembered her inability to tell him about her club modeling job. She was withholding from him, too. She had to change that. She had to tell him. They didn't have a future if she wasn't honest.

Lord, please give me the strength to tell him.

Of all the horrible mistakes she had made, choosing to bare so much of her flesh was the most awkward for her to come to terms with.

She understood what Nick had said when he explained how giving your life to Jesus was like being born again. It hadn't been an instant change, and she still struggled with so many things. But the longer she spent in His will, looking to Him for the answers, the more Jesus changed her. It wasn't about religion, it was all about relationship.

Samara decided to take her time and walk back to the cabin along the beach. Her father was being looked after — Patty had decided to stay on for a few days.

Huge white clouds raced by in the blue sky, and the wind blew in fresh gusts as she made her way along the bay. She hadn't bothered to tie her hair back and the wind picked it up, whipping it around her face. The salt spray filling the air felt fresh on her skin. Wet sand squelched between her toes, and moderate waves provided a resonating thud as they collided with the shore. Samara reveled in her surrounds. Resolution Island was one of the most beautiful places she had ever seen. She realized she was a country girl and not a city dweller.

Movement at the top of the beach caught the corner of her eye and she turned to see Jed get to his feet and come down to meet her. He had been sitting on the grassed area beyond the beach, near her cabin.

Sam watched his progress. Her heart skipped a beat as he reached her. "I was about to send out a search party."

"I went over to see Cassidy. We lost track of time."

"I'm pleased you did. She would have loved to see you." He stopped close to her. "Bob told me you were out. I decided to wait outside. He was interrogating me."

Sam screwed up her nose. It didn't surprise her that Bob would take the opportunity to question Jed. "Sorry. I hope you haven't been waiting long." She had been gone for over two hours.

Jed shrugged. "A while." His blue eyes locked with hers as he reached up and took hold of a stray lock of her hair the breeze had blown across her face. He tucked it behind her ear and let his fingers run through its length.

Samara felt her body sway towards him.

The moment was broken when Jed looked away. "I've thought a lot about what you told me last night. It was hard to understand, but I want you to know that none of it matters to me." His eyes searched hers. "I'm in love with you, Sammy. I never stopped loving you. The past is gone and it's a new day. We'll deal with whatever comes next together."

She reached for his hand, his words giving her

the confidence to touch him.

"There's more. You may not like what I have to say." Jed ran a hand through his hair, as though he was stalling. After a long pause, he continued. "Flynn gave me the letter you wrote to him. He and Bay pushed me to read it. I didn't until last night."

Samara had forgotten the letter she had written when she was at the shelter. She tried to recall its contents. She had resolved to be honest and the revelation of her feelings for him pricked her memory and made her blush.

She gave Jed a reassuring smile. "I don't mind you having read it. Not now, anyway." She would have thought differently when she had arrived on Resolution, but now it was a piece of the puzzle that fell into place.

Samara remembered her resolve to tell Jed everything. "There's something else. Something I didn't tell you last night."

All of a sudden a booming voice intruded upon their conversation. "Sam, have you seen my phone?" Bob's megaphone question bombarded. They both turned towards the command.

He was standing on the veranda of the cabin meters away and yelling down at her.

Samara frowned and shook her head. His timing couldn't be worse. "No," she yelled back, then remembered having thrown the phone on the chair last night. Maybe it had fallen down between the cushions.

"I can't find it anywhere. Can you come and have a look for me?" He wasn't going to take the hint.

"I'll be up soon."

She hoped the promise would satisfy him. Bob didn't move inside, choosing instead to remain on the veranda, watching them.

Great. His request was a ploy to get her away from Jed.

Jed laughed and squeezed her hand. "Perhaps this isn't the best time. I have something important I need to discuss with you as well." He looked out to the ocean. "I have to take Cassidy back over to Kiisay Point in an hour. She's going to stay on the mainland for the night and get the early morning flight tomorrow. Bay and Flynn are coming over, so we thought we'd take her for an early send-off dinner at the hotel bistro. Come with me?" His blue eyes pleaded with her.

"I'd love to." She confirmed without hesitation, relieved to finally be able to accept an invitation from him. "But Jed, it's important for me to tell you all that happened in Sydney. I don't want there to be anything between us."

A bellowing call from the cabin interrupted her. "Samara Jade, I need my phone." Bob was out of line, but it didn't look like he cared.

She frowned up at him to see Patty stepping out onto the verandah. She said something they couldn't hear, then turned and lifted her hands to signal her defeat.

Jed gave her a lopsided grin. "He's not going to give us a break, you know?"

"Anyone would think we were a couple of teenagers." Samara shook her head in exasperation at her father's behavior.

"We'll have plenty of time to talk later.

Hopefully alone. Can you be down at the boat in an hour?" Jed squeezed her hand.

"I'll be there."

He let go of her and turned to leave, glancing at Bob who remained on the veranda. He twisted back and pulled her to him, his arms encircling her waist. He rested his forehead on hers. "Father or not, I'm not leaving without kissing you."

Jed smiled, kissed her passionately, and then he pushed her back just as swiftly as he had pulled her to him. "See you soon, Samara Jade.' He called over his shoulder as he walked away.

He threw a casual wave at Bob as he went. Her father gave him the, I'm-watching-you gesture, two fingers to his eyes and then pointing one at Jed.

Sam cringed and gave a groan, then made her way up to the cabin. Bob was about to be put straight.

The bistro was packed to capacity. Samara had enjoyed her meal in spite of the racket made by their fellow diners and the noise that filtered through from the main bar area. Her dining companions had a lot to do with her happiness.

If someone had told her a year ago she would be merrily dining with Flynn and Jed McKenna, Samara would have pronounced them mentally unstable. Yet, here she was not only happy in the men's company, but feeling her heart soar. Chills ran over her spine each time Jed looked her way or brushed his hand across hers.

They had all taken their time with the meal, lingering over coffee, and now had left their table to say their goodbyes to Cassidy. She felt the warm pressure of Jed's hand on her hip as he pulled her to his side.

Cassidy had already kissed and hugged each one of them several times. She lingered for a moment on her. "I can't tell you how good it is to see you two together," she whispered in her ear. Samara flashed her best smile in thanks and put an arm around Cassidy's shoulders to give her an affectionate squeeze.

They stood in the doorway of the bistro for some time, not wanting to make the move outside to end the night.

A loud argument between a drunken patron and the publican in the main bar broke through their conversation. The main pub was separated from the bistro by the T-section of the bar, but they could see part of the public area.

The owner of the hotel, Archie, was giving someone their marching orders. He was behind the bar inside their vision. The person he was speaking to was hidden by a closed dividing wall.

"Get out of my pub. You're not welcome here and never will be. If I see you here again, I'll deal with you myself." Archie's commanding voice promised to carry through with the threat.

"You can't kick me out. This is a public place." The tone was slurred, inebriated. Samara recognized the voice. Ricky Tanner.

She jumped at the sound of his voice, and saw Flynn do the same. Silence fell over their group.

"This is my pub and I say who drinks here. Now get out." Despite his age, Archie was not a man not to be ignored.

"Okay, old man. I'm going." Ricky staggered around the wall and into their line of sight. Gold chains swung around his neck, and several diamond ear rings adorned each ear. His head was down, but as he made his way out of the bar, he glanced in their direction. He looked through them at first before setting his eyes on Flynn. Recognition seemed to inspire a sobering flash to his face.

"Well, well, well." He stopped to lean over the bar separating them. "If it isn't my old friend, McKenna. How was life in the slammer?" He snickered.

Samara had always suspected that if she came face to face with Ricky again she would melt in a puddle of repugnance and fear. But neither of these emotions surfaced as she looked at the pathetic Ricky. In the few moments he stared at Flynn, it occurred to Samara that Ricky was nothing but a man. The only power he had over her was the power she gave him.

All eyes were on Flynn, who had gone red and looked like he was going to burst with rage. Bay reached up and grabbed his arm. 'Don't, Flynn."

Ricky jeered at him. "Looks like you've done pretty well for yourself, hey? Sexy blonde wife, and rich to boot."

He was looking for a fight, and Flynn was sizing up to give him one. Jed touched his brother's other arm with his free hand while still holding Samara around the waist. "It's not worth it."

His comment drew Ricky's attention. He cocked his head to look past Jed and view the rest of their group. Ricky was as still as a statue as his eyes fixed on her. He stared unashamedly, as a slow smirk lifted the corners of his mouth.

"I thought if I hung around here long enough you'd turn up." His gaze held a lecherous intent.

Samara felt short of breath, and her heart raced. A fleeting thought that she could run back through the bistro and escape entered her mind, but she pushed it away, making a conscious decision to draw on her faith and the security of the man beside her.

A wave of empowerment flowed through her. Ricky didn't have any control over her. He didn't scare her. She placed her hand over the one Jed rested on her hip.

"Haven't you been told to leave, Ricky?" Her tone was clear and direct.

Jed strengthened his grip on her. She looked up at him. His face was as red as Flynn's, and his stance inspired full-on battle mode.

Ricky's focus shifted to the arm holding her around her waist. As he looked back and forth between her and Jed his demeanor changed from offensive to mean. His eyes screwed up and his bottom lip jutted out past his top one.

Archie moved out from behind the bar. "You heard the lady. Out!" Archie yelled in his ear and pointed towards the door.

Ricky glanced at him then turned back towards them, maintaining his stance over the adjoining bar T-section separating them.

"Lady?" Ricky snorted. "She's no lady. Besides, I'm here for some entertainment. How about getting up on the bar and giving us a show, Samara. I'd love to see you shake it like you did in that club in Sydney."

There was complete silence as Samara felt every person in the bistro fix their gazes on her. A hot flash flooded her body, making her legs warp and her skin prickle. She wished it had the power to melt her into the floor.

Ricky staggered up onto the bar. He reached into his pocket, pulling out a ten dollar note. 'I'll give you this if you take it all off." He stood on the bar and waved the money in the air, jeering at her.

Archie scrambled to climb the bar. "You low-life." Several curse words exited his mouth as he attempted to scale the elevated surface.

Ricky scrambled to avoid Archie's approach. He then fixed his eyes squarely on Jed. "Or maybe I should show you who the better man is."

Samara didn't have time to think further because Ricky jumped off the bar and was running at them, a vicious expression on his face.

Sam felt herself being pushed away. A hand closed around her arm to stop her from falling. Once she stabilized she looked to see Bay holding her on one side and Cassidy's horror-filled expression close to her on the other.

Ricky punched at Jed, who was somehow managing to duck and weave like a boxing pro. Ricky grunted and spat in a furious rage as his fists flew through the air.

Flynn reached out to grab Ricky from behind in an attempt to stop the assault. He had gained limited control when Ricky broke free from his grip and lunged back at the bar, grabbing an empty bottle and smashing it against the surface. He waved it around in the air, wielding his newly acquired weapon.

Ricky's eyes scanned the men as he swayed from side to side in sync with the bottle. His grin stretched his face to maniacal proportions, and his low chuckle clearly stated his intent.

Archie had joined them, along with an audience from the main bar clamoring for prime viewing space.

"Put the bottle down, boy." Archie warned Ricky in low, commanding tones. "We don't need this to get any worse."

Ricky didn't even bat an eyelid as he looked between the two brothers.

Samara held her breath and seized Bay's arm. She could feel herself squeezing it hard, but couldn't relinquish her grip.

Ricky let out a sudden war cry and charged Jed, wielding the bottle in attack position in front of him.

In one fluid movement Jed reared back to miss the bottle and kicked at Ricky's legs, crippling him on the spot.

The force of the kick sent Ricky to the floor. The bottle sailed in the air as he hit the ground. The bar patrons whooped and hollered.

"Get him again."

"Kick him harder."

"Get in a few for me mate."

Jed kept his stance as Archie and another barman pulled Ricky to his feet.

Ricky wasn't putting up any fight. His short, stocky build was subdued by the combined bulk of the two massive men. His face held a shocked expression and blood ran from his nose.

"I'm gonna get you for assault, like I stitched up your brother," he yelled.

"Plenty of witnesses this time, fool." Archie's retort was followed by a chorus of support around the bar. Ricky had clearly made enemies among the locals.

Archie released him to the care of the other barman who put his charge in a firm lock. "Take him out the back." He turned to a waitress. "Call the cops to come and get him."

Ricky turned to them as he was pulled out the door. "I'll get you, McKenna. Both of you," he called.

Jed looked down at his hand and flexed it several times.

Archie left in the direction of the kitchen. "I'll get you some ice."

Samara ran to Jed, turning his hand over, cringing. It was already red and swollen. He didn't have to say a word to her, his eyes said it all. Sam could see the confusion and hurt he was feeling.

It was Flynn who spoke first. "I didn't know you could spar like that, little brother. He didn't manage to get one hit in. All those kickboxing lessons Dad gave us clearly kicked in." He chuckled as he patted Jed on the shoulder.

Jed tilted one corner of his mouth.

Archie arrived back and leaned over the bar, holding out a small towel filled with ice. "Put this on it."

Samara reached over and took the towel, wrapping it around the swollen hand.

Jed looked up to address Cassidy. "Looks as

though there's a bit more work to do on my anger, Cass."

She sighed. "This isn't like before, Jed. You had to defend yourself and subdue him. He had a weapon."

"Don't beat yourself up, Jed. I'd say my husband wasn't far behind you." Bay moved forward and gave her brother-in-law a quick hug, then did the same for Samara.

Flynn gave his brother a swift pat on the back "You stay here. Bay and I'll go and get the car."

"Will you both walk me back to my room first?" Cassidy asked them. They nodded.

Cassidy gave her final hugs. "I'll be back to visit again soon." Her sunny smile was infectious and Samara couldn't help but smile back.

She and Jed moved outside with the other three, stopping outside the door as they left.

When they waved their final goodbye Jed turned to look at her. He still held the iced towel on his hand. "Is it true? Did you really do that, Sammy?" His eyes searched hers for the answer.

Samara felt his pain. She had wanted to tell him herself. For him to discover this way was agony. "I was never completely naked, but that was just a technicality. I may as well have been." She looked away before continuing. "Jed, working in that club was my rock bottom. If I had my time again I wouldn't make that choice. But being so low forced me to look up and see Jesus. I don't believe I would have seen Him if I hadn't been there. Because of it, I made the decision to trust in Him. He turned it around, and I'll never regret that."

She had made the destructive choice, but in His love God had lifted her out. "It's part of my story, and because it led me to choose faith, it's actually a great part of my testimony."

Jed reached for her, pulling her close with his undamaged hand and kissing the top of her head. "I understand." He gave a long sigh. "I have a long way to go with the whole blessing your enemy stuff."

Samara could see he was truly upset with having injured Ricky, regardless of the necessity to defend himself. She recalled what Nick had once told her. Becoming a Christian doesn't mean you become perfect. Jesus constantly works on you, bringing all the things keeping you from him to the surface. Sam repeated Nick's words.

"There are times when we will fail, but if we take it back to Him, He then has an opportunity to heal, teach and love."

"You don't understand." Jed pulled away from her. "I let my anger get the better of me again."

"It was self-defense, Jed. Who knows what Ricky would have done if you hadn't stopped him. Besides, we'd all be guilty of wanting to hit him." She laughed, trying to lighten his load.

"I did the same thing at the camp. You think I would have learned my lesson." He readjusted the towel before continuing. "I haven't only been on holidays, Sam. I did something really stupid and I've been under investigation."

The incident Cassidy had mentioned.

He took some time to collect his thoughts before continuing. "The security forces were stationed around the perimeter of the camp to protect us and the people using the facility. There was this one soldier who was constantly in my face. Most of the servicemen were great blokes, and we all appreciated the protection they gave, but this guy was different. He was cocky and downright cruel."

He looked out into the night and shook his head. "He terrorized everyone he came into contact with, all the Afghanis who came into the camp, even to the point of kicking a pregnant woman. He loved to see the fear in their eyes." He shook his head. "I asked more times than I can remember to have him reassigned, out of the camp. Unfortunately, his fellow soldiers didn't want him around them either, so I was stuck with him."

Jed stopped to squeeze the towel, firming it up. "It got to the point that each time I saw him I wanted to hit him. Cassidy told me he was just an outlet for my anger, and I should pray about it. She was right, but I didn't take her advice. One day he grabbed a small boy under my care and stuck the end of a gun in his mouth to scare him. I lost it and jumped him."

Sam felt her eyes grow wide. "How can you blame yourself? He could have killed that child." She could see how the situation would have riled him.

Jed nodded. "Yes, he could have. But I didn't just stop him. I tore off his helmet and beat him. They had to pull me off him." He kicked at the edge of the footpath. "Besides, medical staff can't interfere with the security, and I went about it the wrong way. I should have followed the system and reported him. Instead I took matters into my own hands and ended up being the one under investigation." He shrugged. "Even though they've cleared me of all wrongdoing this week, the whole thing still upsets me. Instead of taking it back to God, I let my anger get the better of me. I know it's different with Ricky. At least he was the one being pulled back. It's just a disappointment to have it happen again."

"You're right, this isn't the same. You kicked Ricky once in self-defense. You can't compare the two situations."

Sam felt a little confused at his story. Having grown up knowing the McKenna boys, she was aware that a bad temper was something they both struggled with. As children both boys were self-assured and never backed away from a fight, but Flynn was the more hot-headed of the two. It surprised her Jed would have trouble in that area.

"I can completely see why you reacted the way you did in Afghanistan, but it doesn't seem like you to lose your cool so dramatically." She voiced her confusion.

Jed looked at his feet. "Cass had a theory. She thinks I've spent the last three years angry at myself over what happened with you. I haven't been able to get over you. It was slowly tearing me up. Looking back now, it was only a matter of time before I blew up. Especially considering how much emphasis I had on perfection. The frustration caught up with me."

Samara felt her stomach drop. She reached up to cup his face in her hands and tenderly looked him in the eyes. "I'm so sorry, Jed." She kissed him.

He took her in his arms and held her tight. Samara rested her head on his shoulder. It felt good to be free from the burden of her past. She felt truly blessed he had understood her mistakes.

They broke away when the lights of a car shone their way. Flynn and Bay were there to pick them up.

CHAPTER 14

"There's no way I'm ever going to agree to this." Jed stared at them both with steely resolve. Samara glanced across at Trevor. She could see they were fighting a losing battle.

Trevor continued the argument. "Jed, we know Ricky's had a crush on Samara for a long time. He's boastful, and there's a good chance he'll implicate himself or others in drug activity in an effort to impress her. I know we can get some information out of him, especially if she goes to him. He won't expect it, and it'll throw him off."

He wasn't moved an inch by Trevor's plea. "We're not talking about some little crush. He's obsessed with her. You told her that yourself. Now you want her to go and act as though she's interested in him so you can get the information you need?" Jed's voice got louder and louder as he addressed the detective. He turned to Samara. "Doesn't this whole scheme sound crazy to you?"

When Trevor had first put the plan to her, it had sounded like madness. Why would she put herself in harm's way to help with his investigation? Now, the more she thought about it, the more she was convinced it was worth a try.

"He's not asking me to play up an attraction to Ricky. Just the opposite. I pay him a visit to assure him I'm not attracted to him in any way. Trevor thinks Ricky will attempt to impress me to change my mind, and I think he's right."

Sam could see the opportunity. In the few days since the incident at the pub, she had had to change her mobile phone number due to a series of hang ups they suspected were instigated by Ricky. If she could somehow get Ricky to slip up, she could help put him away. With Ricky in jail, the threat he posed would disappear.

Samara could tell Jed wasn't convinced. "He's attacked you once. That much we know for sure. He's come at me with a broken bottle, and he's likely the man who gave you that." Jed pointed to the scar on her chest. "What if he attacks you again? He could kill you."

Trevor leaned over to him. "Hey, we don't know for sure Ricky was involved in the second assault on Sam. He's still only a suspect. We'll have her wired and we'll be meters away if Ricky tries anything. He won't get a chance to hurt her."

Jed gave him a decided stare. "I don't care. She's not doing it."

Samara sighed. It was a long shot, but she felt like her life was on hold until Ricky was in custody and far away.

"Could you give us a moment alone?" she asked the detective. Trevor got up and left the cabin.

Sam readjusted her position on the couch where she was sitting next to Jed. She faced him and took his hand. "Jed, I have to do this. I have to give it a try."

He shook his head.

She continued. "Ricky doesn't scare me. I'm not saying I can handle everything he throws at me, but

I feel protected. Safe. Like this could be the catalyst for something good. It's plagued me that I wasn't around for Flynn's case. I knew Ricky had a knife. I could have testified. This is my chance to face up to him. I can't keep running away. I have to do this for me. For us. And because I know in the depths of my spirit this is the opportunity I've been praying for. Don't tell me how I know, I just do." She closed her eyes knowing she couldn't do it without him. "Please help me."

Jed scanned her face several times before looking away again. After a deep exhale, he finally looked back to her. "If you're determined to do it then I'll support you."

Samara smiled in triumph.

"But don't think I won't put a stop to it if it gets too dangerous."

The whole scheme was madness. Jed still couldn't believe they were sitting in a van on their way to execute the dangerous scenario.

He felt as though he was sending her into the lion's den. Even up to an hour ago he had tried to convince Samara she didn't have to go through with it, but she was determined to proceed.

It had been heartbreaking to discover her previous occupation. Jed couldn't believe she had fallen into such degradation. It was beyond his understanding. He had to admit that the thought of her wearing nothing but lingerie in front of a jeering crowd made him sick to his stomach, but she had found her faith from the experience.

He also knew he wasn't exempt from the miraculous way God used mistakes to change hearts. It didn't matter what place he was in, or how many times he had failed, he believed God was there to all who looked for Him and sought His help.

As the police crew hooked up the wiring device to Samara, Jed prayed for her safety. He would prefer her not to do it, but had to admit he had a strange peace about the plan.

Ricky was staying at a hotel in the nearest city. The drug dealer hadn't grown up at Kiisay Point, but his reputation for being a troublemaker spread far and wide. His earlier crimes indicated he tended to be a stupid criminal rather than a calculated one. Jed was surprised he would have the capability to run any sort of organized crime syndicate. It was entirely plausible he was the lackey for someone big.

It also rang true that if the cops were going to get a break in the case, Ricky would be the one to provide it. He was a fool in a high position. Jed prayed that any information Samara obtained would be substantial enough to put him away for good. He wanted them to be free to live their lives, not having to look over their shoulders or have Ricky intrude on their happiness.

The van came to a halt and Trevor gave Samara his final brief. "Now remember, we've got men stationed in the next room and across the hallway. We know he's alone right now." He motioned to his fellow plainclothes officers. "If you need us to get you out, say the word 'talent'. It should be easy to work into a sentence without Ricky noticing. We'll orchestrate some sort of distraction to get you out. If he pulls a weapon on you don't hesitate. One scream or yell for help, and we'll be there."

Samara nodded and swallowed hard.

"We've got a lot riding on this. Without a significant break, this case will be completely stagnant."

Jed wished Trevor hadn't reminded her. The last thing she needed was pressure to perform. She looked over at him. Her big brown eyes were wide. She jiggled her leg up and down, nervous tension reverberating through her body.

He took her in his arms. "It'll be okay. Just do your best and, if you need to, get out. Don't stay for anyone's sake. Your safety comes first, and I want you back." He kissed her before reluctantly releasing his grip.

She stepped out of the white van and looked back once before walking into the hotel reception.

God has not given us the spirit of fear, but of power and of love and of a sound mind. Samara recited the verse over and over in her head as the elevator clicked up each floor. Six, seven, eight. The doors opened and she stepped out into the corridor.

Her heart pounded double with every step she took. *He's just a man. He's just a man.* Her internal dialogue ran in continuous repetition.

She stopped at his door to wet her lips and gain some composure. Her mouth was so dry she wondered if she would be able to talk.

She reached up and rapped on the door. Footsteps sounded inside of the room, then stopped.

Samara could see a huge eye in the peephole. *No turning back now.*

The clicking of the safety lock and turning of the door knob seemed to take forever. Samara pulled her posture up and steeled her body and mind for action. She hadn't considered what she was going to say, thinking it best to improvise—so she would sound more natural. Now she had to get her brain into gear with an opening line.

Ricky was dressed. It had occurred to her that going to his hotel room posed an array of uncomfortable scenarios. He could be half dressed, in a robe, or naked. Samara wouldn't put it past him to open the door in any of these fashions. Fully dressed, gold chains and all, was a relief.

He looked her up and down before speaking. "To what do I owe this pleasure?"

His lecherous smile reminded Samara of Jamal the pimp. It made her shiver with revulsion. Ricky still wore the injuries Jed had inflicted on him a few days ago. His leg was bandaged and his posture lopsided.

He leaned against the doorway and lifted one side of his mouth. "Come to see how I am?"

She let out a scoffing breath. "I want to talk. Mind if I come in?" She worked hard to maintain a firm voice.

"Sure, babe." He stood aside but kept a hand on the door so Samara had to duck under his arm to enter the room. She gritted her teeth and proceeded.

The room was a complete mess. Beer, wine, and spirit bottles littered every surface, some full, some empty and some in between. Used towels and clothing were strewn on the floor and Samara could see a room service tray full of dirty plates and uneaten food on the floor by the bed. She stood in the middle of the room and surveyed the mess with horror, momentarily forgetting the beating he had given her, and recalling what a slob he was.

"Ricky, this place is disgusting. You live like a pig." As soon as the words exited her mouth Sam realized her resolve to play it cool hadn't gone as planned.

Ricky sat on the edge of the bed and leaned back, his arms behind him propping up his body. "That's what I love about you, babe. You're feisty." He wiggled his eyebrows at her.

Samara turned from him and took a deep breath. The last thing her statement was meant to do was turn him on. She remained standing where she was. There wasn't a clear chair even if she had wanted to sit. Besides, standing gave her the upper hand. She took another deep breath before plunging into the purpose of her visit.

"Ricky, I'm here to tell you I'm not interested in you. Not in the past, not now, not ever. You have to leave me alone." Samara stared at him, hands on hips. Her delivery was a little more aggressive than she had planned. The emotion of the situation was getting to her, and she had overlooked the point of her visit— to draw him out.

Ricky dropped his bottom lip like a spoiled child. He soon recovered and frowned before squinting and pursing his lips. "It's the doctor, isn't it?"

Samara raised her eyebrows. *Yeah, Jed's the problem.* It didn't surprise her that Ricky wouldn't consider his own pathetic shortcomings.

He gave her a sinister grimace. "'Cause I could take him out. I owe him big time. Then you'd be available again."

"Who are you kidding? You don't have the authority to take anyone out."

"I worked you over pretty good a few years back."

Samara froze. *Help me Lord. Give me the words.*

She pushed the fear away and took a deep breath. "You only do what Karl tells you to. You're just his little lackey. He ordered you to attack me, didn't he?"

Ricky recoiled from her words. She had hit a nerve. He didn't like to be touted as Karl's underling. He sat up straight.

"I didn't like having to hit a girl, but you made us do it. If you hadn't talked to the cops we wouldn't have had to pull you into line. Anyway, I made sure each hit was clean. I know you didn't have any serious injuries."

Samara could tell he was on the defensive. She pushed a little further. "What about the second time, Ricky? What excuse do you have for that? You could have killed me."

He raised one side of his top lip and frowned. "What second time?"

"The attack outside the club. I was in hospital for days."

"Not us." Ricky shook his head, then sat up a little straighter. "Hey, is that why you disappeared? I had a hard time tracking you down. I staked out that flat for weeks."

Samara felt sadness overwhelm her at the reminder of her flatmate's fate. She had to find out what part Ricky had played in Layla's death. "What did you do to Layla? What happened to her?"

Ricky reached for a half empty bottle of scotch on the bedside table and took a deep swig. "She was a junkie. What do you think happened?" He took another swig. "I had some real pure stuff and she got all greedy and took too much."

Samara closed her eyes. *Poor Layla!*

"No great loss. Another junkie choking dust. She was good fun for a while." Ricky mumbled between swigs on his bottle. He belched loudly.

A mixture of disgust and fury fought for control of her insides. "You and Karl deserve each other. You're both a pair of heartless, selfish pigs. But at least Karl had some brains."

Ricky got to his feet and took a step towards her. His cheeks were growing red, and his eyes looked like they were going to pop out of their sockets. Was he going to hit her?

"I'm the one making it all happen," he shouted. "Karl sits up in his office smoking and hitting on chicks all day."

Samara took a microscopic step back. She had to find a way to run with this. "Come on, Ricky, I know who the boss man is. What have you ever done to make it big?" Samara threw out the challenge, hoping he would take the bait.

She wasn't disappointed.

"You haven't been around for a while, Samara. You don't know how I've expanded the operation." He remained standing, swigging on the bottle.

She gave a snort and hoped it had sounded like genuine belittlement. "Well, come on, Ricky. Impress me with your business skills. What could you possibly have done that Karl wasn't behind?"

Ricky threw up his hand. The bottle of scotch splashed onto the carpet. "I'll tell you what I've done. I've expanded the business back into this area. I've got contacts all over this place. How do you think I knew you were here?"

Samara felt a chill run up her spine. "Like who?"

"Ray Fisher. Pete Mitchell. Just to name a few."

Samara had heard of both men. Lowlifes who had already been caught dealing.

"What a great crew. Those boys couldn't run a choko vine up a chook house." Her father's expression. She had clearly spent too much time in his company.

"You don't know nothing. I've got both of them running labs for me. Pete's uncle's property is the perfect location. He's got a whole underground setup, and Rob's running a show out of a hotel room up the street. We're churning out thousands of tablets a day." Ricky puffed out his chest at his accomplishments. "I can take you and show you if you like."

Samara couldn't believe it. Trevor was right. Ricky was out to impress her.

"No, thanks," she said. "You expect me to believe that Karl has nothing to do with this? This is your plan? You're the mastermind?"

Ricky looked sheepish. "Well, no. Karl's got the contacts. He's organized the buyers. You know Mr. Wong?"

Samara nodded. She had heard of the man, but had never met him. Ricky obviously assumed she knew more about Karl's operation than she did.

"His crew's got the south covered. They're raking in millions as we speak. Check this out."

He sat on the edge of the bed, pulled a sports bag out from underneath, and unzipped it. Wads of hundred-dollar bills were stuffed inside along with several ziplock bags full of pills.

"This is small change, babe. Think of all the pretty things I could buy you with it. And there's a whole lot more where that came from. Karl's got a warehouse in Britton Street full of stuff good to go. We're gonna haul millions in the next few weeks. You can get in on it. We can live the high life together." His lopsided smirk was full of glee.

Samara stopped herself from recoiling. She had to get out. Surely Trevor had more than enough to pin something on him. Samara was also concerned with where Ricky was heading. If she rejected him now he could turn nasty. He thought she was someone he could buy. When it became clear she wasn't, he could explode.

"Looks like you've acquired some talent since I saw you last." She dropped the key word into context.

"You could say that." Ricky puffed his chest out again and patted the bed beside him, indicating she should sit.

A loud rap on the door signaled her escape. "Room service."

"I'll get it." Samara moved to the door, opening it as Ricky called out.

"Tell them to bugger off. I didn't order nothing."

The cop was dressed in hotel uniform and signaled with his eyes for her to exit.

"I'm going anyway, Ricky. I'll think about your offer and get back to you," she called over her shoulder as she took off out the door.

She was halfway down the hall when she heard him bellow. "You do that."

Samara turned to see Ricky's head poking around the door frame. The cop had strategically blocked the entrance with an enormous trolley.

She reached the elevator, which was being kept open by another plainclothes policeman. The doors closed behind her. She leant on the wall of the elevator and rubbed her face. Relief surged through her making her slump.

"You alright?" the cop asked. She closed her eyes and managed a nod.

Sam was escorted out of the hotel and back into the safety of the van. Jed grabbed her as she stepped up into the back, and the van took off.

He held her close, kissing her head. "It's over. You're safe." His breath was warm and reassuring.

"You did an awesome job, Sam. We've got so many leads I don't know where to start." Trevor looked gleeful.

"What do you mean leads? Aren't you going to arrest him right now?" Jed's voice was so direct Samara pulled away from him to see his face. His thunderous expression was aimed at the detective.

"We can't blow it now. There's more at stake here than Ricky's arrest. He's just given us Karl Somers' entire operation. Not to mention the gang

Wong heads. If we arrest Ricky, now we'll miss the big boys. We have to play this out."

Trevor's enthusiasm didn't put a dint in Jed's disgust. "Are you telling me she went through all this for nothing? We still have Ricky breathing down our necks. Worse now that he thinks he has a chance with her."

Trevor took a seat across from them. "I'm sorry, but we have bigger fish to fry than Ricky. We'll organize some protection for you while it all goes down. Is there somewhere you can go where you'll feel safe? I don't recommend going back to the island."

"We shouldn't have to do this." Jed's eyes locked with hers. Samara shared his anguish.

Trevor shifted in his seat, leaning forward and putting his forearms on his knees. He looked thoughtful as if trying to ascertain how to proceed. "Ricky didn't find you while you were at the shelter. Perhaps you could go to Sydney for a few weeks? I can protect you better down there than here. I don't anticipate it will be long before we can organize raids and get them all into custody. Remember, we'll be watching them closely. They won't be able to contact you without us knowing." He sat back up and gave them a closed-lipped smile "Believe me, I'm sorry to have to do this to you, but we can't let the big ones get away. You must appreciate that."

Samara looked back and forth between Jed and Trevor. She did understand his drive to catch the bosses. What was the point of putting herself in danger for a small-time criminal like Ricky when they could bring down the entire organization? She could see from the resignation on Jed's face that he also appreciated the detective's motivation.

"Okay. You win. We'll disappear for a while," Jed said.

Samara nodded.

"Great. I'll make the arrangements." Trevor retrieved his cell phone from his pocket.

Samara reached up and gave Jed a kiss on the cheek. He squeezed her around the waist in appreciation. "I'm so proud of you."

She sighed. "I had a few dicey moments."

He grinned and raised his eyebrows. "I could tell. My personal favorite was the colorful analogy — couldn't run a choko vine up a chook house?"

"It's one of Bob's favorite sayings." She shrugged. "I couldn't help it. It was all that came to mind."

They both laughed.

CHAPTER 15

Nick was ecstatic to see her, especially as she had brought another volunteer to help.

"It's a pleasure to meet you.' He gripped Jed's hand in a firm shake. "We don't have much to offer in the way of accommodation, I'm afraid." He turned to address Samara. "You'll share with Ronnie, and Jed will have to stay in one of the single men's rooms."

"Fine by us." She picked up her travel bag. "I'm thankful you can give us a place to stay."

Nick threw an arm around her shoulders. "It's great to see you, Sam. It's also a bonus to have two professionals to give Ronnie a break. She's overworked. Taking the pressure off her will be a huge help."

Nick wasted no time getting them to the clinic. Ronnie had been running the show single-handed with limited help from volunteer doctors, most of whom breezed in and out with little concern for the patients. Samara could see she was a wonderful nurse and a proficient organizer, but clearly stressed.

Ronnie welcomed them, and put Sam to work as clinic nurse, with Jed filling the doctor's duties. Ronnie was left to attack the mountain of paperwork spilling over the plastic trays in the reception.

"I can't tell you how much I appreciate you both being here. You're an answer to prayer," Ronnie said as they all took a ten minute coffee break. Samara and

Jed leaned up against the desk and Ronnie sat in the office chair.

Sam liked the older woman very much. Ronnie looked like the model for a Mrs. Claus cartoon, with white hair pulled back in a neat bun, a plump, happy face, a round, cuddly physique and bifocal spectacles perched at the end of her nose. Her jolly demeanor added to the comparison.

"Looks like you've been struggling to keep up." Jed looked wide-eyed at the stacks of paper lining the wall of the reception desk behind them.

"You could say that." Ronnie chuckled. "But I've got some help now so I can get up-to-date."

They were interrupted by the swinging of the main door as it opened. Ronnie had put up the closed sign for five minutes to give them a break, but she hadn't locked the door.

Samara recognized the man who entered—Dr. Vega. His stout body shook as he maneuvered his way through the doorway. He was as slimy as she remembered. His thinning hair and beady eyes did nothing to improve him. Samara was surprised Vega was still here—he'd never been good with the patients, and seemed to like the idea of volunteer doctoring more than the actual job.

Samara frowned as he looked at her, first with astonishment, and then with an intensity that gave her the creeps. Jed must have also picked up on the vibe because he put an arm around her shoulders.

Ronnie stood to address him. "Dr. Vega, I am so sorry. You obviously haven't received my messages. I left several at the hospital for you, as well as on your mobile. You have a day off." She motioned to them.

"We've got Jed and Samara visiting, and they've been kind enough to give me a hand."

Dr. Vega reached into his pocket and pulled out a handkerchief, wiping his forehead. Strange. Why was he sweating so profusely? It wasn't hot in there.

"I had such a busy morning I didn't get to check my messages." Vega's voice was shaky.

"Well, we've got everything under control here. After such a busy morning, I'm sure it will be a relief to have an afternoon off." Ronnie opened the door and motioned for him to leave.

Vega's eyes scanned the room before he abruptly turned and walked out the door. Ronnie shut it firmly behind him. To their astonishment, Vega turned back and peered through the glass. He scanned the room once more, his eyes settling on Jed, then Samara, before he swung around and left.

"That was bizarre." Jed looked at Ronnie for further explanation.

"It was, wasn't it? He's a strange man. I expected him to blow his stack when he was told his services weren't required. He's not known for his good nature."

"He's a weird, obnoxious little man." Samara forced away the shivers running up her spine. "I thought Nick was going to get rid of him."

Ronnie looked at them over the rim of her glasses. "Believe me, he's tried. Vega won't go. We thought he'd give us the flick when the promotion he was up for didn't eventuate."

"He thought volunteer service would make his application look good," Samara said to Jed.

"We've stopped using him, but he keeps calling

wanting to volunteer." Ronnie looked at the door. "We're forced to call him in when we're desperate, which I was today. That was before you arrived. Nick's suspicious. There's something strange about him. It doesn't sit well in my spirit."

It didn't sit well with Samara either.

Ronnie frowned and pursed her lips. "Nick told me a few weeks ago that he thought he saw Vega coming out of a strip joint a few blocks away, but he couldn't be sure. The night was dark and the man was wearing a hooded raincoat."

Samara bolted upright. She knew where she had seen Vega before. "He's Mr. Hood." Ronnie and Jed gave her their full attention. "I've seen him in the club where I worked. He would always sit in the same dark corner not moving and peering out from under his hooded raincoat. He'd tighten the strap at the bottom of the hood so he never showed his entire face, but I remember his beady eyes. The girls called him Mr. Hood."

Jed and Ronnie both wore shocked expressions. "I'll go and tell Nick right away. He'll be interested to know his instinct was right. I don't think we'll be getting him back again." Ronnie got up and left the room to go next door to the shelter.

Jed walked over to the window and peered outside before turning around. "So if he knew you from the club, why didn't he ever say anything when you were working here before?"

Samara shrugged. "Maybe he didn't want me to know he was a patron."

That was plausible. Vega didn't want anyone to know he frequented clubs, considering his efforts to avoid being recognized.

Jed raised his eyebrows. "I've seen the worst of human nature in my work overseas. Nothing would surprise me."

Samara didn't know what motivated Dr. Vega, but she was certain it wasn't something decent or righteous.

A chilly draft entered the room from the vent in the ceiling. Samara closed her eyes once more. She was having trouble sleeping.

They had been at the shelter over a week, and today was the first time Trevor had called with positive news. They were closing in on Karl's organization. Trevor wasn't able to give details of the investigation, but he did say he didn't expect them to have to hide out for much longer.

It was great news. They were enjoying their stay with Nick and could see their presence was a great help to Ronnie, but they knew it wasn't where they wanted to be permanently. They had both been told not to leave the shelter under any circumstances, and a police car patrolled the perimeter as an extra precaution. Despite the constant activity Samara was starting to feel the effects of cabin fever. She was itching to have it all resolved so they could get on with their lives.

She and Jed hadn't had the chance to talk about their future, and Samara hadn't given much thought to their life after Sydney. It seemed a long way off, considering their current enforced wait. She only knew that whatever happened, she and Jed had a strong foundation to build upon.

She twisted and turned in her bed in an effort to get comfortable. The clock read after midnight. She looked over at Ronnie. The older lady was sound asleep with her hands clasped together on her chest.

The narrow room was at the back of the shelter. It had high ceilings, bare walls, and built- in vents designed to provide air flow also allowed the cold night air to infiltrate the room.

Ronnie's desk had been removed to accommodate the spare bed Samara was sleeping on. Nick was in the room next to them, and Jed was down the hall. Their rooms were even smaller than Ronnie's.

Samara tried to force her mind to quiet. She felt her body drift in and out of a twilight sleep when a noise made her jerk awake. She opened her eyes to see movement above her. At first she thought it must be Ronnie, but when a gloved hand clasped hard around her mouth her eyes shot open, jerking her wide awake.

A rush of fear struck her, sending numbing tingles from her toes to her head.

The figure standing above her was wearing a large black raincoat. The hood tied at the mouth was a dead giveaway as to who it was.

Vega.

Sam could see his beady eyes set on her. Black, lifeless eyes. Evil eyes. She let out a muffled cry and grabbed his forearm, trying to push him away. But his grip was too powerful.

Samara struggled under his control. She tried to move, tried to kick, but he had her head locked down. He flashed a scalpel, its shining surface catching every flash of light in the room as he played with it between the fingers of his free hand.

He leant down close to her ear and whispered. "You got away from me before. You won't again." His voice was clear and menacing. Nothing like the insignificant Vega Samara knew. "Get up slowly and don't make a noise, or I'll slit your throat as well as the old lady's."

Samara felt her shock subside and a surge of adrenalin flow through her body. She wasn't going to allow this evil man to end her life. *Jesus, give me your strength.* She pulled her legs up to meet her body and thrust them both straight at him. Her feet connected with the side of his chest, sending him reeling backwards.

Samara jumped to her feet to find him on all fours and attempting to get back up. Behind him stood Ronnie, her old fashion nightgown blowing in the draft.

As Vega rose on his knees Ronnie let out a loud, "Yah!" and gave him a swift and hard karate chop to the side of the neck, her long white hair whipping around her head with the force of her movement. Vega dropped back onto the old carpet, hitting it hard face first. The scalpel dropped to the floor with him.

Ronnie grabbed his arm and secured it behind his back. She plunked herself down on top of him. "Go get Nick and Jed. I'll hold him."

Samara ran from the room and rapped on Nick's door. "Nick. Hurry." She heard movement inside and ran down the hall to do the same with Jed. He opened his door and stepped out before she could get there.

"Sammy, what's wrong? Are you alright?" He frantically pulled a dressing gown around him.

"It's Vega. Quick."

Nick was taking over from Ronnie as they entered. "There's a zip tie in my tool box, Ron." Ronnie ran from the room.

Vega was still unconscious.

"What happened?" Jed bent down to help Nick.

"He attacked me. He was the one who jumped me in the alley. It wasn't Ricky. It was him." Samara pointed to the unconscious heap on the floor.

Ronnie re-entered the room holding a handful of long plastic zip ties. "I knew there was something fishy about this guy."

Nick set about securing Vega's arms and legs.

"Did he hurt you?" Jed grabbed her by the shoulders.

Samara shook her head. "No."

Jed pulled her to him and held her tight.

Vega lay unconscious for another ten minutes while Nick called the police. Ronnie fetched Sam a glass of water.

The police were there within minutes. Vega stirred and came to as they arrived.

Samara, Jed and Ronnie left the bedroom to sit in the safety of Nick's office. Nick helped the police get Vega into custody and out the door.

Samara relayed what had happened once Nick and the police had re-joined them.

The men smiled when she told them about Ronnie's spectacular intervention.

"I've spent many years nursing in mental health and rehab facilities. You get pretty good at defending yourself after being in those places." Ronnie positioned her hands on her hips, Wonder Woman-style. The stance was so humorous they all burst out laughing, including the detective.

"I'll let Trevor Delaney know about this new development. He's tied up at the moment with other things." The detective moved towards the door.

The police took everyone's statements, then left. Nick and Ronnie opted to go back to bed to try and get more sleep. Samara and Jed stayed in Nick's office. Sam was far too worked up to sleep.

They both sat on one side of Nick's desk and sunk into the office chairs. Samara pulled her fluffy dressing gown around her. It was cold now the adrenalin had subsided.

"I hope this is the end. I'd like nothing better than to live simply. For the next few years, at least." Jed put his hands behind his head and stretched back in his chair.

Samara saw the opportunity to discuss the future. Their future. "What do you propose we do after all this is over?" She cringed. It came out sounding a bit bossy.

Jed took a while to respond, leaning back further in his chair and grinning broadly. "Well, I propose to propose . . . if I ever get some peace and five minutes alone with you."

Butterflies fluttered in her stomach as he leant forward and reached over, pulling her chair to him. Her legs sat between his.

He took her hand, his eyes never leaving hers.

"Samara, will you marry me?"

She felt like her chest was going to explode as happy tears clouded her vision. "Yes, of course I'll marry you."

Jed looked sheepish. "I don't have a ring yet. I haven't been able to get anywhere near a jewelry store." He searched Nick's desk, picking several objects, only to discard them. He then settled on a paper clip. He twisted and turned it, fashioning it into a ring. Jed placed it on her finger and smiled. "I don't think it's a good idea to leave it on permanently, you may take out an eye, but I guess it'll have to do to signify the moment."

Samara wiped away the happy tears as they trailed her cheeks.

Jed picked her up and put her on his lap, cuddling and kissing her.

"I love you, Jed McKenna."

"I love you, too."

Jed couldn't believe the range of engagement rings lining one entire wall of the jewelry shop. The most spectacular pieces were way out of his price range. Thankfully, Samara hadn't looked twice at the larger settings.

Jed still marveled at the differences between the Samara he had known before and the woman she was now. The girl he used to know would have expected him to give her the biggest, most expensive ring she could find. This woman wanted something special to both of them.

It was good to be able to leave the clinic and feel

safe. Liberating. They had received the all clear from Trevor yesterday afternoon. His operation had been successful in apprehending both Ricky and Karl. Both men were being held under a variety of drug charges. Their entire organization had fallen, along with Mr. Wong's drug syndicate. Trevor assured them both men would be very old by the time they got out of prison.

Vega had been charged with Samara's assault, along with the murder of the other stripper. The fact that his other victim had connections with Ricky turned out to be a complete coincidence.

Vega, as Mr. Hood, had targeted Samara from when he had first seen her in the club. Vega's volunteer work gave him an acceptable excuse to be in the area in case he was ever caught and questioned. It was the reason he refused to quit.

When his attack on her failed and she disappeared, he continued to scan the clubs for her. It was by pure luck that he found her again at the clinic.

He spent the subsequent months planning his next attack on her. Her move back home thwarted his plans again. He gave up and moved on to his next victim.

When Samara surfaced a third time, Vega neglected his careful planning to stop her getting away again. His eagerness was his downfall.

Jed looked down at a small box off to the side of the huge cabinet. The sign on the top read Antique Rings. One caught his eye. It wasn't a huge diamond, but the quality was superb. It caught the light in so many angles the shine made it glisten as if it were wet. Two smaller yellow stones sat on each side of the main one. Their color was intense.

Jed scanned the room for Samara. She was at the other end of the counter, being monopolized by the sales assistant, who was eager to sell them a ring from the range of new arrivals. The assistant manager came to stand in front of him. "Can I help you with something?"

"Can I have a look at that one?" Jed pointed to the ring.

She put on her glasses and opened the case. "You have excellent taste. This is a beautiful ring. Diamond and yellow sapphire—a rare combination." She removed it from the cabinet and handed it to him.

He held it up to the light. It was even more spectacular outside the glass. The price tag surprised him. It was well worth the money.

'"Oh, it's beautiful." Samara stood next to him looking at the ring as it shone.

"It's an antique though," Jed told her. He expected her to reject something another person had worn.

The manager interrupted before she could respond. "I know the story behind this one. My boss acquired it himself. It belonged to the wife of a missionary. They went all over the world and served in all sorts of places. They were happily married for over fifty years. They both died of natural causes within a week of each other. This was one of the only possessions they had. Isn't it lovely?"

"It's perfect." Samara looked up at him.

Jed handed it to the manager. "We'll take it."

EPILOGUE

A set of swells glided into the shore, producing rapidly breaking waves. The fresh salty breeze flowed in a constant stream, ensuring their spot under the coconut trees was pleasantly cool.

Samara watched the island women. She had done her best to copy them, but her coconut leaf basket looked more than a little wonky. She held it up in an effort to figure out where she was going wrong, inspiring one of the young women beside her to giggle. Samara couldn't help but laugh with her. "It's pretty bad isn't it?" Basket-making was definitely not her forte.

The other women stopped their banter to laugh along with them.

She and Jed had been stationed on Thursday Island for the last six months. It was the largest in a group of islands sitting off the top of the Queensland coast. The hospital was small and in need of updating, but still managed to serve the community well. The island locals were friendly and hospitable. Jed and Samara had been welcomed with open arms and hearts.

They had been provided with a cottage that was small, but perfectly suited their needs. Its position on the beach ensured they didn't miss Resolution too much. Jed's desire to live simply had been fulfilled. More often than not they dined on local produce — home-grown tropical fruit and vegetables, and a variety of fresh seafood. They had also been given the use of a tinny to travel to the other islands, although most of the time it was being borrowed by the locals. They were thoroughly enjoying themselves, and most days couldn't believe this was their work.

Ricky and Karl were a distant memory. Trevor didn't anticipate her having to testify, as the evidence they had acquired was substantial enough. The case against Dr. Vega was another matter. It was vital Samara give her testimony when the case was tried in a few months.

Sam marveled at how the Lord had used the mistakes of her past to bring down a mass of evil men. If she hadn't faced Ricky that day, Trevor wouldn't have had the information he needed to bring them to justice. Following that encounter, she wouldn't have been in Sydney, and Vega wouldn't have attacked her. More women would have died at his hands.

Samara knew she wouldn't have had the ability to face Ricky without the strength of her faith. Looking back, she could hardly believe she had once been the girl who lived in fear, ran away from her mistakes, and tried to be someone else.

"What is it?" Jed cocked his head to the side and frowned as he looked at the basket from over her shoulder.

Samara faked offence before throwing the pathetic attempt back into the pile of materials. "You certainly didn't marry me for my basket-making skills. I think I'd better stick to my day job."

Jed laughed and held out his hand. "Want to go for walk on the beach, Mrs. McKenna?"

Samara smiled and allowed him to pull her to her feet. She still loved the way her new title sounded, and the claim Jed now had on her for life.

They had been married on Resolution Island six weeks after getting back from Sydney. Bay had launched into full wedding mode the minute they stepped off the boat, helping her organize every aspect of the day.

Bob had initially complained about the time frame for the event. He would rather they had a long engagement. Samara talked him around. Neither she nor Jed wanted to wait a minute longer to be together. Bob eventually put aside his disgruntled attitude and gave Jed his consent after having a little talk to him. Samara could imagine what that had been like for Jed. But he took it all in good humor, saying it was a small price to pay for having her.

The day was so much fun. Bay had organized huge arrangements of tropical flowers and hung Chinese lanterns in the trees, which formed a mass of color as the night fell. Bay had spent much of the day behind her camera.

Sam had found the perfect dress online. It was silk, floor-length, sleeveless, and with a high neckline which covered her scar. The fabric clung to her body in all the right places.

They had married on the beach. Jed and Flynn had both gone to the trouble of dressing up in sleeved shirts and long pants, although neither wore a tie. Bob had given her away and her brothers and their families had attended. They had celebrated long into the night.

The day after the wedding, they received a call

from Esther asking if they would be interested in a position on Thursday Island. They had jumped at the chance to work in a remote community again.

As they walked hand in hand along the shoreline, Samara recalled their Bible reading that morning. *I sought the Lord, and he answered me; he delivered me from all my fears.*

She thought back to her life before her faith. She was lost, alone, running, and scared. Now here she was with her best friend, safe in the knowledge that love had replaced her fear.

She looked at the man beside her.

God had given her more than His peace. He had given her a life, a faith in Him that grew day by day, and the desire of her heart.

NOTE FROM THE AUTHOR

If you are interested in reading a three-monthly devotional, like the one Samara read, I highly recommend *'The Word for Today'*. This publication is available as a daily email and, in many countries (Australia, New Zealand, UK, USA, Canada etc.), in a magazine format that can be sent to you free of charge.

In Australia go to:

www.thewordfortoday.com.au or phone: 1800 00 777 0

Or see:

www.ucbmedia.com for contact details in obtaining 'The Word for Today' in your country.

Xo Rose.

Anika Deumer looked at the white stick on the bathroom vanity. She couldn't believe her entire future hinged on a piece of nondescript plastic.

She was late. Three weeks late. *What am I going to do if it's positive?*

The thought she hadn't yet dared to contemplate entered her head. She sat down on the edge of the porcelain bathtub and put her head in her hands.

Seventeen was too young to be a mother, even though she was twelve months older than her own mother had been when she was born. *And that's gone great, hasn't it?* Her mother had been absent for a large part of her life.

A knock sounded on the door. Anika held her breath, fearing discovery.

"Ani, I need to brush my teeth."

It was Ronald. The shy six-year-old was the most recent addition to the clan of foster children that included three girls and four boys. Ani was the eldest. She forced her breath out in a relieved rush.

"Give me a few minutes," she said. "I'm almost done."

The brush-off seemed to work. Silence fell on the other side of the door. Ani looked at her watch. *Two minutes gone, three to go.*

She perched on the edge of the bathtub and hid her face in her hands. A peek through her spread fingers. The stick hadn't magically disappeared. With a heavy sigh, she straightened up and tried to avoid its overpowering presence by focusing on the framed photo above the laundry basket. It was an old picture of Aunty's family.

A long line of brothers and sisters, ten in all, stood outside the family home in Kiisay Point, around nine hundred kilometers south of Aunty's home here in Cairns. The face of one brother stood out. Uncle Amos. Her unlikely hero. He had a mass of curly hair, a wide grin, and he wore nothing but a pair of faded shorts.

But Amos, Aunty's older brother, was indeed

Ani's knight in shining armor. He had rescued Ani from her mother's partying lifestyle. Despite being only distantly related, Ani had always referred to the members of her Pacific Islander family as Aunty and Uncle.

Another soft thud at the door interrupted her thoughts. Ani bit her lip and waited for further communication from the other side.

"Aunty says I need to clean my teeth now. She says to tell you your hair looks fine. I think it looks good, too."

She couldn't help but smile at Ronald's shy compliment. "Thanks, Ronald. I'll be two more minutes."

She stood up and looked in the mirror. Her hair was the bane of her existence. Any other day she would have been standing there, brushing, clipping and applying any and every product available in an effort to tame the dirty blonde corkscrew curls that fell below her shoulders. Aunty's assumption that she was holed up in the bathroom doing her hair was usually accurate. Today she was barricaded in due to a life-changing matter which entirely trivialized her hair issues.

Ani picked up a long-toothed comb and did her best to run it through her curls. Her bright blue eyes stared back. She lost count of how many times people commented on their brilliance. Perhaps it was because the color was so unexpected for her Island heritage. Her dark olive complexion and curly hair were the only Island heritage features she possessed.

Her physique was also different from her peers. Ani envied her friends with their curves and womanly hips. She always thought her curves were more lumps than bumps.

"Eat up, Ani. Got to get some meat on those bones." Aunty used to say when Ani first came to live with her. She had been a scrawny ten-year-old at the time.

"You take after your father," her mother would spit at her. "We're all cursed." Ani hated when her mother spoke of the family curse. Fathers without faces had been the fate of each woman before her. Left pregnant and abandoned by her rich married lover, her mother believed no Deumer woman would be cherished by a man.

Ani was convinced it was all rubbish and nothing but bad choices had placed her family in this recurring historical predicament. She was determined to be the one to break the curse.

Now, here she was, one drastic mistake later, wondering if she would end up being part of the cycle. Young, pregnant, rejected, desperate, traumatized, substance dependent. A family tradition passed down from generation to generation.

Ani looked down at the white stick. She closed her eyes, taking a few deep breaths. *Please, don't let it be positive.* She sent up a silent prayer to the God Aunty told her existed, hoping He had a moment to hear her plea.

BUY NOW at Amazon or www.rosedee.com

ABOUT THE AUTHOR

Rose, who holds a Bachelor of Arts Degree, was born in North Queensland, Australia. Her childhood experiences growing up in a small beach community would later provide inspiration for her first novel, *Back to Resolution*. *Beyond Resolution* and *A New Resolution* are the second and third books in the Resolution series.

Back to Resolution won the Bookseller's Choice award at the 2012 CALEB Awards, while *A New Resolution* won the 2013 CALEB Prize for Fiction. She has also released *The Greenfield Legacy*, a collaborative novel, written in conjunction with three other outstanding Australian authors, and has recently released the standalone novel, *Ehvah After*.

Her novels are inspired by the love of her coastal home and desire to produce exciting and contemporary stories of faith for women. Rose resides in Mackay, North Queensland.

BOOKS BY ROSE

The Resolution Series:
Book 1: Back to Resolution
Book 2: Beyond Resolution
Book 3: A New Resolution
A Resolution Novella: A Christmas Resolution

Other books by Rose Dee
Ehvah After
The Greenfield Legacy (A conjunction novel).

Visit Rose at:
www.rosedee.com
https://www.facebook.com/Rose-Dee-Author-172886062810998/

www.ingramcontent.com/pod-product-compliance
Lightning Source LLC
Chambersburg PA
CBHW060954120726
47910CB00002B/632